"Original and finely nuanced . . . many delicious and revelatory moments . . . a fresh and witty perspective."

—*The Washington Post*

"Breaks new ground for American-Jewish fiction . . . Ms. Abraham may be the first Chasidic-born female writer to depict the inner life of an ultra-Orthodox girl imaginatively and critically. She does so with great aplomb and a fierce lack of sentimentality."

—*Forward*

"Wry and poignant . . . a rare visitor's pass to a cloistered Hasidic enclave."

—*Glamour*

"An unflinching portrait of a world not open to outsiders . . . an intelligent first novel—poignant and thoughtful—from a writer to watch."

—*Kirkus Reviews*

"Hypnotic power . . . [a] wonderful first novel."

—*The Jewish Standard Guide*

"Intense, sensitive prose . . . vivid scenes and memorable characters."

—*Publishers Weekly*

"Stirring . . . Rachel's free spirit and courage make her an endearing character . . . entertaining."

—*San Francisco Jewish Bulletin*

"An extraordinary look at the realm of the Hasidim."

—*The Arizona Daily Star*

D0109550

(continued on next page)

Praise for Pearl Abraham's international bestseller,
The Romance Reader . . .

"Wonderful . . . immensely charming and original . . . often hilarious, often moving and always absorbing."
—Hilma Wolitzer, *Newsday*

"That rare work of fiction, both a coming-of-age story and a brave, beautifully rendered exposé of a hidden, insular world . . . heartrending."
—*Elle*

"An assured, smoothly written book, narrated in a muted voice that seems to whisper secrets into the reader's ear. . . . [A] smart, appealing heroine."
—*The New York Times Book Review*

"This story, dealing as it does with guilt and God, is about a journey as brave as Huck Finn's, as difficult as Holden Caulfield's, as stark as any I've read."
—Anne Roiphe, *Los Angeles Times Book Review*

"Compelling throughout . . . we don't want to leave Rachel without knowing everything that happens to her for the rest of her life."
—*San Francisco Chronicle*

Giving Up America

Pearl Abraham

RIVERHEAD BOOKS

New York

RIVERHEAD BOOKS
Published by The Berkley Publishing Group
A division of Penguin Putnam Inc.
375 Hudson Street
New York, New York 10014

Quote from the Kabbala on page 39 is excerpted from *The Essentials of the Kabbala,*
by Daniel C. Matt (New York: HarperCollins, 1996).

Quotes on page 144 are excerpted from *Miracle at Philadelphia: The Story of the
Constitutional Convention, May to September 1787,* by Catherine Drinker Bowen
(Boston: Little, Brown & Co., 1996).

First Riverhead hardcover edition: August 1998
First Riverhead trade paperback edition: September 1999
Riverhead trade paperback ISBN: 1-57322-752-8

The Penguin Putnam Inc. World Wide Web site address is
http://www.penguinputnam.com

The Library of Congress has catalogued the Riverhead hardcover edition as follows:

Abraham, Pearl.
Giving up America / by Pearl Abraham.
p.   cm.
ISBN 1-57322-121-X (acid-free paper)
1. Jews—United States—Fiction. I. Title.
PS3551.B615G58   1998   98-22695 CIP
813'.54—dc21

Printed in the United States of America

10   9   8   7   6   5   4   3   2   1

לך לך מארצך וממולדתך ומבית אביך אל הארץ אשר אראך
בראשית-לך

And God said to Avram, Go to yourself, from your land, from the
country of your birth, and from the house of your father, to a land
that I will show you.

Genesis 12:1

What then is the American, this new man?

—Crèvecoeur

Acknowledgments

Thanks are due to many.

To my editor, Cindy Spiegel, without whom this book would remain unfinished. To Patricia Chao, Cassandra Garbus, Stephanie Grant, and Mona Simpson, early readers of the manuscript. To the people at Georges Borchardt, who make this writing life possible. To my co-adventurer and good friend Margaret Van Sicklen. To Stephen Spewock for his love and sometime patronage. And to my youngest brother, whose wisdom always helps.

Prologue

They met where she was working and where he had once worked. He stopped in for a semester's supply of notebooks and to say hello to his old bosses, the Bluths.

From behind the counter, she watched him walk up and down the aisles, his hips moving just enough, his shoulders stiff and straight. Then he was out of sight and there was only the long stride of his boots.

Leaving, he waved and ducked into the seat of his brown Civic, which suited him somehow.

An hour later he returned to leave his number. Will you use it? he asked.

She looked at his name and number on the sheet of paper in her hand, the narrow D and disappearing A, the crabbed male handwriting. How could he think she wouldn't call?

He hesitated; she smiled. He smiled and she hesitated. Until Mr. Bluth threw him out because the phones went unanswered and the books unkept.

Six months later, the Bluths declared themselves the fortuitous matchmakers. We deserve a gratuity, they said.

Her father disagreed. The engagement had been announced, already there were plans for the wedding, and still he warned against it.

The Hebrew letters of the boy's name add up to ninety-five, he said. Yours come to sixty-nine. Together they make 164, the value of the word בעצב, which is what this marriage will bring you: pain. If you add the three numbers you have eleven. One and one are two. Within a mere two years, he concluded, you'll know it was never meant to be. But it will take more than two years to correct your error.

She countered with some of her own numerics. Nine and five come to fourteen, six and nine to fifteen; the difference is one, or aleph, the first letter of the alphabet, the first letter of the ten commandments—holy beginnings. Also, she argued, both names contain within them Hebrew acronyms for God. This marriage, she announced, is stamped with godliness.

The power to interpret numbers is not granted to just anyone, her father said. He presented her with another warning: The difference between ninety-five and sixty-nine is twenty-six, a year in your life that will prove to be an unhappy one. You live in a country that believes differences among people can be overcome. This marriage will quickly teach you otherwise.

She dismissed his warnings and calculations. Numbers could be used any way you wanted, as good or bad signs. It depended only on your intent. Patterns could be read and recognized, or not. There were their alliterative D's, for example, which seemed perfect, meant to be. For months she traced with her finger the names on every smooth surface. She filled the white pages of a small notebook. She tested the combination in print, in script, in bubble letters, in English and Hebrew alphabet, on fogged windows, frosted hoods, fresh snow, and wet cement. Daniel and Deena. Deena and Daniel. They went together.

Six years later they were still together; in the seventh they bought an old house they could love, took two weeks off from work, and started restoration.

Part One

September

The first morning Daniel unhinged the living-room doors and windows, which were sheathed in smoked mirrors. Old glass and leaded glass, all of it had been covered. For privacy, the previous owner explained. People were seeing right into our living room.

With a heat gun Deena tried to melt the glue that held the mirrors in place, but she was impatient with the scraper, and the mirror soon cracked. After that, the glass came up in strips and pieces, and she had to work with gloves.

Seeing the slices of broken glass, she understood the use of the word *ribbons,* a description so accurate there was beauty in it. Daniel worked on the windows.

At the end of the day there was so much broken glass, edges and corners and shards in every jagged shape, it was difficult getting rid of it. They would have to rent a Dumpster.

They drank wine and ate pizza and looked at how little had been accomplished.

So much broken mirror is bound to be a curse, Daniel said.

Only if you believe in it, Deena said.

Coming down the stairs the next morning, she noticed a triangle of light on the dark wood floor. It entered the house through a leaded glass window, and the pattern, narrowed and elongated, lay repeated on the floor. She stood outside the triangle sipping coffee and watched the light shift with the shifting of the sun. They had after all done something. They'd allowed the sun into their house.

Daniel appeared on the landing above and paused. Deena looked up. Was he seeing what she was seeing? This was their house; they owned a house with bedrooms upstairs, night separated from day. This was the world: the sun in their house. If he came down and stood beside her, she'd let him have a sip from her cup.

He took a step down and groaned. Ouch, my legs.

Deena flexed her toe and pointed. My legs are fine, she announced. But my shoulders and arms.

Perfect. With my arms and your legs we'll have one whole person working. The other can sit on the sofa and direct.

Deena offered her cup. It would go down bitter, she knew. She drank it black; he needed milk. In everything else he was the purist; she diluted things.

Outside the air was sharp and the light clear. The world was at work, and they were here sipping coffee. But this wasn't meant to be a vacation of leisure. They had days of stripping paint ahead.

They worked, Deena on the windowsills, Daniel on the doors, hours of only the noise of the heat gun and the smell of burning paint.

Near the thin leaded glass, slow paint remover had to be used. Deena straightened, inhaled and exhaled, yawned. At her desk what she craved was permission not to focus on a particular product, to not always be in search of words that sell. For the next two weeks, waiting for the paint to soften and relinquish the wood underneath, she was free to think about anything. But it wasn't working quite that way. For free thinking, the body too requires liberation. To truly wander you have to lie on the sofa, or stare out the window. There should be no specific subject, no goal in sight.

She worked too hard for what was ultimately too small. The best ad was still only an ad; and it was disposable. A month later the client would request another one and again the achievement would be for the short term, no chance at greatness.

Nothing of this world is great, her father would say. It's what you achieve for the next world that counts.

But she lived in this world; she was a slave to this world.

Daniel came to see how she was doing. You're pushing too hard with the scraper, he said. You're not allowing the heat to do the work.

He took the gun and scraper from her hands to show her, and she stood watching his capable hands, his patience. She stretched the cramped bones of her fingers. It was good to be empty-handed, but it lasted only a moment.

Here, Daniel said, and went back to work on the door frames.

She counted. There were twenty-three windows, thirteen doors, eight rooms altogether, and each one would take at least a week to do. And they were just starting on the living room. But there was only one way to do the work: to stay with a window or door, thinking with god-like patience of only the next inch, the next hour. The world wasn't created in one day.

After scraping, stripping, sanding, and painting every day for two weeks, they were ready to show what they'd done.

Daniel wanted to invite the new secretary at the office and her roommate, two southern girls just up from North Carolina.

They don't have to worry about finding a baby-sitter, he said. And they're fun.

Deena proposed dinner on Friday night, Daniel called to ask, and the evening was scheduled. They planned the menu together and went out with a list.

Metropolitan Avenue was still new to them, and although Deena hated supermarket shopping, she liked shopping here. With the train overhead it was always dark. In the summer, it was cool. The dark and the noise kept things unchanged. It was a neighborhood no developers thought to renovate. Store signs were yellowed, store windows blackened, but inside there was always someone at work. And it didn't seem to matter to these shopkeepers that they lived and worked on a street in a borough of New York City, that every twenty or thirty minutes there was the possibility of taking the J or M train overhead and seeing the world. They could be living in a village in southern Italy, in an alleyway of Shanghai, or in a shtetl in Eastern Europe. The neighborhoods here resembled the places they'd come from. They lived among their own people, spoke their own language, went from home to work and home again. Life wasn't so different after all.

Walking in the dark under the tracks, with here and there the shafts of harlequin light, Deena remembered the old souk in Jerusalem, dark and cool after the dry, hot sun. She would walk there on the way to the Western Wall, she and her sisters, with their mother or aunt, the sound of their shoes too loud on the cobblestone street. From the feet of Arab women and children, bare feet slapping against cool rock, came a seductive sound. Deena wanted to take off her white polished shoes and her socks and slap like that, barefoot on the cool, smooth rocks.

Like an Arabke, her mother said, and her words held all the scorn of the Europeans in colonial Palestine.

Arab mothers harden their children's hands and feet with olive oil from the day they're born, her aunt said. Your feet would start bleeding after two steps.

Arab hands and feet. They were dark, encrusted, not the soft, pale skin Deena knew. She rubbed olive oil on the soles of her feet every night for a week. But after oiling her soles, she couldn't get out of bed to wash her hands, which didn't need hardening. She wouldn't be picking and peeling cactus with bare hands. She wouldn't be walking the cobblestone streets of Jewish Jerusalem, a heavy basket of fruit balanced on her head, chanting, *Sabras, sabras,* then stooping to bring the basket to the floor, take from the folds of her dress a dirty knife, and with bare hands hold and slice open the thorny fruit.

Overhead Daniel and Deena could feel and hear a train coming, and by now they knew that with a train coming you didn't talk. Everyone who lived or worked here knew. Behind the counter, the owner would stop talking and wait, and when the train stopped, brakes screeching, he'd continue, curt and dry, as if there'd been no interruption. You had to remember what had been said and connect it with what came after.

Daniel and Deena quickly learned the way of things and tried to make friends with the local hardware man, the locksmith, the girl at the cleaner's. Only the shoemaker responded, and only after Daniel had all his soles refurbished.

Now I won't need shoes for another year, he said.

He was always happiest saving money. Although it was true they'd have to save, Daniel liked doing it for the austerity of the thing.

Let's put a moratorium on spending, he'd say, and for him complying was easy.

Deena hid the things she bought. If only she could do without. On Daniel's side of the closet there were only necessities: suits, two pairs of jeans, shirts, and two sweaters. Everything about him was spare, disciplined: his narrow face, his angular nose, his leanness. His lips, however, were full and sensuous. If we have a child together, he liked to say, it will be all lips.

On their way home, they walked up Sixty-eighth Street even though it was out of the way. Deena was convinced you could find good things on the street, things people threw out. The house was empty. They needed chairs, tables, dressers. They needed beds.

One thing we don't need is other people's junk, Daniel said when Deena came home with an old leather suitcase just out of someone's attic. It was full of cobwebs and spiders, but the leather had seasoned to a golden ocher. She brought the vacuum cleaner out to the patio.

Now that she had this suitcase, she knew what colors to paint one bedroom. An off-green on the woodwork, and on the walls an ocher wash. This house, painting and furnishing it, had invaded her life, her brain, like a disease. She was always looking. Running after work, she went up one block and down the other. A pile of junk around the corner, a patch of color somewhere within the pile, everything beckoned and called for a stop. She was seeing from blocks away what before she wouldn't have noticed. She was drawn to all possibility, to the warmth of aged color, to anything old.

When she came home with an old iron garden chair, Daniel said, You're starting a garbage collection.

You sound like your mother, Deena said.

Mrs. Binet threw out all the junk her husband carted home, old baby carriages, mattresses. The sleds he found, wooden sleds with the letters faded, were kept out of sight under the porch until the snow came. There were American Flyers, Flexible Flyers, Speedys, Cherokees.

I'm continuing a tradition, Deena said. I'm doing what for years your father did so you could be more of your mother.

Lay off my mother, Daniel said. What do you have against her?

Only that she's not my mother.

On her desk at work was a requisition for point-of-purchase advertising on the Swanson fried-chicken account. Three years before, her first day on the job, she was handed the same assignment, and so far six pieces had been approved and produced, but every year the client came back for more. Couldn't they for a change assign this to another copywriter? She was down to second- and third-best lines. She'd have to do better. It was September; a back-to-school poster might work. Kids love fried chicken, heat-and-eat appeals to mothers—but how best to say it?

They set the table together. In this house, setting the table had become something even Daniel liked doing. Opening the paned glass doors of the white cabinets in the pantry, taking the dishes out, and carefully setting them on the tiled counter below, stoneware on stoneware, was a reminder of what mattered. This was the best of life. They looked at one another in silence and gloated.

From Daniel's mother, Deena had learned to set a table. There was civilization in sitting down with all that was necessary in place and no jumping up for a forgotten spoon. There was time for a woman to sit and eat with the others, not between runs, not in the kitchen after. At her parents' house the spoons arrived with the soup, the forks on the plate with the meat. Knives, implements of destruction, were kept off the table. One was brought in to cut the bread and removed soon after.

Deena chopped and Daniel stood over the stove, stirring, frying. It smelled good and there was room for two in this kitchen. Bumping occurred only when intended. He looked over her shoulder and reminded her that what he needed was thin slivers not chunks. Deena pushed him away. Mind your own pot, she said.

He went back to the stove. She brought the chopped vegetables to him and leaned against his shoulder.

Ow, he said. That pointy Stern chin.

How would you know a Stern chin?

I've seen your family, Daniel said. You have your father's chin and it's pointy.

You mean his beard, Deena said. You've never seen his chin.

Daniel smiled. If you shaved you'd know that the natural shape of the beard follows the line of the chin. Another thing women don't know.

One thing. Tell me what Jill's like, Deena said.

She's really nice, Daniel said. And friendly. She's been in New York since July. She was a department-store model in North Carolina. Here she takes acting classes, and her agent wants her to try for the Miss America contest. Her schedule is pretty hectic. She works out twice a day, rehearses and memorizes parts, plus she temps at the office full time.

Deena made a face. A Miss America wannabe? Does she have a chance?

She is pretty. Blonde, leggy, sweet in a southern, Miss America way.

I hate her already, Deena said.

You'll like her, Daniel said. She asked about you and I told her you two will hit it off. You're alike in many ways. She's a runner too.

Deena poured a glass of water and sipped. She watched Daniel gather the chicken wrap, put it into the garbage bag under the sink, wipe the counter, wash and dry his hands. His cooking always took longer because he cleaned as he went. Now he stood in front of the open cabinet of spices deciding what to use. He was making chicken-pepper stew, but he didn't follow recipes. Sometimes the food was good.

No cinnamon, Deena said, reminding him of an unsuccessful dish.

Do not tell ze chef how to cook, he said.

He moved from sink to counter to stove easily. This kitchen was designed for cooking. She'd start entertaining more.

In the shower, with hot water running down her back, she pinched her stomach. Were the handfuls too full? She was in good physical shape, but she'd never be model-thin. Her collarbones and wrists would never break hearts. She wasn't made that way.

Jill and Ann arrived. They both wore their jeans tucked into short boots, and they walked with long-legged certainty. Deena would never wear her jeans in her boots like that. Still she admired them. Cowgirls. She watched Daniel watching them and wondered about what pleases men. In bed, he liked holding her in the crook of his arm, torso to head. He liked knowing he could hold her like this within the length of his arm. She was so compact.

You're small like my mother and sister, he said. But you have grace.

Deena appreciated the *but*. Today she wore a short charcoal dress that stopped just above the knee. She liked simple, one-colored things.

Daniel liked knit dresses with waists, or skirts with sweaters. He'd bought her some things, a taupe knit dress with polka dots and another one with blue stripes, but they remained in the closet. Deena wouldn't wear them.

Why not? he wanted to know.

When they met she wore pleated wool skirts with clogs. Everyone else on campus wore jeans, but she'd grown up in skirts, she knew how to wear them, and he'd liked that.

But Deena wanted jeans, the simplicity of jeans, the ease of never having to think about what to put on. There was a kind of democracy in the very fabric. Denim. The material of the peasantry, her father called it. What he liked to see her wear was a suit of fine dark blue wool, a skirt and a jacket, what he remembered his mother wearing, what all educated women in Europe wore. If he saw her in the baggy denim jeans she wore, he'd call her a farmer. The heavy boots she trudged in would also disturb him. What are you studying in college? he'd say. The art of herding sheep?

Daniel took her to a warehouse where they stocked every style of jean ever manufactured.

She tried Levi's and Lees and Wranglers. They didn't fit right. She tried Sassoons.

Designer jeans, Daniel said, is an oxymoron.

Men have it easy, Deena said.

But there were women who could wear jeans, who knew something about the era of jeans, the nature of the fabric. Maybe you had to have grown up in them.

Give it up, Daniel said. You look good in dresses.

But she didn't give up. She wore her Levi's baggy.

Jill and Ann had long legs and long torsos, and hips that didn't interrupt too much. Bodies like Daniel's. They sat, three pairs of denim legs under the table; Deena wore tights.

Daniel uncorked the wine, a kosher cabernet, and poured it into the silver kiddush cup. He had to recite the blessing aloud. He looked at Deena, shrugged, and started, first atonally, then the chant crept in. That was better. His voice strengthened and he finished with a flourish.

Amen, Deena said.

Amen, Jill and Ann responded.

Daniel and Deena smiled. Jill and Ann looked up, alarmed: had they done something wrong?

And now for the famous Jewish delicacy called gefilte fish, Daniel said.

He brought from the kitchen the four plates with the fish already on them. Deena heaped three teaspoons of horseradish onto her plate and passed the jar to Ann.

Don't do as she does, Daniel warned. She eats some fish with her horseradish.

Ann tasted and sneezed. Careful, she warned Jill. This stuff is dangerous.

Jill put a piece of fish in her mouth, chewed, swallowed. She nodded and ate a larger piece.

It's okay, she said. Kind of bland. Not at all fishy.

She dipped into the horseradish and continued eating. Ann finished hers.

You like it, Daniel said.

There isn't really anything to dislike, Jill said, and brought another piece to her mouth. It doesn't even taste like fish. It's odd.

Deena nodded. The color doesn't help. Cement.

In grade school, Jill said, my best friend was Jewish, or, rather, is. I guess she still is. Remember Beth? Jill asked Ann.

We used to have sleepovers at her house. But I don't think her family ever did this; they didn't have traditional meals.

Daniel nodded. Most Jews in America don't. If it were up to Deena, we wouldn't either.

Do you eat only kosher too? Jill asked Deena.

Daniel snorted. Only when I'm around. But she comes from a Hasidic family; she's used to bending and twisting laws at will, finding and using every loophole, the way people do with taxes.

You really believe that? Deena asked.

It's true, isn't it? Daniel said. What time in the afternoon does your father finish the morning service?

Jill laughed.

These people have lateness built into them, Daniel explained. They can't help being late.

He exaggerates, Deena said. But Hasidism is different from Orthodox Judaism. Custom and ritual are sometimes more important than law. Legend and myth have as much influence as fact. It's a way of life rather than simple, strict adherence to religion.

That seems more pleasant to live with, Jill said.

Daniel laughed and stood to clear the plates. When he returned, Deena went to toss the salad. From the kitchen, she listened to talk of work. Ann was probably bored, but it couldn't be helped, it was what Daniel and Jill had in common. She brought in the salad.

Daniel brought in the stew, and the red and yellow peppers glistened.

Mmmm, Ann said, sniffing.

Wow, Jill said, her eyes on Deena.

Don't look at me, Deena said, I was only the sous-chef. Daniel is the cook in this family.

Daniel? Jill asked.

Deena nodded. He stands in front of the cabinet and chooses ingredients.

Last weekend, Daniel said, I made a tuna salad that tasted and looked like chopped liver. It wasn't bad.

Perfect, Deena said, if what you wanted for lunch was a liver sandwich.

Jill and Ann laughed.

The only thing Mike ever does in the cooking department is barbecue, Ann said.

Yes. He'll barbecue anything, including cheese, Jill said and laughed again. He claims grilled cheese is a Greek thing.

Who's Mike? Deena asked.

My husband, Ann said. He's back home. He didn't want to move here.

Well, Jill drawled, he wouldn't get to do much barbecuing on Broadway.

Yeah, Ann laughed. Mike's not a city person.

Deena looked at her. She was shorter than Jill, not as pretty, older. She laughed less or not as freely, not with that extra something of someone who knew she had places to go. Was it marriage that did that to women? And what was it like, married but living separately? Did they talk on the phone late into the night?

Daniel started clearing plates and Jill stood to help.

Deena watched her. She was different somehow, softer than women in New York City. She looked down chastely one minute and was flirtatious the next.

When the table was cleared they went into the living room. Deena brought in cookies. Daniel poured tea. They watched the fire burn.

Daniel checked the time. It was after eleven.

I'd drive you home if I could, he said. If it weren't Friday night. You should probably call a taxi.

The subway is fine, Jill said. I have a new recording I want to hear.

We can walk them, Deena said. I can use the exercise.

Jill agreed. A walk after all that food would be good. I ran this morning but I didn't have time for the gym.

You work out twice a day? Deena asked.

It's not really twice, Jill said. I work different muscles. Running is aerobic. For my upper body, I lift weights.

She took out her Walkman for the ride.

She has her Walkman with her everywhere, Daniel explained. If you want to talk to her at work, you have to go to her desk, because she doesn't hear a thing.

Jill laughed. I know Pat doesn't like it, she said, but I get more work done this way. She and Joe can't call me for just anything. It has to be important enough for them to get up and get out of their chairs, and for Joe we know that isn't easy.

Daniel and Deena laughed. It was the way she pronounced and emphasized words. Daniel mouthed and mimicked: *git up* and *git out*. And *Jeell,* not *Jill. Jeell* and *Aahnn,* he said.

Jill and Ann laughed.

Jilly, Ann said and a hand was clapped over her mouth.

Jeelly, Daniel said. You look like a Jeelly. Do you two go dancing?

Sure, Ann said. All the time.

We could go some night. I'll find a place that has good music.

This man has never danced in his life, Deena said.

Never? Jill said. Not even in high school?

I didn't go to that kind of high school, Daniel said.

With three women, you'll have to dance, Jill said.

At the station, Daniel wanted to wait until the train arrived. Then he and Deena walked home, holding hands.

That was fun, Daniel said.

Deena nodded. He'd been unusually lively. It was good to see him laughing. She remembered him like this only in the beginning. They'd gone out one night and then almost every night after that. It was summer, they were taking classes, and after classes they were free. There was no one to say what was too early or too late, no one to mention tomorrow. Late afternoons they went to Smithpoint Beach, built a fire, put foil-wrapped potatoes underneath and juicy steaks on top, or fish if they were lucky that afternoon. After dusk they drove back to the dorm and filled the bed with sand.

Sunday they painted the woodwork in the small bedroom. When Deena looked up, there was a smile on Daniel's face. He sat on the floor not painting, the paintbrush in his hand wet and idle.

You're dripping, Deena said. What's funny?

I was just thinking.

Deena waited.

I like the way they laugh. So high and happy, Daniel said. He dipped his paintbrush and painted, the spell broken.

They're fun, Deena said. We don't have enough friends who are just plain fun.

Jeelly, he said.

Jeell and Aaahn, Deena said.

They continued working. There were three doors and two windows, too much woodwork for such a small room, Daniel said.

This room will be the guest bedroom, Deena said, and suddenly thought it likely their first guest would be Jill. This room would suit Jill, especially with the walls washed in color, something bright, something that would work with green. A pink. Salmon pink.

She stopped painting. Pink walls? She'd always liked neutral colors: black, gray, white, the colors of her clothes. Also navy. She dipped her drying brush, painted, and watched the white sill turn a dark olive green. She liked color when it was off: off-gray, off-black, off-blue, off-green.

Daniel stood to pour more paint into his tray. He stretched his legs and back.

You better be sure about this color, he said.

The woodwork will look great, Deena said. It looks great already.

What about the walls? Daniel asked, delaying, his body resisting going back into a crouch.

I'm still debating the walls, Deena said. If I use color, it will be a wash. So we'll have to paint it flat white anyway. Then we'll decide.

Double work, Daniel said.

No, Deena said. The book says a wash rolls on easily and dries quickly. I can't wait to see how it looks.

The one good thing about a wash is that it works with uneven walls. These walls look like they were plastered by a drunk. And see this crack; it started in the living room and traveled up. This house settled crookedly; it's leaning toward the chimney. That's why the stairs are crooked. Basically, the chimney is holding up this house.

It's an old house. What did you expect?

You won't feel so comfortable when you find out how much fixing it will cost, Daniel said.

What do you mean fix? This house has been settling for seventy-five years. It's not going anywhere.

How do you know that? Daniel asked.

She didn't answer. He was always seeing the bad, always pointing out the expense and risk. It had been difficult enough leading him through the purchase of the house. Before they signed, he couldn't sleep thinking that someone would make a higher offer. After, he got cold feet. Now they were here she would just let him talk. He was a worrier; he warned, worried, and insured whatever he could. He insisted on more insurance than the bank required. He insured the house, the mortgage, himself, her. Even his stereo equipment was covered.

She minded his caution. It slowed them down; it made every decision a tortured one. She minded that what was in high demand signified value; what he owned was always questionable. She minded this in herself, when after purchasing the very thing she'd spent days wanting, the questions began. It made for a life of debate, vacillating, regretting, then debate again. It made her head hurt. She wouldn't buy another thing.

But with this house she was certain. She was in love with this house the moment they drove up to it, parked under the oafish oak, and walked through the front double doors held open for them by the young owner. Inside, Deena trembled. If only the price were negotiable. She didn't want to lose this house for five or even ten thousand dollars. Of the sixteen houses they'd seen, this was the only one that looked the way it was built to look. This house had entrances worthy of the name, windows with wavy, shimmering panes made to be thrown open. The framing of every lintel and sash was in place, all the wood generously wide, honestly worn, true. Everything in this house was perfect. The fireplace had its original mantel, the banister its spindles. There was chair railing in the dining room, and adjoining, a small—the original—butler's pantry. This house still showed its first intentions; it needed only encouragement.

On the second floor, there were demolition and construction to do. The owners had taken down a wall between two rooms and built other walls to create walk-in closets. One back window ended up in a closet, illuminating hanging clothes. The effect was complete distortion. When Daniel lifted the carpeting, he could trace on the wood

floor the mahogany trim that formed the outline of the original layout. There had been two small closets, too narrow to hang a dress.
Still Deena leaned toward complete restoration.

With shelves, she said, these narrow closets will be dressers. For
hanging, we'll buy old wardrobes.

She remembered in her grandmother's house in Jerusalem a tall
mahogany *shraenke* with mirrors set into the doors. Inside, her grandmother's dresses hung on the left and her grandfather's striped caftans on the right. Deena remembered her mother's younger colors
like flimsy vagrants between the deep blues and browns. They didn't
have the distinction required of dresses hanging in such a closet.
Her grandparents' thick brocade and heavy satin belonged.

Even in traditional Jerusalem, the modern world has some influence, and every generation changes a little. Deena's mother and aunts
wore prints and brighter colors, which was more than their mother
had ever dared. But a woman wearing pants, that remained unheard
of. When Deena visited, she wore only skirts.

Looking at her clothes, she wondered whether anything she
owned deserved a place in a wardrobe. Daniel's suits would look fine;
suits had dignity.

Your suits will do better stored in wood, she said.

There'll never be enough space, Daniel argued. My suits alone
would take up a complete cabinet.

We'll learn to fold more, Deena said. And we'll keep out-of-season
clothes in the attic.

This is not the 1800s, when a woman had two dresses to her
name.

I'll throw away extras, anything I haven't worn in two years. I'll
pare down. It will be easier to get to the good stuff.

You're dreaming, Daniel said.

.   .   .

In the afternoon, Daniel was restless. I need fresh air, he said. Let's get out of here.

Deena looked at him. It wasn't like him to want to stop halfway. He was usually the one who pressed toward completion.

Let's finish up first, Deena said.

They worked for the next three hours without stopping, caring less now about perfect coverage. They would finish turning the white woodwork this grotesque green. Touch-ups could be done later.

It's grueling work, Daniel said. I work hard enough during the week. Weekends I want something else. This house can wait. We have the rest of our lives to work on this house. I'm twenty-nine, next year I'll be thirty. In high school people in their thirties were old farts.

He arrived at the corner of one wall and met the painted corner of the other. Finally. He stood and rubbed his knees. Human beings weren't meant to spend the day on their knees, he said.

Deena finished the last door. The green glistened; it was fresh. Nothing helped like fresh paint. But here and there white still showed through, and while the paintbrush was wet, while the cans of paint were out, she might as well. She walked around the room and added paint. A dab here. A stroke there. She spent another half hour dabbing and stroking.

Come on already, Daniel said. You can schedule a day just for touch-ups.

Okay. Let's go, Deena said.

They washed their hands and went out.

It was late afternoon; the sun was low. They walked east, with the light at their backs. They didn't yet know much of the neighborhood.

There was the German bar that was said to have photographs and maps of the area when it was still all dairy farms. The Tudor building, low and dark, was so forbidding they'd never actually entered. And somewhere near the tracks, they'd heard, was an old ice-cream parlor. Jahn's. They were headed there now, hoping they'd find it.

I hope they serve egg creams, Daniel said.

At the end of the avenue, they stopped. There was only a flower shop on this corner. Daniel went in to ask. Deena bent over a pot of geraniums. She loved the smell, and it was a plant that could continue flowering through the fall and winter. The windows in the house needed pots and pots of flowers. What she wanted was a gift of several hundred dollars' worth of plants and flowers, enough to fill the house at once. Buying like this, one pot at a time, the house would remain bare for years.

Daniel grew impatient watching her stoop over every pot, finger it, desire it.

Let's go already, he said.

She paid for a pot of red geraniums.

Daniel led the way across the street and across an abandoned parking lot. They stepped around pools of broken glass, and rusting car parts, but suddenly there was Jahn's, the Gothic script sign hanging in the dark window.

Inside, the walls were paneled in mahogany. Daniel and Deena sat in a booth, strangely quieted. They didn't know what to say. A few blocks from their house was this ice-cream parlor from another century: red stools with ornate black backs; tables with round marble tops.

The waitress, in pale green uniform and cap, took their order, and when the drinks arrived, Daniel and Deena sipped and eyed the ice cream and toppings behind the curved glass counter.

A banana split would be perfect, Daniel said.

A waffle with plain maple syrup sounds better, Deena said.

With scoops of vanilla and chocolate, Daniel said, still imagining the banana split. Melted dark chocolate topped with nuts. A royale.

Deena shook her head. Just waffles. Maybe some fresh strawberries and whipped cream on the side. She closed her eyes. Mmmm. Let's, she said, eyes open now, daring him.

He laughed. You have no restraint. If it weren't for me, you'd eat anything, everything. We can bring Jill and Ann. They'd love this place.

Deena nodded. She'd been thinking the same thing: Jill and Ann would like this. They could sample anything: hot chocolate with melted marshmallows, waffles with whipped cream, a double fudge sundae.

Deena continued eying the menu.

None of it is kosher, Daniel said again, his voice resolute, denying her. It's not for you, his eyes said.

We need more friends like Jill, Daniel said. People who are single and know how to have fun.

It was true. The couples they knew all had babies or were about to have them. They needed friends with whom you could have a drink and not talk about the baby's first tooth, first step, first word. When you called, you reached not only your friend, but her kid, her baby-sitter, her cleaning lady, and her husband. They were all there, and they heard what was said and responded. The conversation took place at the other end; you were simply filled in. Then the kid wanted to say hello. Hello, hello, hello. Susie, are you there? Can you hear me? And Susie would nod, and nod again. Then, bored with nodding, she'd return the phone and her mother would be back, but by now you too were tired, and you'd forgotten what you were saying, or what you'd called to say or ask, and if you'd forgotten it couldn't have been that important in the first place. You'd hang up and wonder what had happened. You'd called your friend, but you hadn't spoken to her. You'd spoken to a mother and wife, the employer of a baby-sitter and cleaning lady, but not to your friend.

What are you thinking about? Daniel asked.

I don't know. Everything, a thousand things, Deena said. Life, friends who are fun.

Daniel nodded. There was joy in his thin face. For a moment, he too was alive.

Yes, he said and he looked good saying yes. With his eyes sparkling, he was once again the man she'd met and married.

They smiled. After so many years together, going to school to-gether, studying, they knew each other. They knew what was there, what could be counted on, and what was missing. With more experience they would grow more complete.

They walked out of Jahn's and slowly home.

A corner lot is larger, Daniel said. You get a larger house and more garden space. Look at this one.

Deena agreed. But they don't have a sunroom.

They hadn't yet gotten out of the habit of weighing and judging every house they passed, its advantages and disadvantages, as if they were still looking to buy.

A black squirrel ran up their driveway, and they followed the squirrel to the back of the house, their patio.

I noticed the gray squirrels fight him; they don't accept him, Deena said.

They're racist. They belong in this neighborhood, Daniel said.

Deena laughed. After the closing, they were informed—warned, Daniel thought—by the previous owner that the neighbors weren't happy about the sale, about Jews moving into this Catholic neighborhood.

No one stopped to say hello when they pulled up to the house in the mover's truck and started unloading. On their right, in the brown house on the corner, the lights went on every evening, but the residents used a side entrance; Daniel and Deena didn't see them coming or going. On their left lived an old man whose daughter visited every other day.

The black squirrel leapt up the tree. No one bothered him now; he had the place to himself.

Deena sat on the back step and rubbed a geranium leaf between her fingers. She'd had a good, full day. Work in the morning, egg creams in the afternoon, sunset on the stoop, and also the geranium.

It smells like an old lady, Daniel said. Like my grandmother.

I love the smell, Deena said. She traced the red-brown stripe that scalloped an inch from the edge.

This was a perfect day, she said. Work, play, and rest. A little of everything. If we could live only such days.

You'd lose your appreciation for them, Daniel said. You'd get bored.

Deena shook her head.

Trust me, you would, Daniel said. I could use going out more. Like tonight. A club would be fun. After two long days inside, going out would be welcome.

It's funny. When we were first married, you never wanted to go anywhere. Now that I'm satisfied not going, you're interested.

We didn't have money then. Now I can order a drink without worrying.

But now there's the house, Deena said.

Still, things are different. I bring home a good salary. We're both earning decently. We don't have to worry.

Well, make plans to go out, Deena said, and we'll go.

He picked up a twig and scraped at a crack in the concrete. Black ants poured forth in every direction. Ants in the pants.

You're driving them out of house and home, Deena commented.

Daniel threw the twig aside. There, he said, bending over the crack. They're headed back in.

They sat silent, feeling the wind, listening to the dry leaves rustling. It was growing darker now; in the surrounding houses lights came on, and still they didn't move.

What should we have for dinner? Daniel asked.

Leftovers. Let's go look at the room.

They got up. Daniel unlocked the back door and Deena bent to pick up the pot of geraniums. A nut dropped off the tree and they turned to look. The black squirrel looked back.

Don't move, Daniel said quietly.

They remained still, the squirrel, paws empty, body wary. All three jumped when the alarm went off. It was deafening. Daniel rushed in, through the kitchen, to the top of the basement stairs and fumbled. The neighbors would have a reason to complain. Jews making noise. Jews protecting their wealth with alarms. The damn thing was loud.

Three five nine seven, Deena shouted. I told you not to turn it on. We were out for less than an hour.

He turned off the main switch; Deena was right behind him, and they stood looking at one another, the pot of geraniums between them. Deena looked at the pot, ridiculously still in her arms, walked across the kitchen, and set it down on the windowsill. The green and bright red were perfect, but it was hard to love it right now. She pushed it to the left, then the right, to center it.

Should we get a cat? Daniel said, attempting to retrieve the calm of the stoop, the squirrel stillness of the previous moment. A cat and a pot of geraniums, they'd keep each other company. Or kittens, *two cats in the yard,* he hummed. Who sang that?

I don't know, Deena said. She wasn't yet ready to swallow her irritation.

Come on, Daniel said. Name that tune.

Crosby, Stills and Nash.

Pretty good, he said. You're getting better.

She shrugged to show she didn't care, which wasn't true. She was pleased. She'd learned a few things. After twenty years of not having heard of the Beatles or anyone else, she'd caught up a little. Still, she'd never know rock and roll the way he did. She wasn't interested enough. Even when they listened to the same station and heard the same announcer, Daniel knew more because he paid attention to music trivia; he absorbed it.

They went upstairs. What do you think? she asked.

Dark, Daniel said.

And dull. It needs color. White walls are too stark against this green. We'll do the walls next weekend. By then the paint will have hardened.

What color? Daniel asked. Have you decided on the color?

Deep salmon pink.

Daniel looked at her. You're joking, he said.

It will be cheerful, happy. With no furniture to speak of, we need color.

Whatever you say. Remember, you won't get a second chance. At least not for a while. You'll have to live with it.

We'll put the Amish quilt in here. It'll look good. Pinks and greens. It will be a bright room.

It certainly will, Daniel said.

· · ·

Daniel announced that this year he would become a member of a synagogue. The high holidays were coming, Rosh Hashana was only a week away, and since they owned a house in the area, they ought to belong to a congregation. There wasn't one in their neighborhood, but between Bushwick and Atlantic Avenue or across a stretch of Forest Park into Woodhaven there were temples. Either one would be a walk. Daniel chose Woodhaven, met with the rabbi, paid the membership fee, and received two designated seats: one for himself in the men's section, and one for Deena in the women's section, even though she said she wouldn't go.

She questioned his sudden interest in membership. It was true he prayed every morning; he'd probably never missed a day, but he didn't attend services, not even when they were living several blocks from a synagogue. Only when they visited his parents did he go to services with his father. His mother went on Saturday mornings and she expected her daughter-in-law to accompany her.

At first Deena went; later she resisted. Living at home with my parents I didn't attend services, she argued. Hasidic women were never expected to. On regular Saturdays only old grandmothers sit in the synagogue.

Rosh Hashana isn't a mere Saturday, Daniel said. For the high holidays you could make an exception.

What does Rosh Hashana mean to you? Deena asked.

He didn't have an answer. He didn't repent, or promise, or form resolutions, but every year he was there, in the synagogue with other Jews, the way he'd been the year before and the years before that.

Why do you go to the synagogue? Deena asked.

Some things you just do, Daniel said. What's wrong with following a tradition simply because it exists, because it's what Jews do, and you're one of them? I know one thing: people at work respect my integrity. I follow certain laws and I'm consistent. I always wear my yarmulke and I always eat kosher. On the high holidays, I go to the synagogue, which is better than nothing.

I spend the day thinking about things, she said. That's something.

You do that every day of the year, he said. On Rosh Hashana you could try something different. For thousands of years Jews fought and died for the right to gather in the synagogue and pray. And you give it up just like that.

But it wasn't just like that. She used to look forward to the Sabbath and holidays. She liked the preparations: the purchasing of exotic fruit, the hurried cleaning of the house. She liked the white cloths and silver candlesticks, the special chants and prayers. But somehow she and Daniel couldn't replicate that, she didn't know why. Maybe because they had no children. What did remain were the things she couldn't do. She couldn't run or shower, she couldn't listen to music or watch television, she couldn't travel anywhere; there was nothing she could do. Although she'd grown up with all these don'ts, now they left the day empty. Daniel woke up late on Saturdays, prayed and ate, read a little, went back to bed, woke to pray and eat again. For Deena, that wasn't enough. The mechanical way he adhered to laws made transgression imaginable.

Orthodoxy without the delight of Hasidism, her father warned, is a very dry thing. The commandment is to serve God with equal parts of love and fear. Orthodox Jews incline toward fear. Hasidim err perhaps on the side of love, which is emotional and therefore more powerful. You were brought up with this love; without it, I fear for your soul. As a child, you were an excellent student only if you loved your teacher; if not, you weren't merely less than excellent, you were miserable.

Two years into her marriage, Deena wasn't observing the Sabbath.

A letter came in the mail, a response to the pictures she'd sent of the house. Yes, she and Daniel were still together; they'd even bought a house.

A house? her mother wrote. You aren't having children, what for do you need a house?

Her father quoted from the Kabbala: *The purpose of marriage is union. The purpose of union is fertilization. The purpose of fertilization is giving birth. The purpose of birth is learning. The purpose of learning is to grasp the divine.*

The purpose of marriage. It wasn't that her father wanted her to have children with Daniel. He was just pointing out that not having them indicated some failing, that things must be less than idyllic.

The letter ended with the blessing for a sweet new year, and reading it, Deena felt her father's humid breath, as if he were right there, his heavy hands on her head. For a moment she wanted to be in Jerusalem, which was beautiful in September. You didn't need a calendar to know that a holiday was less than a week away. On the streets of Mea Shearim you smelled the green leaves of the willow and the lemon scent of citron imported from Morocco and Algeria. Every month, every day even, was distinguished somehow. You knew it was a Thursday and Friday by the fat carp in the market and by the hurried comings and goings of housewives. Before sunset on Friday night, the sound of a gong informed you that it was time to light candles.

.   .   .

On the eve of Rosh Hashana, Daniel and Deena dipped apples in honey, drank wine, and ate dinner. In less than an hour they were finished, rituals included. Then Daniel wanted to go to bed. Whatever you do on the new year, you do all year.

But Deena didn't want to find herself going to bed early all year. She wanted to stay up late, all night even, and avoid the death of sleep. Daniel's way of suddenly putting down the magazine he was reading, rising abruptly from his seat, and announcing that he was going to bed bothered her. He meant it as a request that she come with him to bed and she minded the flatness of his request, as if he were making an appointment. She disliked also the ease with which he ended the day. He went to bed too willingly. They were opposites that way. At nine or ten o'clock in the evening, with only a couple of hours left to the day, she came wide awake with a sudden need to tackle everything she hadn't done in the course of the day. She hadn't finished more than a chapter of the book she was reading and already Daniel was asking that she put it aside and accompany him to bed. It's quiet, it's Friday night, this is what Sabbath is for, he said.

When she asked him whether he wanted sex only because that's what one ought to do on Friday nights, he shrugged.

I want sex every night, he said. Friday night happens to be convenient, he said. The television is turned off, the phone is unplugged. We've had dinner and wine. What else is necessary? You can read all day on Saturday.

But on the night of this new year she continued to read, and he looked at her, at her head lowered over the book, and she felt him looking, but she didn't look up. She finished the sentence and began the next sentence, and Daniel started walking to the stairs. Only then did she lift her head and watch him walk across the room, then up the stairs on his way to bed. Seeing the force in his stride so intent on carrying them both up to bed, and the expectation in his stance when he paused at the foot of the stairs, she remembered all the early bedtime curfews in her life, and all the years of trying to postpone the final hour, which called for the closing of the eyes, for sleeping and acknowledging the passing of another day. She'd always dreaded bedtimes. She sat behind the kitchen door and listened to the sound of teaspoons against glass: her mother stirring tea, her father sipping it, and the tea passing through a square of sugar held between the front teeth. Even when there wasn't a single giveaway sound, her mother knew that Deena was behind the door. She had eyes in the back of her head. Without turning round she'd suddenly say in a calm, even voice, Go to bed, Deena. Tomorrow is another day.

In bed, Deena's eyes had crept to the shadow on the wall and focused on the distortion that occurred where the shadow folded at the end of the wall and climbed onto the ceiling, an animal. She was afraid of this shadow. She stayed awake watching it, making sure it did not come closer. She heard the quiet of night, the sleeping sounds of the others in the room, the sounds of water running through pipes, heating the room, and from farther away came muffled the same soft sounds. Everyone slept. They liked sleeping. When the alarm clock rang in the morning, they didn't want to stop sleeping. They would sleep all day if they could.

Daniel liked going to bed and being in bed. He went to bed early and slept late. He spent half his life sleeping. And he wanted her with him. Even in death there was to be no parting.

Some nights she went with him. After, she put on a robe and came downstairs again and read and there would be the relief of having delivered, of knowing she would have to herself the following night and maybe the next one, until it became necessary to think again about her obligations, her duties. She was a married woman, Daniel was her husband, he wanted from her what husbands expected to get from their wives. She should provide what other wives regularly provided. But were other women also simply obliging? She enjoyed it. Once started, she liked it. Why didn't she remember that? Daniel wanted to know. Why wasn't she drawn by the memory of pleasure, the way he was?

She liked his brown skin next to her skin, his hands on her body. But then there was the pressure of its having happened, of its insignificance, of how it left everything unchanged. She'd spent an hour in bed satisfying needs. Then she was downstairs again, and he was upstairs snoring.

Married people average four times a week, he said. According to studies. We, he said, are bringing down the average single-handedly.

Averages, Deena said. People lie for reports, everyone knows that.

Daniel wasn't satisfied. It was important to get closer to the average and always they fell short.

Deena wondered sometimes. She wondered whether what people in old age regretted was not having had more sex. What did dying people think about? If they were like Daniel, they'd think about all the times they could have and didn't have sex. How was it she'd ended up with someone so intent on numbers?

I'm normal, he argued.

In the morning, with a cup of coffee in her hand, she watched from the window Daniel's tall, straight back. It was the first day of Rosh Hashana, and he was walking to the synagogue in Woodhaven. He walked well, a rare thing in a man. He knew how to carry a suit. It was one of the first things she'd noticed and liked about him. But when you live with a person, looks stop mattering. Or they matter occasionally again, for a moment, when you see him from a distance, or when someone else notices. He's a good-looking man, she had to remind herself. Still she could look at him, watch him walk away, and feel nothing. Was this married life?

He arrived at the corner, then turned the corner, and walked out of sight. It was good to have him out of sight. Now she had the house to herself. She had several hours of quiet, with no one around. She liked the calm that descended the minute he walked across the sunroom and out the front door.

It was misting outside. She'd promised to go with Daniel to the synagogue if the weather was fine, but it was a rainy day and she knew just what to do. She walked up the stairs to the attic and breathed and smelled wood, an ancient cedar forest on a fresh morning. She ran her hands along the thick beams and rafters aged to red honey, four times the thickness required by building codes today, the engineer had said. A structure built to last.

This house would outlive them. It had outlived several generations already.

Although she kept only emptied moving boxes up here, she liked having an attic. This was her first time up here alone. When she was thirteen or fourteen, it wouldn't have taken so long. But she was twenty-six, and every morning she went to work and every evening she ran; then dinner, and dishes after dinner. Weekends she scraped and painted. She needed more free time.

She walked end to end. On the wall above a vent was a spider spinning a wide, fine net, an intricate, sticky web. She watched. It moved up the thread, shortening it, as if eating it. Sliding down, it regurgitated the thread and ended with a centimeter more than before. It shuttled up and down, weaving and wending forward and back, like sewing a hemstitch, like life, one step forward, two despairing steps back, making, finally, for greater tensile strength. Spiders were said to have destroyed the temple in Jerusalem, therefore, spiders in your home should be destroyed. But hanging from the rafters was this industrious spider spitting and spinning, turning spit to flax, a fairy tale. She wouldn't bring it down. She wouldn't respond superstitiously.

She went down the steps and walked from room to unlived room, a tour of the second floor. Whose house is this, she wondered, and repeated aloud, Whose house is this?

They slept up here, but she didn't yet know these rooms. She stood at the front window, learning the view. From up here she could see the top branches of the oak tree. The leaves were just turning red, bits of yellow here and there. In the spring, she'd know precisely at what stage the buds were. If she looked, that is. If she remembered to look.

She turned back to the room. The dresser wasn't placed well. The beds either. After all these years they were still sleeping on the beds her parents had left behind for her when they moved back to Jerusalem. Twin beds for a marriage that observed the menstrual laws, an area Daniel's religious discipline didn't cover. This was his weakness. He wanted sex whenever he could get it. It didn't matter whether or not she was bleeding. They never separated the beds.

Deena turned the beds so that their long sides faced the door and pushed the dresser into another corner. She stood the old leather suitcase up against the foot of the two beds and folded a wool throw over it. That was better already. It left more open space. She leaned the mirror on top of the dresser in the corner and the room looked pulled together.

Daniel would have something to say about this change and about the general frequency of Deena's changes. During the night he'd stub his toe against an unexpected leg of the dresser. Once used to getting his socks out of the third drawer, he expected to find them in the third drawer. Discovering in the morning when he was tired or late that his socks were no longer where they had been the day before was upsetting. Why couldn't things stay put? He looked in the drawer below and it wasn't there either. He opened and closed the one above, then gave up and started at the top, opening each drawer with a quick pull followed by an angry shove. One drawer would slide off its track and he'd have to stop to correct it. He'd have to pull the whole drawer out and carefully fit it back into its metal slot. Meanwhile the alarm clock on the dresser would tick to seven forty-five and still he'd be standing barefoot, not yet dressed, not yet on his way to work. And all this time his socks would be sitting in the bottom drawer, where he should have looked first, if only he'd known.

But why should socks be so far down? he asked. Like underwear, they're something you change daily. Women like organizing and re-organizing, but they have no principles of organization. Not that I care where things are, so long as they remain in the same place.

Deena shrugged. Change helped her see things anew, like coming home after a long trip. A new point of view gave a sense of life thrusting forward. Yes, it required adjusting, but you remained agile. You adapted. Getting out of bed in the dark during the night she'd have to learn to turn left instead of right. To dress she'd have to stand near the window. Standing near the window while dressing would give her an opportunity to know the view. And winter, when the big oak lost its leaves, she too would lose cover. She'd have to put up a shade and remember to draw it.

But Daniel didn't welcome adjustments. Stay away from my clothes, he said. What is it about women?

I'm not like your mother, Deena said.

She does exactly what you do, Daniel said. My father complained until finally she agreed to lay out his clothes the night before.

Your mother lays out your father's clothes?

That way she can sleep half an hour later. Then she gets up to make his breakfast and lunch.

Daniel too liked oatmeal or Wheatena in the morning and he wanted Deena to cook it. That's what his mother did for his father; that's what he wanted of his wife.

Deena cooked Wheatena the first year of their marriage. She stared into the saucepan every morning, at the cereal going round and round, sinking toward the center, a trap. Then she started buying cornflakes and bran flakes and Rice Krispies, cereals Daniel could pour into a bowl and eat with cold milk.

He wasn't satisfied. What about lunch? he asked.

I'm not your mother and you are not your father. Make your own lunch, Deena said.

At the kitchen table with a second cup of coffee in front of her, Deena wrote on a blank page, "Resolutions of 1987." She underlined it. Then underlined it again. She formed resolutions twice a year: in January and again in September. September included a review of her achievements in the last nine months, followed by renewed resolutions to accomplish what had been left undone.

Always on the list were the regulars: to exercise, to read more, to do better at work. Five years ago studying French was on the list. Now she didn't write down what was unlikely; she didn't pretend she'd ever get to it; she wouldn't even try. Every year the list became shorter, and what remained changed less. She could turn to last year's list, erase the 6 in 1986 and fill in a 7. Did it mean that nothing had been achieved? She'd run, she'd read, she'd attempted improvement, but they required continued effort. They would remain on the list forever.

In college her list had been longer. But it wasn't that she now wanted less. She still wanted change, but where, and in what? You had to acknowledge that there was something you wanted. Then you had to define that something. If she didn't know to name it, it would remain unachieved. In the beginning there was nothing, and the blowing of the wind to the south and around to the north, and round and round went the wind. Then came the making of the heavens and the earth, their naming, the words. In the naming was the cognizance. She had to name what it was she wanted.

She looked at the heading on the page, underlined it again. It was now triple ruled. She was turning twenty-seven. She had a house, a job, a husband. She had enough. Then why wasn't she happy? She didn't have enough time to enjoy the things she already had. She needed more free time, the freedom of time, freedom from the tyranny of work every morning. She wanted to wake up and lie in bed thinking, remembering dreams, an hour of lying there every morning, no rushing, just knowing herself. Companies paid you to forget yourself and become only their agent, but there wasn't a salary high enough to make up for what was taken.

She wanted more than just the walk from work and back every day. She wanted to wake up elsewhere some days, so that going out in the morning for the paper she'd tread on the cobblestone streets of a strange city; at the corner, she wouldn't know which way to turn, left or right, and it wouldn't matter, there'd be no one expecting her anywhere. Turning, she'd come upon the Pantheon or the Wailing

Wall, and the knowledge that, thousands of years before, human beings stood on the very stones that were now under her pedestrian
feet.

She couldn't begin writing down what she wanted. It would have
to be enough to think it. If holding a pencil in her hand helped her
think, that was enough. She wouldn't fill pages with her scribblings.
In the last years, her handwriting had gone from fat loops and wide
spaces between words and letters to a mature, paper-saving style.
She'd read *The Ciderhouse Rules*. And she liked her new script: long
l's and tall t's, which she'd consciously lengthened because greater
length was said to indicate height and character. She couldn't change
her height, a compact five-two, but she could write like a tall person.

She ought to go somewhere. She ought to call a courier service,
leave a note for Daniel, and take off. That was the way to do things,
last minute, without much thinking or planning. Just doing. She was
always wanting to go. In school, she'd wanted to just take off, freely
and alone, as if unmarried, as if there weren't classes to attend the
next day, books to read, papers to write, money to worry about. When
she'd finished school, she'd worried about finding work. And also she
was a married woman, a wife. Daniel would have a fit if she booked
a flight, wrote a note, and found herself up above the clouds, flying
freely, thinking of nothing and no one. She wouldn't be home to hear
his outrage. Was it Daniel who held her back all these years? Somehow marriage didn't go with traveling alone. You had to be single. If
she arrived in Jerusalem alone, her father would know more than
she wanted him to know. You're not happy, he'd say. I can see in your
face that you're not happy.

She stood up. Singlehood, a 1987 resolution? Is that what she
wanted?

But what about the house? She wanted this house, and with it came the need for togetherness. They'd bought the house together; they'd inhabit it together.

Resolutions or not you never knew what would happen. There was luck or fate or even God, if you believed. Every Rosh Hashana the inevitable prayer hummed in her head: Who will live and who will die; who by water and who by fire; who by disease and who by sword.

She stood still and heard from miles away her father's chanting. She chanted with him, her voice barely audible, and at the end, after the final word, attached an unmouthed prayer.

She didn't know what was best. She prayed for what was best.

October

A Thursday night was agreed upon and Daniel made reservations for four. When he and Deena arrived, Jill and Ann were already dancing, Jill in a short black leather skirt.

First a drink, Daniel said, and ordered a scotch for himself and a sloe gin fizz for Deena. Before his first sip, he put his hand up to cover his head for the blessing. He'd taken off his yarmulke for the night. Wearing one while drinking and dancing at a club, he decided at the last minute, was inappropriate. He left it in the glove compartment, then changed his mind and slipped it into his pocket.

Deena shrugged. She didn't think it mattered whether or not he wore it. She didn't care.

They looked at each other above the rims of their glasses, and sipped. This was odd. They hadn't been out for drinks in years, not since their Saturday-night dates. And they'd never danced.

Liquor is quicker, Daniel said and finished the last of his scotch.

I'll get up if you get up, Deena challenged.

They stood. The floor vibrated. You could feel the music and dancing in your feet. The rhythm was inciting. It made you want to move.

Jill and Ann looked good on the dance floor, smooth.

Deena hesitated. Could her body move like that?

Daniel was determined. Let's go, he said.

They edged onto the dance floor, bumping into people. Daniel moved awkwardly. The length of his stride, which looked good when he walked, was too long for dancing. His feet seemed too large. He would have to take smaller steps; he would have to learn to shuffle.

Deena looked away and tried to feel the rhythm. She moved, stopped. Then Jill saw them, waved, and made her way over, hips rocking. She took Daniel's hands and led him to the center. Her excitement helped. Daniel seemed to forget himself. He danced. It didn't matter that his knees were a little too bent, or that his shoulders were too far back. He didn't know it.

Deena listened. She could feel the music through her shoes, the thumping bass. She swayed, shuffled. It wasn't so hard once you started. But you had to start. She made her way to the center. She needed a partner. That would help. She looked at the musicians, and the guitar player winked. She smiled and moved her feet, and it was all right. If she didn't think so much, if she forgot herself, if she let the music take over, she could do it. If she allowed the music into her neck and arms and legs, if she allowed the music into her stomach, she'd come alive. To feel herself alive, she needed thumping bass.

When she saw Jill and Daniel again, the music had slowed. Jill's arms circled Daniel's neck; Daniel's hands were on her waist. They moved together, a couple.

Then the music changed, and everyone was alone again. The floor rocked. Jill pulled her in, Ann joined them, and then the four of them were in a circle, dancing together but separately.

They stayed till 3 A.M. Then up the black stairs to the street and out into the night.

Deena inhaled the crisp October air, pure air for this month of high holidays, the month of repentance. Aspirin would help, but even without it she felt clear-headed. The music was a shofar calling her awake. It could do what praying and fasting were meant to. It reminded you that every day must be lived like a holy day, fully awake and aware. She looked at Daniel. Did he know this?

Jill and Ann took the first cab, Daniel and Deena the next one.

At the house, Daniel rushed to disable the alarm. An anonymous note had been left the last time the alarm had gone off. If it blared at three-thirty in the morning, people were sure to complain. Deena stood on tiptoe looking over Daniel's shoulder, made sure he remembered the code, then hurried up the stairs to the bathroom.

Daniel sat on the bed, unbuttoned his shirt, sniffed it. Smoke, he said. That's the problem with bars and clubs.

He took the shirt off, bunched it up, and threw it on the floor. Take everything off, he said. I'll take them down to the washer. They reek.

Deena undressed. Even her underwear smelled of smoke. Daniel, still in his jeans and socks, gathered everything up in his arms and went down to the basement, where they had a washer and dryer, a laundromat in their own home. She felt under her feet the vibrations of his descent down the slanting stairs from the second floor to the first, then around the corner to the narrow, steep stairs of the basement. She could follow without following. He was setting the washer to half load, pressing start, pouring in detergent, and closing the lid. In the morning, he'd load the dryer. After years of laundromats, he could wash his clothes at home. He could stand in front of the washer in his underwear and stocking feet, and decide while standing there to add what he was wearing. Naked, he could run up the stairs in the dark, the cold air on his bare skin letting him know that he is the owner of this house, and if he's running, it is only because of the cold.

She shivered. It was cold. It would be cold between the sheets. But on reeking skin and hair, a clean T-shirt? Daniel always slept naked. When he turned to her, first thing he removed all her clothes. After, she fell asleep, warm beside him, until he turned in his sleep, took the covers with him, and she would wake with the cold night on her skin.

She got into bed and tucked several inches of blanket beneath her as insurance against the cold. The sheets were crisp cold. If only Daniel would hurry. He was on the stairs now.

Brrrr, he said, and came into bed, and then closer beside her. This was good, her body against his warm body, nothing between them. She bent her knees and he put his knees into hers. They would fall asleep like that, spoons. She could feel him wanting her, but he didn't move to do more and she liked that. Not starting was the way to start. It brought her round without effort. She pressed in toward him, he came into her, and they moved together in the dark, cold night.

I can smell the smoke in our hair and skin, Daniel said.

We'll strip the sheets in the morning and wash another load, Deena said.

I had fun, he said. Did you?

Yes.

Did you see me dance? Daniel asked. I thought I was getting the hang of it by the end.

You looked good, Deena said. It's easier to dance when you don't think about it.

You were great, he said. Jill says you're a lively dancer. Your Hasidic blood, I told her. I was thinking we should take ballroom dancing. What do you think?

Mmm, Deena said. A good idea. We'll talk about it tomorrow. I'm falling asleep. Goodnight.

But she'd slept only minutes when something woke her. She pulled up the sheet and blanket and dropped back to her pillow. She'd forgotten something. She looked up in the dark at the white ceiling. The spider, how far had it gotten? That's what woke her. The spider's web over her eyes, nose, and mouth. Her throat was dry. She'd forgotten to fill a glass of water. The membranes of her mouth were dried out; she didn't have a mouth. But it would be easier to fall asleep if she didn't get up. She closed her eyes and slept.

At work the next morning, Deena sat at her desk, her fingers on the keys of her silent black Panasonic. She had copy to write, but her mind wasn't on it. She didn't give a damn about chicken. Last night she'd been alive; she had to find a way to live like that, fully alive every day. There were ten offices in a row, and in each one a human being sat, simmering, holding back, holding off living until after hours. People grew old like this, pushing days. But they had to earn a living. In the sweat of your face shall you eat bread. Adam's curse.

If only she were sweating. Along with sweat comes the knowledge that your body is alive; you feel your heart working, the muscles and bones in your body stretching and straining, your blood rushing. At her desk in her office she didn't sweat. There was only the numb hum of the air-conditioning. At the end of the day, she stood and stretched to feel her bones and muscles, cramped for lack of use. She'd worked but there'd been no sweat. The thought of the next eight hours was unbearable. She couldn't stand the white walls or the careful sound of modulated voices heard through them. It was unnatural. She wasn't made for this. This wasn't the way her family lived. Better to sit like her mother, swollen legs up on a stool, to sit like that peeling eggplant and mending socks, and rise now and then to stir and taste the soup. Better to spend the day the way her father and brothers did, in study and prayer, fervently, at high pitch. How did they sustain the urgency day in day out? There were stories of Hasidic ascetics who submerged their bodies in ice water and walked on hot coals with bare feet. Pain was what kept them alert and alive. She would run. She'd fight this half living with something. She left work early.

Walking to and from the train, seeing blue sky and trees, feeling her legs moving, she felt better. At home, she pulled off her work clothes. She hated these clothes, the skirt that shortened her stride, the jacket that allowed for only so much movement. She had extra energy; it wouldn't be restricted. She started running quickly, her body free and strong. She'd slept only five hours, but with full living she needed less sleep. With her body alive, she could do anything. She would change her days, she would give her days the promise of nights.

She ran through the park and the trees overhead shaded her, the breeze kept her dry. She was healthy and strong, not the sickly child her parents raised. She stretched the length of her stride, reached harder. She would make her legs grow longer; she would will growth. Already her shoulders were expanding; her neck was reaching higher. She came to the end of her run before she felt it. She wasn't tired. She was surprised to be at the end. Had she run those miles?

What are your resolutions? Deena asked Daniel before Yom Kippur night.

I don't make them and I don't break them, he said.

You don't even think about it?

He shook his head.

Not even in January? Deena asked.

I don't know why you bother, he said. You make resolutions every day of the year. Every day in your life is Yom Kippur. Why can't you just live? That's a good resolution.

Deena nodded, agreeing. The purpose of life is to live. That was the answer to her father's letter. She was always trying to make herself over. A life of self-correction. There wasn't much time for living when you were always starting again.

Sunday they painted the small bedroom white. Daniel used a roller on the ceiling and walls; Deena worked with a paint brush at the edges and corners. They spent most of the day painting and still the room was white, no change. They walked away disgusted.

At least it's clean, Daniel said.

Let's take out our bicycles, Deena said.

They rode to Forest Park, Daniel in the lead in traffic, Deena ahead in the woods. Today she wanted to ride slowly, to take in the trees, fat old trunks you couldn't circle with your arms.

Come on, Daniel said. I've had enough standing around. I want to move.

They raced. He had a headstart. Deena bent low over the handlebars. In this, her size was an advantage; she offered less resistance. The trees on both sides of the paved path formed a natural tunnel, and she centered herself on the path, the tops of the trees high above her. The wind fanned the thin hairs on her arms, her eyes watered. There was rustling, the leaves. Stirred by Daniel's tailwind, they caught in the spokes of her wheels, rode with her, and then dropped off. Hitchhikers.

Daniel was still ahead. She held her breath, thought light, her head and shoulders low, and rode past him. All she saw was the blur of his wheels, then she was ahead. She sat tall and her body cooled in the wind. In the old days, people did this on horses, she thought. In parks then you would have seen horses' legs rushing, four thin limber legs moving as if at once.

She could hear Daniel approaching behind her. He was strong, his legs were all lean muscle. She would let him overtake her. Today she was happy enough coasting. They were always competing. Growing up, one of six, she'd never felt the need. Married, she was always proving she could. She didn't know how it had started. Maybe it came with modern marriage, with couples better friends than lovers.

She remembered learning to ride. Ten-year-old Arye Werner, her brother's friend, held on to the seat of his blue Schwinn bicycle while she climbed on, fumbled, swayed, and found that if she pedaled hard enough she didn't waver, but miraculously stayed up and stayed straight. She pedaled so furiously Arye couldn't hold on. He let go and she kept moving until suddenly, feeling his absence, she looked behind her to confirm it, veered, wavered, and fell over. He ran to help her up, and before she could remind him of his promise to hold on, he said he'd never seen anyone learn so quickly. After that, she wanted his help only getting on. He ran alongside and they talked until, several visits later, Deena's brother said something about playing with girls and reclaimed his friend's attention. Deena continued to borrow the bicycle when Arye came to visit, but he only nodded when she asked; he didn't come out to be with her. Two summers later, when she was almost twelve and Arye's bar mitzvah was less than a year away, they saw each other only from afar.

Bicycles are for boys, her mother said. Boys wear pants, boys ride.

Fifteen years later she was on a Fuji, wearing black leggings, and following Daniel on his old British Raleigh, which by a curious intersection of human lives he had purchased from Deena's cousin Natan just before Natan and his family, the Engels, had moved back to Israel. It was possible that at the age of twelve she saw her future husband. Daniel didn't remember seeing her; he'd had eyes only for the bicycle, he said.

For years he went everywhere on his Raleigh. Then he purchased the Civic, and the bike remained in the basement until Deena asked for a bicycle for her twenty-fifth birthday. If they were going to ride together, he would refurbish his bike. He demanded Deena's assistance.

I wouldn't be doing this if not for your sudden interest in bicycles, he said.

I'm interested in riding, not bicycles, Deena said.

But everything Daniel did he had to do to perfection. His bicycle had to be overhauled, the various parts brought up to date. He installed new gears, new brake pads, a new chain, and wondered whether a new bicycle would have been the wiser choice.

Deena wasn't attentive on the job. In one hand she held a magazine, in the other, limp at her side, a metric wrench. When Daniel asked for the screwdriver he got the metric wrench. For the metric wrench, she handed him the screwdriver. It happened often enough to develop into a joke.

Scalpel, he'd say.

Scalpel, she'd answer and hold out a hammer. In college, they'd watched *M*A*S*H* together.

It was good to be on wheels. They followed paths, doubled back, turned and came upon a winding road they didn't know. They took it and were surprised to find what looked like a country road in the city. They rode uphill, then down, and suddenly came upon signs for the Interboro.

We'd better turn around, Daniel said.

But they continued until they saw the traffic and breathed the dust and fumes of thousands of cars a minute. This was still New York City. Watching the cars going east and west, Deena remembered the Williamsburg apartment on Rodney, where the Brooklyn-Queens Expressway ran below street level. Whichever window you looked out, at whatever hour or day, cars sped by at sixty miles an hour. In America, her mother said, there is no day of rest. Even on vacation, people constantly come and go.

The return trip was faster. They pedaled hard. The breeze picked up and the sun was setting. Coming out of the park, they weren't yet ready to stop. They went up one block, down the next. They saw a sign for a yard sale and rode over to 101st. Under a table, Deena found an old watering can for three dollars. Daniel put it under his arm and rode home one-handed, something Deena still couldn't do. She followed, worrying that Daniel would drop the can, or, worse, crash into a car or tree.

Monday morning she was back at work, at her desk, hating the four walls. Walking into the lobby of the black glass building, waiting for the elevator, riding it up to the twenty-second floor, she felt a certain dread. She knew this dread, a familiar heaviness. It weighed on her eyelids and on the skin between her brows. It settled at the base of her neck. She would spend the next eight hours sealed in this black tower, a prisoner with other prisoners, all of them trying to work, a community of workers. She worked better at the kitchen table at home. Here, through the walls of her small office, she could feel the anxiety festering in the office next door. It impregnated the thin Sheetrock and entered on her side, alive and anxious and all too willing to breed.

On the surface everyone was calm, friendly, supportive. You poked your head into your neighbor's office to say hello. If encouraged, you stepped in and sat, for only a few minutes, you said, and stayed a quarter of an hour. But the air was damaging somehow, and when you stood to go, with a sigh of back-to-work, you felt incapable of doing work and continued to hope for help, for the beginning of an idea, and if not that, then just to be detained, to be saved from the blankness of your office, from the white sheet of paper to be filled. You walked back to your desk, in worse shape, guilty for the time wasted, for having tried to escape what only you could and should do:

your job. On your desk was the thin carbon sheet, the yellow work order. When it arrived, you were relieved. Another assignment meant you were still needed in this business, and would therefore manage to keep your job awhile. But when you read the sentence or two that described what was wanted, the work requested turned out to be less than what you'd hoped for of your next project. You looked at the bottom of the page and found yesterday's date. This job was overdue. At the top of the sheet, the work order was predated by a week. It was past due even before it arrived on your desk.

There is only one remedy for the anxiety of work: to do the work. The longer you wait, the worse it gets.

She'd started the day with the best intentions. She left home half an hour early, took the train, stopped at the deli for coffee and a roll, walked through the revolving door of the lobby, hoping not to meet anyone. She was early. The elevator lurched upward and continued rising forever; it seemed to take her past her floor, past the roof of the building, up, up, into the open sky, to freedom. But no, it stopped, and the doors slid open with a hot puff. She stiffened her shoulders, swiftly crossed the lobby, and mouthed a good morning to the temp at reception. She had the keys to her office in her hand, ready. She turned down the hall, passed two open doors, and without looking left or right, unlocked her door, and she was in her office. She left the door open enough to reveal that she was in and closed enough to indicate interruption unwelcome. There was one good thing still ahead this morning: coffee. After the forty-five-minute ride to the office, it would go down like a first cup. She would sip, eat her roll, and thumb through *The New York Times,* the pleasures of a morning at her desk. Her high school history teacher once warned against eating and reading simultaneously, indulging in two pleasures at once. But why is it sinful to enjoy more than one thing? They didn't detract from each other.

She finished her coffee and wanted another half cup to accompany her first attempt at sentences.

In the kitchen people were waiting for the pot to fill. They grumbled and talked. Deena waited with them. She liked this, the shared grumbling.

What would you be doing if you weren't doing this?—the question people in advertising ask themselves at least once a day.

Running and sweating, Deena said.

Paul Herz, the director, looked at her. Wouldn't you do something academic like teach? he said. Something closer to what a scholar does, to what your brothers do?

No, Deena said. The last thing I want to do is teach. I got this job to avoid teaching, which, my father claims, is the worthiest profession in the world. I want to do something unworthy.

She looked at Paul, who every day looked more like a professor. He no longer wore the navy and gray suits of an ad man. Ever since he'd been invited to do public-service work for the upcoming bicentennial celebration of the Constitution, he came to work wearing brown. Today he was dressed in tweeds with suede patches at the elbows. For the D.C. meeting with Ted Kennedy, he had to be asked to change, and a Brooks Brothers suit was delivered via messenger to his office.

This is what I've been training for all my life, Paul said. I've been writing ad copy for twenty-five years. I know how to simplify complicated concepts.

He had an idea that he could make the Constitution more accessible to the public: he would rewrite the United States Constitution.

The argument that the ambiguities and complications in the document were there for good reasons didn't stop him. He came back from the library and bookstore with stacks of books, and for hours at a time the door to his office remained closed. Inside Paul read and took notes.

Because I like and respect you, he said, I am offering you a piece of the pie. Her assignment, if she wanted it, was to write short biographies of the founding fathers, which would be printed on bookmarks and distributed to schoolchildren all over the country. He presented her with her own copy of *Miracle at Philadelphia*.

She was halfway through the book, which was quite interesting, but still she wasn't enthusiastic about the project. In fact, she wanted nothing to do with it, not because the notion of rewriting the Constitution was completely off the mark; not even because of Paul's misguided attempt to use his adman's skills to accomplish meaningful work. She just didn't want to spend days and weeks sitting in his airless office, inhaling his smell, and discussing his dream come true. She didn't want to see him with his hair on end, his eyes far away. She was afraid of this man who was so desperate for work that had meaning.

And it was no advantage to be known as his protégée. There was talk of his uselessness as creative director and his strange obsession with the project. At the Kennedy meeting, university professors with doctorates in American history and law were horrified by the idea that the language of the Constitution be simplified. There was practically a scuffle over it, the account executive reported. Somehow all this had escaped Paul; he continued working behind his closed door.

Deena continued requesting regular assignments. She was a copywriter, that was her title. She would do her job. She would live without worrying about how she was living. Every day you made choices without the certainty that this was what you wanted, without

even the feeling that they were choices. And this was how you became, in an incidental and incremental series of moves.

And mostly work was good; she liked what she did, and the people with whom she did it. They laughed and complained, but were
back at their desks the next morning. It was up to her to do more with
her days. One good line and the day would be worthwhile.

She would get into the right mood for work. There was a certain
rhythm and tone you had to take doing this kind of writing. The sentences had to remain short and the jokes easy and light. There was
no room for regret and resignation in ad copy. Reality didn't draw
buyers, optimism did. Selling required only your upbeat side. Anything else was yours to deal with in unhappy privacy. This was perhaps why you were given more than most employees had at work. You
had an office with a window and door. You could close your door and
open your window and eye the sidewalk twenty-two floors below.
Every day you could lean out the window and contemplate the distance, but you couldn't put that in your copy. Consumers bought
your product as a way to escape their own gravity.

It was easier to sustain the necessary levity in the morning. Afternoons were impossible. Maybe it was the poor air circulation. The
closed-air systems in office buildings pumped out the same stale air
all day long. There were two hours when all she wanted was sleep. Instead she drank another cup of coffee. Today she would postpone
lunch until one-thirty and extend the morning. She had the next
three hours to work. She typed.

Volvo. Revolve. The sun revolves around the earth. The Volvo 240
as a sun? But a Volvo doesn't revolve. It drives, it's driven by a driver
who appreciates safety over revolutionary technology. But this issue
of staidness, even staid safety, wasn't what the client wanted to ad-

vertise, because the product they sold was in fact an unrevolutionary automobile. One doesn't acknowledge one's faults in one's own advertising. For what was the car named? She'd have to ask. With an idea in her head she wouldn't be spending her day revolving around the word. She'd be writing. She could start the way every piece of copy started: with the name. The Volvo 240. You began by naming the product and circled back to naming it again. The client liked seeing the name repeated. Repetition brought product recognition. The other words hardly mattered. But the name must have meant something at one time. God made the firmament and then he called it heaven. Adam named the animals after they'd become what they were. And when in the thirteenth century surnames became necessary, people were named for what they did, not for what they would become. Miller, the man who milled wheat and corn. The Rosenbergs, the family who tended hills of roses. The Shoemachers made shoes. If the sons followed in the steps of their fathers, they fulfilled a predetermined role.

She reached the bottom of the page, pulled it out of her typewriter, crushed it, and tossed it at the garbage pail under her desk. The crumpled sheet fell on the silent carpet and unfolded, an attempt to continue life despite Deena's judgment. There was after all something worthwhile on the page. It revealed the bend of her mind. She followed ideas that were of interest only to her; she didn't focus on the task at hand, on the given problem. She diverged so far, coming back took a while. Sometimes her meandering led to unique solutions, which were labeled different, and which gave her certain advantages. In a world where new ideas are what matter, even impossible ideas, a reputation for the offbeat is good. You could count on Deena for an unusual solution, but you couldn't expect her to make deadlines.

Sitting at her desk, trying to produce copy, she was aware only of the fact that if she didn't come up with something she couldn't call herself a copywriter. You had to prove yourself every day. Yesterday's decent sentence didn't serve today. When your work finally made it into print, by the time it was acknowledged, it had nothing to do with how good you were just then. What you'd written a week ago didn't reflect your current ability to write. You had to sit at your desk and start all over. Every day was a first day.

She put a new sheet into the typewriter. There was something in the idea of circles: Volvos were known for tight driving circles. They had the ability to complete a 360-degree turn with a radius the length of the vehicle. That was something. It made for tight maneuvering and parking.

Karen's head appeared at the door. Lunch? she asked.

If it's late and cheap, Deena said.

That's what I was thinking. How about soup and salad? She pulled up the sleeve of her jacket to look at her watch. Is after one o'clock all right?

Deena nodded.

I have some running around to do, Karen said. I have to go to the bullpen, then to Ron in traffic. I'll be back.

She smiled, adjusted her skirt, and went. She was tiny, and today she wore very high heels. She'd walk long corridors, to the elevator and back, up and down, in those heels. But she looked good. Her skirt was short and her legs long. She was thirty-five and still single; she wanted to attract attention. She wanted to have a baby before she turned forty.

Deena sighed. Everyone wanted something. She kneaded her eraser and sniffed it. From every city she visited, she brought home a pencil, an eraser, or a plain grade-school notebook. She had a collection of pencils and notebooks, but when she was really writing, she typed. It had taken months to get comfortable writing directly on the keyboard, but it was important, it was how admen and journalists work, Paul said. And she'd come to like the typewriter. Working, she could look away and keep her fingers going. She could turn her head toward the window and see the blue sky, and the cloud that floated across the expanse of blue. The light on the brick of the building across the way would turn golden and glow, and suddenly the shadow of a bird would dart across the brick, and she would see and not see all this because in her head the words of the next sentence would be forming.

She turned back to the waiting page. No matter how many pages she filled and threw away, the sight of a fresh sheet in the typewriter still presented possibility. On this page, she might prove herself again. On this page, she might produce something great.

After lunch Deena stopped into an art-supply store and purchased a tube of pink paint. She'd start the wash that evening. Daniel would be working late, and according to the book, it was an easy, quick job, something she could do on her own. She'd surprise him.

At home she skipped running, changed into work clothes, and mixed a dab of pink into one cup of white paint and two cups of water. Too pale. She added more pink. The mix was watery. She checked the directions. It did say two cups of water. She poured the mix into a fresh paint tray liner, wet the roller, and began. Pink drops splashed everywhere. She stopped stricken. Something was wrong. Long drips were forming on the wall and running down to the floor.

She grabbed a rag and mopped up the dripping paint. She tried a paintbrush. That was better and now the work went quickly. The room turned pink around her. She stood in the last section of white. She was cornered, but pleasantly, pinkly cornered. She would have to do another coat, but already you could see how the room would look. She had something to show tonight. She soaked and cleaned the brushes and liner in the bathroom sink, then she stood in the doorway looking in. She stepped farther back and smiled. The pink and olive together were an invitation, the colors beckoned. She wanted to hug herself.

Daniel arrived home with an expensive Walkman and two packs of blank cassettes for recording. He spent hours deciding what groups would combine well, what to record on sides a and b. He was excited and Deena sat with him, helping him choose. She offered suggestions: The Who goes with The Stones. The Dead with Bob Dylan. And with Roy Orbison? Daniel asked.

Paul McCartney, Deena suggested.

Daniel said no, then maybe.

They talked about the music. They didn't mention the moratorium on spending. Or the fact that a year ago he'd ridiculed Walkmans as just another fad, and called her frivolous because she'd wanted one for running.

He looked at her. So I've changed, he said.

Deena nodded. She wouldn't criticize; she didn't want to stop him. She wouldn't mention money when spending it brought pleasure. She liked seeing Daniel excited. She didn't mind him breaking his own rules. Now she could show him the white shirt she'd bought; she'd worn it to work, but he hadn't yet seen it.

I have something to show you too, she said.

Oh no, Daniel said. What did you buy this time?

It's not that, she said.

She led the way to the pink bedroom and inhaled the smell of fresh paint.

It looks like a girl's room, Daniel said. But it's not half as bad as I expected.

The next day, he came home with a Walkman for Deena and offered to make copies of his tapes, but she didn't want to listen to more of his music. She wanted to hear the new female vocalists, the singers Jill was excited about: Suzanne Vega, Natalie Merchant, Edie Brickell.

I'll borrow Jill's tapes and make copies, he said.

A continuing education flyer came in the mail, and ballroom dancing was on the list. Daniel signed them up for Thursday-evening classes.

We'll practice on Friday nights, he said. With no furniture to speak of, we have plenty of floor space.

At the first session, trying to hold each other, they were dissatisfied.

Lead with your arms, the instructor advised. She reached for Deena to demonstrate.

Back in Daniel's arms, Deena knew better. Hold me like you mean it, she said.

Let me concentrate, Daniel said. And stop pushing me.

They dropped their hands and the instructor came to see what was the matter.

Deena complained that Daniel wasn't supporting her where he

should, and Daniel said Deena was trying to lead. The instructor danced with Daniel to show him.

At the end of their first session, they looked forward to the next one. They'd learned the basic steps to the merengue, the cha-cha, and the tango, and they couldn't wait to know more. It was tiring practicing the basic steps over and over. Turns and twists, that would feel like dancing.

When they practiced in the living room the next night, they couldn't remember which steps belonged to which dance.

At their second session, Deena became irritated again. Daniel was always a second behind; he waited to hear the music instead of moving with it.

Listen to the music, Deena said. You're way behind.

You have to learn to walk before you run, Daniel said. You keep pushing me off balance.

That's because you're off rhythm. And we're crawling, not walking.

They tried again. Again Daniel was behind, again Deena pushed. They threw their hands down and walked off the dance floor.

Deena looked at the other couples. You could see in their faces the stupidity of concentration and the irritation. You could see in their eyes that they were counting, slow, slow, quick, quick, slow. Then slow, quick, quick. And this was called dancing. She saw the hand of an older man clutch the flesh on his partner's back in an effort to retain control, turned back to Daniel, and they laughed. This was just for fun; they were learning to dance. It shouldn't matter so much.

But it did matter, and by the third week Deena was disgusted with Daniel. He seemed to have forgotten every step. He'd gotten worse, not better.

Daniel blamed her. She wasn't letting him concentrate.

They didn't talk to each other all the way home. Deena wondered about the unmarried couples. Would these classes show them what was missing? Ballroom dancing as a test for marriage potential? If you could dance together, you could live together. If she had tried dancing with Daniel, perhaps they wouldn't have married. Everyone exercised some signs and tests. Her mother, whose marriage had been arranged the way her mother's and grandmother's marriages had been, had her own reasons. She'd had several choices, she could say yes or no, this or that one, and she chose the dark orphan boy who'd come from Poland as a stowaway.

He's not from here and he'll take you from here, her father said. He'll drag you from the holy land and you'll die in a strange country.

Despite the warnings, Gita said yes to the man with black hair and blue eyes. Through years of errands, coming and going on the cobblestone streets to and from the boys' school where her brothers waited for their lunches (it was for such errands that she was withdrawn from school before the fifth grade), she'd heard as she passed the whistling of the local boys, dark-skinned, black-haired boys, and she'd wanted to stop, to answer their call. They muttered under their breath, and although she couldn't make out what it was they were saying, there was promise in their call, a promise of something different, something new, life. But already there were rumors, and she was kept in the house for a week. Still, a desire for a foreigner had been aroused in this girl in braids and long dark dresses with maybe a round white collar, and she insisted that it was the dark Polish boy she wanted, not the pale, red-headed Yerushalmi, so-and-so's brother, an all-too-well-known entity whom her father favored. It was the Polish boy's very foreignness that was the attraction. He would give her a different life. She'd had enough of the everyday: mopping floors in the morning, preparing breakfasts and dinners, cleaning up after dinner.

Besides, she argued, much was said for the boy: he studied hard, was of the top students in his class, and he didn't have a mother. He was an orphan; he needed a wife.

And her father's warning had not materialized, not fully. It was the red-haired Yerushalmi who ended up marrying an American girl and moving away. The Polish boy who'd risked everything to come to the holy land stayed. True, they'd lived in America for a few years, but from the outset it was a temporary move, strictly for the sake of Torah; he was collaborating with another scholar on a book of law. But even this temporary move had cost him. One daughter remained in America.

November

The Binets came to see the house. They arrived all together, in two cars, one following the other south on I-95 all the way from Stamford, Connecticut, over the Whitestone Bridge and Expressway to the Interboro, and left on Myrtle. Mr. and Mrs. B. emerged from one car; Celia and Ben, who didn't want to listen to opera, from the other. They followed Daniel and Deena from room to room and admired the wide windows and doors in the living room, the leaded glass. Upstairs they smiled at the pink wash.

This is so you, Celia said. I don't know anyone else who would paint a room this color.

Does that mean you like it or hate it? Deena asked.

Celia shrugged. I'm not sure yet, she said. She was just finishing high school and it was important not to stand out too much. If no one was wearing corduroy that year, she too didn't wear corduroy.

It's interesting, Mrs. B. said.

Interesting. A polite evasion. So different from her own mother, who said too much too often and later regretted. In the beginning, Deena had liked Mrs. Binet's restraint. She was so civilized. Now, she missed her mother's rudeness, the no-holding-back. You always knew where you stood.

I tried to tell her, Daniel said.

It's gutsy, Mr. B. said. It just takes getting used to.

Gutsy, Ben said and laughed.

Dad, Daniel said. I want to show you the basement.

Wait for me, Deena said.

She wanted to be there to hear what Mr. B. had to say about the white powder on the basement walls, the good along with the bad. Daniel would repeat only the worst. He fastened onto bad news like it was some kind of insurance.

I leave basements to the men, Mrs. B. said. I haven't been in ours since my sciatica.

Deena shrugged and followed the men down the steep stairs.

Mr. B. ran his hand along the walls.

Every old foundation has seepage, Mr. B. said. The tar breaks down over the years. The only solution is to dig all around the outer walls and reapply it. It's a huge job.

In his head, Daniel was calculating how much it would cost to hire people to do such a job. Seepage undermined the value of the house. It wasn't after all a great deal. He'd known all along that there was something wrong. Great buys just didn't happen to him.

Deena looked at his tight lips, the worry between his eyes. She could practically see what was going through his head. She could say it all for him; she could preempt his saying it and not have to hear it so gratingly from him. She couldn't stand his worrying. Why was it that she had to wind up with a worrier? If only he'd turned out more like his father, a man who enjoyed his meals, music, woodworking, and his books on philosophy.

They sat down to lunch: bagels, cream cheese and lox, spinach pie just out of the oven, Golden's blintzes, and salad.

Maybe with this house you'll start looking more like a married couple, Celia said.

We've been married for seven years and we still don't look it? Deena asked.

Celia shook her head. Married people look softer somehow. Maybe because they're not so skinny.

You mean they get fat, Daniel said. With all the cooking Deena does, there's no danger of that.

They laughed.

Daniel has always eaten well and remained thin, Mrs. B. said. Why should he change?

Daniel hardened his stomach and slapped it. Tight as a drum, he said.

He liked being talked about. And with everyone's attention on him, he came back to the subject of high closing costs, insurance, and taxes.

Everything's higher, Mr. B. said. Even banking fees have gone up. You know that.

Speaking of banks, Mrs. B. said, there was a story in the *Stamford Journal* I wanted to tell you about. Who was the writer? His name is on the tip of my tongue.

She paused, thinking.

The story, Ma, Ben said.

Where was I? she said. Oh yes. Union Savings has been trying to attract new accounts, and as a promotion they hired a clown to entertain neighborhood kids. The journal did a feature piece on it, I can't remember the writer's name.

Who cares? Daniel said. Just another local hack writing for a local paper.

Let your mother tell her story, Mr. B. said. He looked at his wife magnanimously. Tell your story, Mom.

He said the word the way he always said it, lips closed on the first m, opened for the o, closed again, and then, still in the pit of the pattern, open again. Mom-o.

Mrs. B. continued. On the cover that day was a photograph of the kids watching the show, and there were Hasidic kids in the group.

Deena looked at her. There was a point to this story.

What struck me, Mrs. B. said, was how stupid they looked with their mouths open. It must have been the first time they'd seen anything like that, a clown doing clown tricks. They're so sheltered all their lives they remain ignorant.

Hasidic ignorance and stupidity. It was what secular German Jews said before World War Two; now American Jews were saying it: Ignorant Hasidim. They don't read newspapers, they don't acquire a secular education, they speak English like foreigners, and their long black caftans, black hats, beards, and *peyes* attract too much attention on the street. In the twentieth century, they continue to look like their forefathers in the Carpathian Hills. They should go back to the mountains where they're not heard and seen.

Deena gathered up plates and went into the kitchen.

. . .

After lunch Daniel suggested a short tour of the neighborhood, then dessert and coffee. His mother declined. It's chilly out, she said.

Celia also stayed in, two genteel stay-at-home women.

Oh good. It will be a man's walk, Ben said. There will be no complaints about the cold and the dark.

I'm coming, Deena said, and put on a jacket.

Oh, the little woman is coming after all, Ben said. Are you sure you can keep up?

She runs six miles, Daniel said. She can outrun you any day, Ben.

Daniel and Deena conferred, then led the way up 112th, past the white pillared house rumored to have belonged to the John Adamses at one time. Around the corner was the old red-maple tree, its roots pushing up against the slate blocks, the sidewalk at different levels, a crazy stepping up, down, and up again. Deena pointed out the Victorian with all the turrets. Daniel led the way to Jahn's Ice Cream Parlor and then back on Myrtle to the house. They walked briskly. It was cold, winter was on its way, but this year she didn't dread the cold. She would come to know the house in every season. Besides, a fireplace was best in the cold.

Inside Mrs. B. sat with a blanket around her shoulders.

Deena suggested lighting the fire.

We're not staying much longer, Mrs. B. said. I don't know whether it's worthwhile lighting it.

Something in the statement of worth bothered Deena.

Daniel and I will enjoy it all evening, she said, and went to put on water for coffee.

She was irritated. Mrs. B. always irritated her. There was nothing carefree about her. When she did speak, it was to say what was proper. Deena missed her mother, who would thank her less, criticize directly, and still be more welcome. Waiting for the water to boil, she saw the kitchen the way her mother would see it. First thing she'd note the lack of two sinks, the missing separation of dairy and meat, indicating that this was not a perfectly kosher home. She'd eye with suspicion the two Rubbermaid basins Daniel used in place of separate sinks. In the pantry, she'd see the makings of a Passover kitchen. She'd wander through to the dining room, which was a room she understood; every room in Jerusalem homes had a table. The living room would seem strangely unnecessary. It was long and thin, and in the middle a gaping hole to the outside. Who would risk lighting an open fire in a house? She would advise Deena to nail a board over the black hole and paint it white to match the walls in the room. It would remain an eyesore but a less noticeable one.

At the foot of the stairs, she'd pause, her hand on the banister, one toe on the first step, the weight of her body still below. So many stairs to go up and down, a good way to tire yourself out before half the day is over. You don't yet know what it is to be pregnant, she'd say. Stairs in the later months are difficult enough; after the birth, they're worse. You will not want a newborn so far from the kitchen, up so many stairs. You wouldn't hear the child crying, or choking if suddenly it stopped breathing. All sorts of things can happen. Croup, crib death, God forbid. This isn't a house for children. This is an American house built for a couple with a dog. Maybe one child, a little girl, the apple of her father's eye. Is that all you want to leave behind?

At the top of the stairs, the water closet. Pink? Why not clean white? Color in a closet feels dirty.

Her mother's rant. Did she really want to hear it?

What about Thanksgiving? Deena heard Mrs. B. ask, and delayed in the kitchen. She'd let Daniel answer. They'd agreed that he would be the one to call and say they weren't coming.

Uh oh, Ben said and laughed. Although older than Daniel, he still lived in the attic bedroom they used to share, and life so far had been no great burden. With no rent to pay or food to buy, he kept what money he had in gold and silver futures and continued to laugh easily.

Daniel allowed some silent moments. He knew how to use timing to his advantage. We're planning our first big dinner here, he said.

That sounds like fun, Mr. B. said helpfully. This is a good house for entertaining. Who's coming?

Friends whose parents live too far away, really the only guests you can get on Thanksgiving. A friend of Deena's with her boyfriend or soon-to-be fiancé, who knows which. And someone from my office with her roommate.

Old Ma is furious, Ben said. Just look at her face.

Of course I'm upset. I like having the family together on Thanksgiving. But I can understand wanting to show the house. It is a lovely home.

There was chagrin in her voice. And resentment, Deena thought. At the age of twenty-nine, her son was earning more than his father had ever earned. He was working in an office, dressing well every morning, experiencing life in the world of business. And his mother and father were growing older. Her once slim waist, of which she'd been so proud, had thickened. Her slender wrists and ankles were no longer what they'd once been. And her husband, a schoolteacher, was counting the years to retirement. He was a good man, satisfied with what life had given him. He'd fallen in love, that was something; it didn't happen to all men. And she had become the mother of his children. She sat at the table every morning, experiencing with him his first cup of coffee even though she didn't drink it. She perked and poured it and watched him warm his hands on the mug. He was a gentle man, a loving husband, and a solid father. He'd always earned a living, but never more than was necessary; they lived frugally, watching pennies in order to set aside for a night of dinner and the opera. Her son, however, her slim, tall, handsome son, was making his way in the world, earning and achieving, and although she had given birth to him, raised and educated him, the rewards went to another woman, his wife, not his mother. Which was as it should be; still she couldn't help resenting.

Pouring Mrs. B.'s coffee, Deena questioned the accuracy of her attempt at omniscience. And was Mr. B. still in love? she wondered.

They bought a turkey. Daniel poked, prodded, and finally picked a frozen twelve-pounder.

For three days, with the turkey thawing in the refrigerator, they talked about how to cook it. Daniel wanted to do it his mother's way, in a brown paper bag.

You can't baste it that way and it is never crisp enough, Deena said.

That's the whole idea. With a bag you don't need basting. It stews in its juices, and the oven doesn't get dirty.

We don't have to worry about the oven; it's self-cleaning. What cook worries about keeping the pot clean? Anyway, your mother's turkey is always dry.

I'll tell her you said so, Daniel said. He sulked. In the end he agreed to let Deena do it her way as long as he had nothing to do with it. But Thanksgiving morning, when she was mixing hot paprika, salt, pepper, and oil, he protested.

Hungarian paprika on a turkey?

Paprika gives good flavor and color, Deena said. What do you have against paprika?

What do you know about turkey? Daniel said. You're not American. Your mother never made a turkey in her life.

Wait till you taste it. Why don't you take care of the cranberry sauce?

When the turkey was in the oven they walked to Metropolitan Avenue for fresh bread and flowers. It was cold and clear out, and the wind cut through their sweaters. The sky was pure blue, it was quiet, and from kitchens on every block, the smell of roasting meat.

They bought two baguettes. And instead of flowers—there wasn't anything worthwhile left—a bag of shiny red apples.

At home, Daniel opened the oven door.

Leave my turkey alone, Deena said.

I'm just checking. With people coming, I want to make sure it's cooking.

It's cooking, all right. You can baste it if you want to. I'll take the pies out of the freezer. Then we can set the table.

She put out a white tablecloth and deep red napkins. Daniel took plates and flatware out of the cabinets, and they worked together, spreading the cloth, putting out plates, spoons, and knives.

You want to run with me? Deena asked.

Daniel shook his head. No. It's too cold.

She ran down the front walk and up Myrtle, on a road plastered with damp leaves. Running on them, she didn't hear the firm thud of her sneakers echoing. Instead: the swishing and slipping of moist, still alive leaves. She'd pick some on her way back. She'd find some use for them.

On the track, she put on her headphones. Lone Justice rocked in her ears, and she picked up speed, entered the second ring, and made her way in toward the center, one ring at a time. You ran in the innermost ring only if you were sprinting. A month ago, on a Saturday, a runner had challenged her to a race and she'd accepted. He was stocky and she thought she could keep up, which she did until the end, when thinking about her legs in rhythm, she fumbled. She'd been thinking; during a race, the mind should be empty. But it was the first time she'd sprinted and she was conscious of her legs and arms pumping like machines. It was exhilarating going so fast, so automatically, her body something separate, moving without her.

She suggested another lap and the man agreed. This time she kept her mind off running. She breathed and ran and came in first. Life unhindered by mind. Mindless life.

She lost the third round; her legs felt sore. That's unusual, she said. I run all the time.

Sprinting uses a different set of muscles, the man said. You put up a good fight, though, he said and smiled, easily sympathetic since he'd won. Later, she wondered whether he'd let her win the second lap.

She began sprinting two laps of every run. If she met him again, she'd be prepared. But she hadn't seen him again so far. He had the paunch, she remembered, of a weekend-only runner, which made losing to him worse.

The music helped, and she sprinted hard and fast in the innermost ring, then slowed down on her way out. It was difficult keeping count when you ran circles. Each lap was a quarter mile; to run three miles she had to do twelve laps. Moving one ring inward on every lap helped her. If she forgot to switch, she forfeited the count of that lap and had to run another. To and from the track was one mile. Saturdays, with plenty of time on her hands, she ran home the long way through the park, a six-mile run.

Today she ran on limited time, purely for exercise before the huge meal. Jill was probably at the gym right now. She and Ann were coming. Karen was bringing Greg, to whom she was either already engaged or planning to get engaged. Altogether they'd be six, which was exactly the number of chairs they had in the house.

Daniel was in the shower when Deena came in. She washed the spinach leaves and put them out to dry. Then she washed the leaves she'd picked up on her way back.

He came down wearing jeans and a new flannel shirt, cuffs unbuttoned and flapping as usual.

Is this all right? he asked.

Perfect, Deena said, spreading leaves on a towel to dry. It takes forever to dry lettuce like this, she said. We need a spinner.

Get one, Daniel said. Tomorrow at lunch, go and buy a spinner.

He came up and kissed her on the neck. She inhaled his after-shave and liked it. And she liked him like this, generous and confident.

He took over at the counter—he was in charge of making the gravy—and Deena went to shower and dress. She would be the kind of hostess who looks good.

.   .   .

Karen and Greg arrived early. They came in Karen's old Toyota and brought a tall red amaryllis, perfect for Thanksgiving. If you have friends with taste, you get good gifts.

As planned, Jill and Ann telephoned from the station, and Daniel went to pick them up.

Deena showed the house, which she thought was at its best that day. In the living room the fire burned, and the table in the dining room was set.

Greg and Karen oohed and aahed.

So much leaded glass, Greg said. You know how valuable that is?

I know that replacing the broken panes will cost us, Deena said.

In the pantry, Karen opened a glass cabinet door. These are wonderful, she said. And so useful right near the dining room.

Deena led the way into the kitchen.

What a beautiful deep blue, Karen said. You told me it had been redone and that you minded, but this was done well.

I'll bet it's fun cooking here, Greg said.

Upstairs Karen loved the pink wash. It's such a happy room, she said.

She would love it, Greg said. Pink is her favorite color. But I like the green because it provides dignity. It balances the pink.

Seeing the bubblegum-pink tub she'd heard about, Karen laughed. And she admired the brass showerhead. It looks like a giant sunflower, she said.

Deena hesitated before opening the room she used as a dressing room. All her shoes were lined up against the walls.

The Imelda Marcos room, she announced.

Karen laughed. You do have a lot of shoes, she said, but you never wear them.

Deena lifted one edge of the carpet and showed Greg the traces of the original proportions. We're planning to restore this room, she explained. We'll get rid of the walk-ins, and expose the window that's buried behind the shelves.

I want a house too, Greg said.

Greg doesn't miss a single episode of *This Old House,* Karen said. He drools when he's watching.

Deena laughed. She knew the feeling, seeing a friend's house, wanting one, but it all seems so far away, so impossible. Before they could purchase a house, Greg needed a better job, Karen wanted a raise, and they were thinking about getting married. But the want was already there, the want before the possibility.

She listened to them talk. They sounded like brother and sister. They'd met living across the hall from one another, become friends, then lovers. From the beginning, there'd been plenty of comfort and too little excitement. Maybe the two never went together. Greg's first proposal was declined, after which he moved downtown, and Karen spent the next months trying for some of the single men at the agency. There were some sparks at first, but nothing developed. Four months later, she announced that she and Greg were getting engaged. They'd started designing the engagement ring of her dreams, a cabochon emerald set in gold.

They heard the car pull into the driveway. Greg perked up. The Miss Americas are here, he said.

Karen and Deena laughed.

I told him, Karen said.

The Miss America hopeful, Deena said. Only one of them is try-ing and she's not that incredible. Daniel thinks she has the right look, middle America.

Tonight I'll be the judge, Greg said. I'll give the thumbs-up or -down.

Downstairs, Daniel was taking coats, and Jill and Ann were warming themselves in front of the fire. Deena served cups of hot cider. Daniel offered bourbon.

This hits the spot, Greg said. Spiked cider and a blazing fire.

It is perfect weather for it, Daniel agreed.

Great for running too, Jill said. She turned to Deena. Did you have time today? she asked.

Deena nodded. For a quick one. I've been running with music and it's fun. Depending on the piece, you run either faster or slower.

Jill nodded. You could put together a tape of pieces designed to start you off slowly and speed up. Running tapes. I'll try it. If it works I'll make you a copy.

You did all this cooking and you had time to run too, Karen said. It took me hours just to get out of bed this morning.

I had some help, Deena said, and nodded toward Daniel.

In the kitchen the turkey was cooling on the counter, and the pies and stuffing were warm in the oven. The gravy was on the stove and the salad was ready for tossing. The bread would be heated at the last minute. She went to check on things, read the menu to make sure nothing had been forgotten. It was time to get people seated. She tossed the salad and went back into the living room.

Jill was telling a story about work, and laughing too hard to finish.

Daniel took over. Deena looked at the others. Ann and Karen were focusing on Jill and Daniel, but Greg, whose arm circled Karen's shoulder, was looking at everything, trying to take in more than was readily apparent. There was a nervousness in his looking. He went from the fireplace to the stairs to the windows, back to the room and the people in it. She caught his eye, and after a moment's hesitation he gave her neither a thumbs-up nor a thumbs-down, but a so-so.

She smiled, met Karen's eyes, and nodded. A so-so was about right.

She tuned in to Jill's story. The office and the boss. The only people who were interested were those who worked there. She waited for Jill to finish before announcing that the turkey was ready, that it came with a warning, hot paprika, and that Daniel had called it un-American.

Jill laughed. Un-American. Like he's General MacArthur. Come to think of it, he is a bit of a tyrant. At the office he makes everyone else feel guilty because he's always working. The consultants at work complain that Daniel makes them look bad. They come back after a late lunch and of course he's at his desk. He never goes out.

That's because I eat kosher, Daniel said. It has nothing to do with work.

Then they were back on the subject of turkeys. Daniel told of his mother's paper-bag method, which had been rejected. That brought forth a recounting of other methods.

Ann's mother soaked the turkey in a bath of brine for twenty-four hours.

Jill's mother put pats of butter under the skin and inside a southern-style corn-bread stuffing.

Greg's mother had a special rack that lifted the turkey up off the pan so it roasted rather than stewed.

Karen's mother, who lived in California, barbecued the turkey on an outdoor spit that turned and produced a true roasted bird, browned and crisped all around and inside all its juices sealed.

Karen swore it was the best turkey she'd ever tasted. Deena said she believed it; anything barbecued was great.

Mike would agree with that, Ann said. He likes everything barbecued.

The many ways to cook a turkey. Next to such complex measures, paprika seemed too simple. It had provided good color, that she could see. Deena hoped the oil had helped retain juices.

Well, bring the Hungarian turkey in and we'll see, Greg said.

I have a feeling your mother's method will lose, Jill said.

Daniel seemed willing to lose. Between the bourbon and Jill's teasing he'd relinquished all loyalty to his mother. He went to get the turkey.

Brussels sprouts, curried yams, roast potatoes, salad, and bread traveled around the table, but all eyes were on Daniel, who was sharpening the knife and enjoying the opportunity for showmanship. He carved into the turkey, skillfully following the bone of the thigh, the way his father, a son of a butcher, had taught him.

A platter full of sliced white and dark meat was passed around the table, followed by stuffing and gravy. Then for minutes there was only the sound of cutlery on plates.

Mmm, Karen said. I believe goulash wins.

I've never had it spicy, Greg said. It's very good.

This might rival southern style, said Jill.

I'll have to tell my mother her daughter-in-law makes a better turkey, Daniel said.

Leave your mother alone, Deena said.

Good idea, Jill said.

·   ·   ·

Stacks of dishes, bowls, and platters, all crusty with the dried juices of turkey, sweet potato, and apple pie, were piled on the counters and in the sink. There were also leftovers. Daniel carved the rest of the turkey to put away. They'd have turkey sandwiches for days. Deena rinsed the plates and stacked them in the dishwasher. Better to wake up late the next morning to a clean kitchen than to fall into bed now, which is what she wanted to do.

Everything went beautifully, Daniel said. And the turkey was great. If I had room, I'd eat more right now.

Deena felt good. She hadn't overeaten. She'd been too busy hosting, and the food would be around the next day and the next.

Finally the table and counters were clear; the twenty-cubic-foot refrigerator was full. They switched off lights and went up the stairs to bed. It was two o'clock. It was time to sleep. Deena heard the dishwasher shift into the next cycle. Daniel was saying something, but she was falling asleep. She responded just barely, she said mmmm and yes, and turned over and sank deep into the mattress, into the bed. Still he talked, he was wide awake, and though she felt him beside her, she heard him only from a distance. She was feeling and not hearing. She felt the center of the house and the rooms all around. Her limbs stretched down the stairs toward the windows and the walls, the ends of the house. Unlike in their old apartment, she had to grow to fill this space.

December

It was warm for December, and in midtown everyone was out walking and eating lunch. Late afternoon, Daniel called.

It's a gorgeous day, he said. Let's spend the evening in the city.

But you never want to stay late in your suit, Deena said.

Today I feel like doing something different.

Deena hesitated. But why wasn't she saying yes? For years she'd wanted to do things after work.

Okay, she said. I'll be working till six. Come at six-thirty.

Forty-five minutes later he arrived; it was only five-twenty, and Karen was still in her office. They moved down the hall to Karen's office to sum up and plan where to begin in the morning.

They had three ideas, all going nowhere. Karen taped the thumb-nails on the wall and they sat looking at them. There was no leap off the page. She'd done nothing good all day. She didn't deserve a night out.

A good night's sleep will help, Karen said, her voice soothing. Great work doesn't happen when you're anxious. We need a break.

If she could allow herself the break, if she could believe in relax-ing, maybe it would help. Early in the morning, she'd try again. She'd fall asleep thinking about Chase Manhattan Bank; sometimes that helped. Sometimes, after a night of worry, the idea came in the shower.

People spend a third of their lives sleeping, Deena said. Might as well do it in the greatest bed, a canopy, or something.

Karen nodded, excited now. We could find out how much time is spent in the shower. How much in the kitchen.

Deena nodded. There was something in this idea. Numbers they could manipulate. They looked at each other, searching.

I know we've said this, but for some reason I keep coming back to it, said Karen. People don't like to borrow money for luxuries. They feel as if it's something they shouldn't do.

It's indulgent. A vacation isn't a necessity.

It's the kind of thing your parents frown on, Karen said.

Or your husband.

There's always someone.

Paul Herz stuck his head in, and the thin, long strands of hair combed to cover his bald crown fell forward. He patted it back into place.

Ladies, he said, smiling. Carry on. Karen, see you in the morning. Deena, better finish the campaign before you give us up and go back to Hasidic life. I am off to good old Yankee Connecticut, where I've never quite belonged.

You look the part in that tweed jacket, Karen said.

A country gentleman, Deena said.

You think so? he asked, and waved.

Karen shook her head, eyes wide. I heard Ron and Todd talking, she said. If he keeps going on that Constitution, he'll soon be in Connecticut full time.

Maybe that's what he wants, Deena said. They'll give him a good severance and then he'll get unemployment. At his level, that could amount to some money.

He doesn't want that, Karen said. He's less than five years from retirement. His pension would amount to a lot more.

Oh, Deena said. She never knew about things like that.

Karen stood. Let's go say hi to Daniel. We've left him alone long enough.

They walked down the hall. In every office, people were clearing their desks, talking on the phone, making plans for the night. Daniel too was on the phone, his back to the door. But with whom? Deena wondered. It was unlike him. He didn't usually chatter on the phone. Unless it was Jill.

Daniel was in her seat, at her desk. Deena sat beside Karen in one of the two visitors' chairs. It was odd for her to be sitting on this side of her desk. And she was squirming. She hoped it didn't show. She hoped Karen wouldn't figure out who it was, and that Daniel wouldn't tell her. But was it wrong for him to be talking to Jill? And if it wasn't wrong, why was she so ashamed?

Daniel saw them and turned away to face the window. He leaned back in her chair and put his legs up on the sill, as if this were his office. Karen rolled her eyes and Deena wondered how much she knew. But what was there to know?

Finally Daniel hung up, spun around, and leaned forward, elbows on her desk.

This is nice, he said. Your own office. At the research center we have cubicles, no privacy.

It was probably Jill who made privacy at work suddenly desirable, Deena thought. Then she was surprised to find herself thinking that way. She held her breath. She hoped Daniel wouldn't mention Jill in front of Karen. Right now Karen was doing the talking.

This is the advertising business, she said. Creative work requires concentration. We need a lot of quiet time.

Daniel nodded. If you can call what you do work.

Karen's eyes opened wider.

Don't respond, Deena advised. He knows better. Or should. But he wants to believe that he's the only one in the world who does any real work.

Karen laughed. So where are you two going tonight? she asked.

Deena looked at Daniel. Yes. Where are we going?

Daniel shrugged. I don't know yet.

Well, if you want dinner, there's a little Italian place Greg and I like.

You mean Aegean's? Deena asked.

That's Greek, Daniel said.

Karen nodded. The name is Greek, but the food is Italian. It's on Sixty-third or maybe Sixty-fourth.

Deena looked at Daniel. Do you want to walk uptown?

He shook his head. We'll have dinner later. We're probably meeting some people from my office for drinks.

They waited for more information, but he didn't continue, and finally Karen stood.

Well, I'll leave you two to figure it out, she said. Have fun.

Deena dropped into the vacated chair.

Ready to go? Daniel asked.

Where to? Deena asked.

I don't know yet, Daniel said. Let's just go.

But where? she said again.

Daniel shrugged. He put on his coat. Come on, he said. Deena put on her jacket.

On the street, he turned west. He knew where they were going. Deena knew too. They walked together not saying what they knew.

Deena untied her silk scarf. She was too warm. What was he trying to do? What was he hiding?

Doesn't Jill live around here? she said.

She does. I'll show you where, he said.

She'd made it easier for him. She'd helped him. She didn't know why.

They continued walking in silence. Jill's building was just off Eighth, a place near enough to Broadway for any girl with stage dreams.

Daniel rang the bell and waited. He rang again. There was no answer. That's strange, he said.

She's probably at the gym or out running, Deena said. That's what she usually does after work. What's strange about that?

I told her we were coming, Daniel said.

Deena looked at him, at the puzzled question in his eyes. You told her? Then why didn't you say so? she asked. Why did you pretend you didn't know where you were going?

He didn't respond. He turned to the buzzer and pressed again. There was a phone booth across the street. He fished a quarter out of his pocket and went to call.

No answer, he said.

Maybe she stepped out for a minute, Deena said.

They walked around the block. Daniel rang the bell again.

He looked at Deena and looked away. He understood now. He was angry. He straightened his shoulders, put his finger on the door-bell, and kept it there.

Deena hated him. Then she pitied him. Then she hated him again. How dare he bring her along? It was disgusting seeing him like this, stood up by another woman.

Stop it, she said. Stop it now. Let's go eat dinner.

I'm not hungry, he said. He released and pressed the buzzer five more times, a series of rings. He kicked the door.

That'll help, Deena said, and walked away.

He followed and they walked to Eighth Avenue in silence. Deena stopped to look at the menu of the Stardust Deli, but Daniel turned away.

It was too early for dinner, but she wanted to get them off the desperate street. She didn't care whether or not he was hungry. They would sit at a table and order; they would do what other couples did.

Then what do you want? she said. I have work to do. I left the office because you wanted to do something. I don't want to walk the streets all evening.

He hailed a cab. Bleecker and MacDougal, he said.

The club. They were going back to that underground club. She leaned back and closed her eyes. She could use a drink.

Daniel led the way in. She would drink but she was in no mood to dance. Certainly not with him. She wanted to hit him. Or kick him, hard.

The juke box was playing. Something hard and fast. That was good.

Daniel ordered a scotch, Deena a sloe gin fizz. They drank quickly and ordered another round. The band was setting up, the music would start, and the drinks arrived. This is what they'd do on this beautiful evening. Drink.

Come on, Daniel said.

Deena looked at him. For years she'd wanted him to dance with her. Now he was the one asking.

They made their way to the dance floor, more confidently than the first time. Or maybe just more drunk, Deena thought. She was off rhythm. She stopped, started again, and felt good to be moving. Everything she was worried about fell away. She was here now, not at her desk thrashing about for ideas, not trying pun after bad pun. She was moving now. She was dancing like she meant it. She looked at Daniel and wanted to tell him, to push him. Enough half-heartedness. If he wanted an affair with Jill he should go ahead and have it. She didn't care now. She wouldn't care if he went all the way.

It was early and there was room on the dance floor. When a slow song started, Daniel put his arms around her for the waltz and they moved together. They knew each other better than anyone.

They separated after the first set. Deena went to the bathroom; Daniel went to make a phone call. When she returned, he was smiling.

Jill's coming, he said. One of the technicians from work is coming too. He lives in Chinatown.

What happened earlier? Deena asked.

Ann had a fight with her husband, she was crying, and Jill agreed to go to the gym with her. She couldn't call to tell me because she didn't have your number at work.

You should give it to her, Deena said.

Daniel nodded. I'm starving now. Let's order some food.

The technician arrived first. Daniel introduced him as Gary.

Then Jill arrived, her eyes large and sad. She didn't say anything about Ann. She didn't repeat the excuse. Was there any truth to it, Deena wondered.

Daniel ordered more drinks. The food arrived and soon Jill was laughing. Hearing her, it was easy to believe that laughing was the only thing in this world worth doing. It was possible, Deena thought, that Daniel was taking the friendship a little too seriously, and if that was true, then Jill's ambivalence was understandable.

The next set started. Gary ordered another beer. I don't dance, he said.

Deena stayed at the table too. Her head was spinning. But when Jill came toward her, hips swinging, Deena responded. Daniel smiled. He was happy. The two women in his life were friends.

In the taxi, Deena focused on the road and the traffic. She rolled the window down and the fresh air helped. But when the car stopped at a traffic light, she couldn't hold her head up.

If you have to, try doing it out the window, Daniel said. Or I'll ask the cab driver to stop. He swept her hair off her forehead.

She inhaled. She wouldn't let go. When the cab pulled up in front of the house, she jumped out, turned the lock, and ran up the stairs. Daniel paid the driver and hurried to turn off the alarm.

Deena ran a bath. It was two-thirty in the morning, and in the bedroom Daniel was picking on the strings of his guitar, composing a lyric about hugging the porcelain.

On a yellow pad Deena sketched eight rectangles. She would work fast, without stopping to judge. She'd fill each mock page with a concept before she got off the train. Brainstorming, it was called. Or stream of consciousness. Sometimes it worked. Moving trains had helped her in the past. Coffee shops too. Anywhere, it seemed, was better than her desk. She scribbled all the way to work. But today the trip was fast, to thwart her, she thought. Everything and everyone, it seemed, was working against her on this Chase assignment. Should she stay on the train, ride to the end of the line and back, and continue working? At the office she became too anxious to think freely.

She looked at her watch. To stay or go? Arriving late on the day of a deadline would be held against her, unless she came in with a finished ad. If she stayed on the train, she couldn't walk in with anything less than the perfect piece. And knowing this decreased the chances of her coming up with anything good. What she should have done was work late last night. She shouldn't have gone to sleep without a finished ad. Shoulds and shouldn'ts. It was too late for that now. And her head hurt. She needed water. And aspirin.

In her office she sat at the black keyboard, a sleek, silent machine. It seemed only minutes since she'd been here yesterday, minutes since Daniel was here on the phone with Jill. But she wouldn't think about last night. She'd focus on work. People spent most of their lives working. Americans are said to have the least vacation time. Averages and numbers. Which could be used both ways. A great luxury bed, since you spend a third of your life sleeping. And a good vacation since it is rare. Europeans know how to live. Why? Does it have anything to do with their proximity to the cradle of civilization? Could the Renaissance have occurred in New York, where people are always rushing? That was an idea. A Chase loan to finance a week or two of becoming, a week in which to contemplate yourself and the world, to stay at home reading and thinking, learning, becoming a Renaissance man. Chase Manhattan Bank as a patron. Palladio also had to be financed.

There was a knock at the door.

Deena continued typing: asdfjkl; asdfjkl; if she kept going, whoever it was wouldn't stay.

Good morning, Deena said, and looked up.

You're here. You're working, Karen said. I have to run down to the bullpen, sign off on some boards, then I'll be back.

Deena nodded. Take your time, she said.

Good. She was onto something. She needed time alone. She pulled the sheet out of the machine, read and underlined. These were still only ideas. She was an idea person, a teacher once said. But someone else had to do the execution.

This is good, Karen said. We'll present this to them after lunch. They're always in better moods after a few drinks, she said.

The first in the series would show the Villa Rotunda; the copy would read: DESIGNED BY PALLADIO. FUNDED BY THE MEDICIS. The tag line would say, CHASE WILL FINANCE YOUR DREAM. Then the bank's logo. Other ads in the series could show paintings, ancient manuscripts, anything. It was a campaign with a long life.

The more they talked about it, the better the concept seemed. They were excited. For lunch, they picked up salads at the deli and ate in Karen's office. She wanted to do good mockups.

They don't have much imagination, she said. The more finished the work, the more likely the approval.

Deena thought the ads would either make it or not; nothing she and Karen could do or say would change anything.

I'm feeling confident, Karen said. The concept is different enough without going over the edge. And it's interesting.

Deena worried that the idea was too unusual for the client. Banks weren't known for creative advertising. And the requisition asked for a hard-hitting campaign focused on rates. That other banks were more competitive than Chase didn't make a difference. For a corporate bank, the rates were low.

So tell me what you did last night, Karen said.

Last night? Deena asked. For a moment she didn't remember the significance of last night. Oh, she said. We went dancing. As you know, Daniel's gotten into that. Several people from his office joined us.

Could two people be considered several? And she didn't mention Jill's name, which wasn't a lie, just an omission. Karen's eyes were calm saucers.

You and Daniel do a lot together, she said. You have the same interests. It must be fun.

It was, but I should have eaten something before drinking. I started feeling awful.

Karen nodded knowingly. You should take some vitamins. Alcohol depletes all your minerals. She stood to reach her second shelf. I have some ginseng. You should always drink this after a late night.

Did Karen ever drink or eat or do anything too much? Deena wondered. She sat in the sun more than she should, but so did every fair-skinned blonde from California. Was her commitment to vitamins, ginseng, and subliminal tapes a way to compensate for other abuse? Deena stopped herself. She would accept the vial of ginseng and drink it. Maybe if you allowed yourself to think that such things worked, then they did.

Karen opened the ginseng vial with her X-Acto knife and handed it to Deena, who swallowed it in one gulp. It wasn't bad. Sweet and pungent simultaneously.

The phone rang; it was Greg, and Karen read the headlines. He didn't get it right away and she had to explain. Deena chewed her lips, which were already down to raw skin. The campaign wouldn't fly.

It's very soft sell, Greg said. It's not the kind of advertising banks do. Even if Paul and Ron approve it, he said, the client won't.

Then he was saying something, probably about what a great copy and art team the two of them would make, from the way Karen was giggling. He worked in the traffic department of a medical advertising agency and he was trying to switch into creative; some days he wanted to be an art director, others a copywriter, but he never completed a portfolio for either position.

Karen giggled again. Despite the deadline, she was lighthearted, she could laugh. She and Greg actually did seem good together. But people always say that about couples; they said it about Daniel and her. In the meantime, standing in front of Jill's apartment the night before, she'd wanted to hurt him, to kick and trample him underfoot. Angry, she was out to kill. Two hours later on the dance floor, they were friends again.

Couples had good moments. That was true enough. It was also true of life. Occasionally there was a good moment.

They put the mockups down on the desk in front of Paul and Ron, and stepped back. Deena looked at the ads upside down. Now that it was in front of new eyes, she found herself capable of reading and judging it the way they would, critically. She knew it wouldn't fly.

With different buildings or works of art, Karen explained, this campaign could have a long life.

Ron shook his head.

This won't work, Paul said. Isn't the client asking for hard numbers? You're headed in the wrong direction.

Deena looked at him. We should give the client what we believe in, she said.

I don't believe in this, Paul said.

Can you say why? Karen said.

It's vague. It's farfetched.

It tries too hard, Ron said.

Deena turned around and walked out. Seconds later, Karen followed, rustling tissue paper in hand.

They sat behind a closed door.

He's thinking about what the client wants, Deena said.

He's a hack, Karen said. He wants numbers, we'll give him numbers. What we ought to do in the future is show our second-best work first. That way the good work will get approved. They like giving us a hard time.

Why? Deena asked.

I don't know. Because we're shorter than they are.

Deena laughed.

Don't laugh. If Charlie and Todd had gone in with this concept, Paul would have approved it because he's afraid of six-foot-seven Todd.

Let's go back to that four-poster bed with the price tag. That's number-oriented.

Karen started sketching. Deena wished she'd stop. If she spent more time thinking, they might get somewhere.

Stop dreaming, for x dollars a month, Deena said.

It's not terrible, Karen said. She wrote the words. There's the play on dream.

A pun, Deena said.

It is crystal clear, Karen said. Paul will approve this.

Would you put it in your portfolio?

Karen lifted the pad, looked at it. If it were a good photograph. If the production were high quality. But I have a feeling I'll end up having to hire an illustrator.

The phone rang. It's Scott, Karen said. The client is anxious. Something has to go to the printer tonight.

Tell him we were shot down, Deena said.

Karen hung up. He's coming up to talk to us.

She looked at Deena. What were we saying?

We were talking about illustration, which gives me an idea. Is there anything we can do with architectural drawings? The product is essentially a home-improvement loan.

Yes, Karen said, sketching again. How about Chase will finance your plans?

For x dollars a month, you can stop planning.

Great, Karen said.

We can do a series of these hokey ads. Divide the page in three and show drawings for a kitchen renovation, bathroom, and the bed. Kitchens, beds, and baths from Chase.

That's not half bad. Listen, Karen said. This campaign is not the best project you'll have in your life. Let's just get the job done. This isn't image advertising. They want to push product. They want numbers, we'll give them numbers. And actually in black-and-white newspaper, blueprints will look good.

Deena watched Karen sketch. By the time Scott arrived she had a series of thumbnails. She tacked the page to the wall. He stood reading.

They're perfect, he said.

Show him our first choice, Deena said.

Karen pulled out the old sketches. They watched him read.

They're arty, he said, but the message is obscure and slow. These are straightforward and simple. They're what the client wants. Can we get them done quickly? Is the art available or will we need an illustrator?

Paul hasn't seen these yet, Karen said.

I'll get him, Scott said and ducked out of the office.

We should have let him see only the first campaign, Deena said. Given nothing else, he might have gone for that.

Paul came in, stood in front of the sheet on the wall, read quickly, and clapped his hand on Scott's shoulder. There are your ads, he said.

Scott asked about another overdue Chase project and Paul suggested nominating Karen and Deena as the Chase team.

No thanks, Deena said.

Then the men were gone.

The mediocre gets quick approval, Deena said.

Karen shrugged. Fight the battles worth fighting.

. . .

The agency was closed for a week between Christmas and New Year's, and Deena wanted to work on the house. Restoring the missing wall between the two bedrooms would make the upstairs more usable. Together, she and Daniel could put it up in a day.

Daniel wanted to postpone the job.

What else are you going to do on Christmas? Deena asked. It's not as if you celebrate the holiday.

Jill, she knew, was visiting family. Everyone else was out shopping, which they could be doing too, but Daniel had suggested waiting.

A week from now, everything will be half price, he said.

He wasn't enthusiastic about anything. He'd been sulking since the day Jill had gone south. But Deena had the week off and she wanted to get things done.

In a manual on wall construction, she read directions that seemed simple enough. First you framed the wall with two-by-fours; over the framing, you nailed Sheetrock. The taping was the hard part. If necessary they could do that the following day.

With the measurements on paper, they drove to Martin's Lumber. Deena followed Daniel up and down the aisles. Near large buckets of plaster of paris were trays and pails for mixing, cans of spackling, rolls of tape, nails, underpaint. They figured out what they needed from what was there.

In the lumber section Daniel requested seven eight-foot two-bys and two ten-footers for the length of the room. He calculated that they'd need five full sheets of Sheetrock. Somehow they'd have to get everything into the car.

The drive home with an open hatchback was slow. And by the

time the material was unloaded it was twelve-thirty and they were hungry.

They ate a quick lunch at the kitchen table.

We should keep the carpet on the floor as long as possible, Deena said. To protect the wood floor.

We should protect the carpet too, Daniel said. We can always use it in the basement.

Okay, okay. I'll put plastic down. But let's go, Deena said. Talking about it won't make the work happen.

First I need another cup of coffee.

Bring your coffee up, Deena said. It's one o'clock already.

Upstairs she asked about the closets.

Forget the closets, Daniel said. It'll be enough to build this wall.

We're wrecking the place anyway. If we do it today, we'll save ourselves another day of cleanup.

I don't want to get in over my head. Come Monday I need a clean suit that's not wrinkled or covered with dust. We'll do one thing at a time.

He stood there, eying the room and sipping coffee. He had a point. The wall would make a difference, the rest could be done later. But if only he'd put that cup down and start moving. She'd moved everything out of the way; she'd brought a tarp up from the basement to protect the carpet he wanted to save. Here, she said, and handed him two corners. But he had only one hand free. He held both corners in one hand. Deena took the other two corners and pulled to spread the tarp. Daniel fought to retain his grip, and drops of coffee splashed on the carpet. He let go of the tarp and Deena fell back against the wall.

Idiot, she muttered.

Daniel laughed.

He asked to see the how-to book and stood reading it, as if they were days away from building the wall.

You couldn't do that yesterday? Deena asked.

Stop it, he said.

Deena placed one of the ten-footers along the length of the floor and started hammering it into place.

Wait a minute, Daniel said. Did you check for level?

He came and checked and it wasn't level. He pulled up the two-by-four with a crowbar and reset it. Hammer, he said, holding out his hand.

As soon as he got started, she was the assistant. Why couldn't he pick up his own hammer? She could be doing more than hand things. She could be taking down the closet walls, for example. But Daniel claimed he needed her right there. Someone had to hold the pieces in place.

She thought he wanted an audience, someone watching and admiring. At work, Jill; at home, Deena.

On the ceiling there were traces of the original wall, indentations where the nails had been. Use the marks as guides, Daniel said. They'll make the job easier. But if the original wall was crooked, this one will be too. Call it authentic restoration.

Deena held up each of the eight-footers while Daniel nailed them in place. Then she held up the Sheetrock. All she did was hold and hand things—a facilitator not a creator. He called it assisting; he built, she assisted, which irritated. Next vacation, when Daniel was at work, she'd take the closets down. She couldn't build by herself, but she could destroy. She wouldn't say anything. She'd organize and execute alone. When he came home from work, the rubble would be in garbage bags in front of the house, and inside not a trace of the closets.

The wall was finally up. Deena dropped her arms.

Finishing always takes more time than anything else, Daniel warned. I have to tape the edges and spackle over the nails. The next step is priming. You can open and stir the can of primer. Make sure you bring the paint up from the bottom, Daniel said.

I know, Deena said. We've painted before, remember?

She watched the thick white paint fold over and in. She liked the smell of paint.

They worked on opposite sides of the wall. Daniel heard the roller. Deena heard the scratch of the putty knife. They could feel and hear where on the wall the other was. It was strange feeling and not seeing. They were separate; they had a wall between them. He couldn't see her hating him. She stuck her tongue out. That felt good. She did it again. It hurt to stretch her tongue like that; still she couldn't stop doing it. She used to be better at it. Angry, she'd turn her back on her mother or teacher and stick out her tongue. When they caught her doing it, she was punished. Still she wasn't sorry. There was satisfaction in having expressed herself.

She leaned her roller against the wall and put her head in at the door. Daniel was patching. She waited. When he looked up, she stuck her tongue out, and quickly disappeared.

What'd you do that for? he asked.

Deena shrugged. She didn't know.

January

For the first snow of the season people left work early, not because there was danger—the storm had been predicted; snowplows were out sanding and salting—but it was a Friday and no one, it seemed, wanted to remain at work. Deena and Daniel met walking home from the subway, and together they saw for the first time their gambrel-roofed colonial capped in snow.

They stood on the cold sunporch, watching the snow fall.

Will it stick? Deena asked. Did you hear any reports?

Daniel nodded. It looks like the real thing, he said. This snow is here to stay.

We could go for a walk after dark, she said.

They sat on the floor in front of the fire, back to back.

We could sleep here tonight, Daniel said.

Without curtains?

How about some full-length sheets of smoked mirror? Daniel joked. That'll give us privacy.

Deena sipped sherry and turned to offer him a sticky kiss. Right away his hand went under her sweater and found the thin white cotton of her T-shirt. Today she didn't mind. This was different enough. They weren't in bed and it wasn't after dinner. He put his glass down and turned to take full advantage of her unexpected willingness.

She felt his long fingers searching and quickly finding what they were looking for. He turned to kiss her fully, and with the weight of his lips on her lips, brought her head down into his lap. Then she was in his arms, responding. It was true he knew where and how to touch her. She just had to give him a chance.

After, he wanted to lie still and sleep through the night and into the next day. He always went to sleep after. She was restless. She wanted to go for a walk. So they dressed and walked to the park, where gliding and tumbling down the hill were kids and teenagers and also men and women their own age. They watched, and regretted not having a sled.

At the top of the hill, a woman with a sled stood hesitating, afraid.

Try going down on your stomach, Deena advised. You can hold on and steer with your arms.

I'm afraid, the woman said. Would you like to try it?

Deena didn't wait for a second invitation. In less than a minute she was on the sled, gliding downhill. The hill was short. She arrived at the bottom too soon, turned ninety degrees and continued coasting.

You're good at it, the woman said. Would you like to try it too? she asked Daniel.

Come on, Daniel said, inviting Deena to ride with him. He turned the sled around, waited for her to sit, then got on behind her and held her tight. He was always nicer to her after sex; she didn't know why she denied him. If only they could remain this way all night.

They pulled the sled uphill, exhilarated. I haven't done this in ages, Daniel said.

The first time he'd taken Deena to visit his family in Connecticut it was winter. Daniel brought two old sleds out from under the porch, and they joined the neighborhood kids on Hilltop. After, his mother had steaming cups of hot chocolate waiting. Yes, this was what young couples in love did: they went sledding together, came back holding hands, and warmed themselves over cups of hot chocolate.

They returned the sled to its owner and walked along Park Drive, inhaling the cold. On a bench overlooking the park was an abandoned half snowman.

He's so small he looks like a girl, Daniel said.

Let's make her a snow woman, Deena said.

They packed and shaped snow. Daniel worked on the torso, breasts, and shoulders. Deena shaped the curve of a seated back. They stepped back to get a better look. She was uneven. One side was thicker than the other. Daniel took off his gloves and chiseled with his bare hands. He shaped a graceful neck.

Help me with the legs, he said. If she sits with her legs together, she'll have more tensile strength.

They gathered and packed more snow. Daniel kept returning to the thighs. He etched the lines with his fingers, a shadowed triangle in the center.

Her legs will have to stop at the knees where the bench ends, he said.

Let's leave her with only half arms too, Deena said. She'll look like the statue of Venus.

We could leave her without a head, Daniel said. A ruin.

Deena agreed and shaped the slim neck at an angle, and left it unfinished, a stump.

They stepped back and laughed.

She needs more stomach, some roundness, Daniel said.

He added snow, formed a small mound, working carefully, one hand on the lower spine to keep from pushing too hard and breaking their fragile Venus. With a fingernail he scraped at the base of the neck to reveal a throat.

Deena stepped back and watched his fingers hover. He worked knowingly; he knew the body of a woman. It was how he worked her body, one hand in back of her head, the other cupping her hip. It was the way he handled tools, with knowledge and finesse. He was good at things. He took pride in doing everything well, driving a stick for example, slipping into gear without a hitch, smoothly, perfectly. She liked that about him. She liked his knowing hands on her body. Even when it seemed that was all he ever wanted: to handle her body. As soon as they were alone, whether in his car or in his parents' living room, his fingers groped. She used to like the attention, except for those times when suddenly, with her clothes awry, she had to sit up on the sofa and pretend that nothing was going on, that all along she had been reading *Good Housekeeping* and learning how to make a perfect broccoli soufflé. Beside her Daniel would be hiding the smirk on his face with a copy of *Stereo* magazine. He enjoyed getting caught, and the pretending after. It was the way things ought to be. For hundreds of years parents have walked in on the scene of sons and daughters smooching. This was part of the fun, this pretending and fooling no one.

They woke up to seven inches of soft snow and stood on the sun-porch watching their neighbors shoveling. Daniel wouldn't hear of clearing the steps or driveway until after sunset, when the Sabbath was over, and they were restless.

Let's get Jill to come over tonight, Daniel said. We could show her our snow lady.

But he wouldn't call till after dark. In the meantime, he prayed, read, paced, ate, read, and went back to bed. After the snowplows came through, Deena went running. Today she was grateful for running. It was the one thing she insisted on doing even on the Sabbath. Sometimes she also showered and gave Daniel more reason to call her a shiksa. If it had been up to her, she would have shoveled the snow and called Jill. It was what Daniel wished he could allow himself to do. Of course, if you broke one law, why not all. It wasn't as if Daniel's observance was entirely perfect either. But she would gain nothing by pointing out that sledding and building a snow woman were also problematic. If you wanted to be a stickler, planning what you would do after the Sabbath wasn't appropriate either.

As soon as Daniel saw two stars in the darkening sky, he dialed Jill's number and left a message. Then he brought two shovels up from the basement. He worked on the driveway; Deena cleared the steps and front walk. She stopped and listened to the scraping of his shovel, long, full, and wide, and the silent seconds as the full shovel was lifted. She could almost hear the exertion in the lifting, then the whisper of snow falling on snow. She picked up a handful in her glove and pressed and pushed it into a hard ball, the harder the better. She wanted to hurt. She passed it palm to palm, calculating the distance, planning. She waited until Daniel bent down for another shovelful and aimed at his back. She threw quickly and turned away.

When Daniel looked up, she was busy clearing snow. He said nothing, but the sound of his shovel had stopped. He was making an avenging snowball, which she'd dodge. In the meantime she pressed another handful of snow against her leg while keeping the sound of her shovel going. She'd be ready; she'd throw as soon as his snowball was in the air. She continued shoveling and watching for Daniel's arm to lift up for the throw.

He took his time. She was ready to give herself away and lob the second ball, and then she saw the movement, the arc of his arm swinging in its socket. She threw too quickly and her snowball landed several feet short. Daniel's snowball crashed smack into the stop sign across the street. He eyed the distance critically. Yes, his aim was still decent, nothing to be ashamed of. He started another snowball. This time, he tried for the streetlight and grazed it.

Deena felt mean; she'd aimed at him twice. Then she felt overlooked. He was more interested in perfecting his aim than in getting back at her. There was something about men and balls: put one in their hands and they had to test the power of their arms.

·   ·   ·

He'd called Jill all evening and again in the morning and gotten no answer. He kept leaving messages, but she wasn't returning his calls.

We can do things without her, you know, Deena said.

He nodded, embarrassed. I was thinking we could go ice skating, he said.

It would be fun, except that it's a long drive. Anyway, why not sledding? We can buy a sled on Metropolitan Avenue.

We went sledding Friday night, Daniel said.

He dialed again. This time Jill picked up.

He suggested lunch and was turned down.

What about dinner? Deena heard him ask.

He was practically begging. The corners of his eyes turned down. She must be saying no. Deena wondered about her. What was going on in Jill's head? Maybe nothing. Maybe Daniel was simply demanding too much of her time.

He went back to bed.

Let's go check on our snow lady, Deena said.

I'm too tired, Daniel said.

You're too tired for a walk but not for other things? she said, and disliked the sound of her voice saying it.

I'm not in the mood for anything, he said. Leave me alone.

Mope if you want to, Deena said.

She put on her boots. She could do things without him. She wanted to do things without him.

Daniel sighed and sat up. Okay, okay, he said.

February

It was Daniel's idea but Deena made the arrangements. She booked a two-bedroom cottage with a fireplace, and after sunset on Saturday they loaded the car and drove into Manhattan to pick up Jill and Ann. Then they were on the road, going somewhere.

The speed, Daniel said, will be thrilling.

I'll try anything once, Jill said.

Ann wasn't so sure or so willing. One thing I'm not prepared to do, she said, is break something. I don't need any more complications in my life. First I move to New York, then I break a leg. That's all Mike needs to hear. If I can't get to work, I'll wind up hobbling back home.

Deena wondered about the arrangement Ann had with her husband. It sounded like she was on sufferance. If anything went wrong, she was finished.

Daniel wasn't worried about anything. We're off, he said.

To see the wizard, Jill finished.

But traffic was heavy. This was a holiday weekend and everyone, it seemed, was on the road. They crawled up the West Side Highway and across the George Washington Bridge. By the time they were on the Thruway it was dark and they were all hungry.

We'll stop at the first HoJo's, Daniel said.

What could he eat there? Deena wondered. In a cooler, he'd packed kosher hamburgers, hot dogs, and steaks for grilling, but tonight they'd arrive too late to cook.

When they were seated at an orange Formica table, Daniel announced that Howard Johnson ice cream had an o-u. Which means it's kosher, he explained to Jill and Ann.

Ice cream is not quite what I had in mind for dinner, Deena said.

Jill laughed.

It's too cold to say the word *ice,* Ann groaned. Hot soup is more like it.

Daniel and Jill were in good moods. They didn't care what they ate. Daniel bantered and Jill teased. His eyes were bright, her lips soft. She was ready to laugh, willing to laugh, and Daniel was trying to make her laugh.

I think I'll stick with the cottage cheese and fruit platter, Jill said. I didn't run today.

That's a good idea, Daniel said. There probably isn't anything unkosher in fruit and soft cheese.

Deena opened the menu. What she wanted was a glass of red wine and a bowl of hot soup.

Ann ordered cream of celery soup and a chef's salad with the dressing on the side.

Ditto, Deena said when her turn came. Soup and salad. And do you serve wine?

Wine at a Howard Johnson's? Daniel said. Besides, it wouldn't be kosher. And that soup definitely has either chicken or beef broth, which no rabbi, Hasidic or otherwise, would sanction.

Deena shrugged. Don't eat it, she said.

Yeah, Jill said. This is the twentieth century. Women are no longer chattel.

Daniel put his hands up to show that he wouldn't hold anyone back. Still, he said, laws are laws. Kosher is kosher. There's no such thing as being a little kosher. It's all or nothing. But I won't say another thing.

Good, Jill and Deena said together, and laughed.

After dinner everyone was quieter. Daniel drove; with a flashlight, Deena kept an eye on the directions. In the back seat, Ann and Jill seemed to have fallen asleep, and they didn't move until the car stopped in front of the main house.

Deena knocked at the door, which was opened with a long grumble.

It's almost eleven, the woman said. I ask guests to arrive before ten.

We encountered heavy traffic, Deena explained and apologized.

It was cold. They zipped up their jackets and stomped their feet. Half asleep, Ann and Jill struggled out of the car. Daniel and Deena carried bags. It was freezing and the snow was piled high.

Inside: the cold and wet smell of closed places.

A roaring fire would help, Daniel said. He put on his leather gloves and brought in three logs from the woodpile outside.

They won't burn well, he said. They're damp.

He went out to look for kindling.

The women looked at the two bedrooms, which were equally small; one had a double bed, the other two singles, and without discussion it was assumed that Deena and Daniel would get the double. At home, they slept on twin beds and someone always ended up in the crack. In the morning they complained, but they'd never gone out and purchased a double.

Folded sheets were stacked on the dresser. Ann and Deena made the beds. Jill was too sleepy; she needed help getting undressed. Ann guided her and they giggled, and Deena wished it was in their room she was sleeping.

Standing in the main room, in front of the fire, Deena and Daniel heard more giggling. They looked at each other and smiled. He prodded and poked the wood, delaying going to bed, hoping for what, another glance at Jill?

Go ahead, he said. I'll stay up a while longer.

He also wants to sleep with them, Deena thought. She undressed and slid under the covers. She wouldn't think about it. She'd sleep and wake up fine. She moved to find a better side of the pillow, but it resisted. It was damp and smelled of mold. Everything in this cabin was damp.

When she opened her eyes, the room was silent and dark. What time was it? And where was Daniel? She pinched her arm and knew she was awake. The door was ajar. She heard steps, then Daniel came in. He was still fully dressed. He started to un-dress.

You're awake, he said.

She dropped back onto the pillow and closed her eyes.

In the morning, the smell of eggs and coffee, and Daniel's morning voice, low gravel. Had he slept?

At the kitchen table, Jill and Ann sipped coffee. Daniel stood at the stove.

Good morning, sleepyhead, he said.

Jill and Ann turned to look and laughed.

Deena pushed her hair off her forehead.

Coffee's ready, he said.

She poured a cup.

The sun was up and the thermometer at the door showed thirty degrees; it was warmer than expected.

It's a good thing they make snow here, Daniel said. Still, we'd better dress warmly. It will be colder on the mountain.

I'm wearing thermal leggings under my jeans, Jill said.

Deena looked at her. Even with thermals, her tight jeans fit. Her hair was freshly washed, blow-dried, and curled; Ann's hair was straight, the bangs turned under. Their faces were in full makeup. Fresh red lipstick lined the rims of their coffee cups. Just looking at them made her tired.

I'm making eggs, Daniel said. Want some?

She shook her head. It's too early for eggs.

These two have been up for hours, he said. By the time I got up they were showered and dressed.

Deena nodded. Yes, she could see that. She shivered. It was cold in here. Even with the fire going it was cold.

It must be warmer outside than in here, she said.

Jill nodded. That's what woke me up. It was too cold to sleep.

Did you bring a blow drier? Deena asked.

Ann did, Jill said. It's in the bathroom. You're lucky. Your hair probably dries in two minutes. If my face weren't so damn large, I'd wear my hair cropped like yours.

Daniel doesn't like my hair short, Deena said.

It's not that I don't like it, Daniel said. I like long hair better.

It's too hip for him, Jill said. He's old-fashioned.

In cold weather, you come to appreciate long hair. I went out and bought a hat yesterday, Deena said. Of course, as soon as I put it on my hair will go flat.

We brought hats too, Ann said. I'll show you.

She went to their room and came out carrying two hats with pom-poms. They laughed. Deena showed them her red ski hat. Next to their pale blue and pink snowflake patterns, red seemed harsh, but in the dirty slush of New York City sidewalks, white had seemed ridiculous.

Don't worry, Jill said. We'll all look bad. What I would have liked to wear is an Emma Peel suit.

Who is Emma Peel? Deena asked.

You never watched *The Avengers?* Ann said.

At the ski lodge, they picked up boots, skis, and ski poles, and Daniel put it all on his credit card, including lift tickets and four beginners' lessons.

Why are you paying for everything? Deena asked.

Because I want to, he said.

I don't, Deena said.

He shrugged.

They put on their boots and goose-stepped out onto the snow.

Jill slipped and fell. Ann followed. Daniel helped them up. They fell again. Deena held on to Ann, Daniel kept Jill standing, then the ski instructor took over. He showed them how to bend their knees, turn, slow down, and stop. They practiced. Deena watched Daniel go into a turn. He was good at it. He did it hips first, with grace and control. She tried it, but her timing was off. She tried again. She practiced steering, stopping, and turning—there, she'd gotten it once. When she turned to say, Watch me, she too went down. Getting up was difficult; the long skis were entangled; she needed a hand. She looked for Daniel, but he was helping Jill; the ski instructor was at Ann's side. Deena struggled and finally stood.

Getting off the lift, they all fell and went down the first short hill on their backs. At the bottom they struggled to stand; then Jill fell again. Seeing flailing arms, Ann too lost her balance and went down, giggling helplessly. Deena helped Ann up. She didn't know what was taking Daniel so long with Jill. When Jill started slipping again and Daniel took her arm to steady her, Deena didn't stop. But she was skiing too fast. She was headed toward a tree. She had to stop, but she couldn't, she didn't. She put her hands out and ran into the tree. She straightened her skis, looked back, and saw the three of them holding hands, struggling to stay up. She wouldn't wait. She'd get some practice; she'd learn. The sun felt good and she was alone. She went down and down, into turns. She tried putting her hips into the movement, fell, straightened her skis, and tried again.

Half an hour later, when Daniel arrived with Jill and Ann in tow, Deena was sitting on a bench quietly, her face turned to the sun. Jill stopped giggling, suddenly self-conscious.

What's wrong? Daniel said.

Nothing, Deena said. I'll go up again in a few minutes.

Wait for us. We'll go together.

Jill and Ann went to the ladies' room. Daniel went to buy hot chocolate for everyone. Deena remained in the sun. What was wrong with her?

They came out with their hair freshly brushed and lipstick reapplied. Daniel followed with hot pretzels and hot chocolate.

They had stories to tell. Every fall had turned into a pile-up because they'd stayed together throughout. But they'd had fun. Jill said she was beginning to get the hang of it.

They snapped on their skis and went to stand in line at the lift. Jill and Ann held hands, wobbled together, but didn't fall. The man working the lift helped them into seats, and then they were on their way up the mountain. Daniel and Deena took the next chair.

What are you so quiet about? he asked. Aren't you enjoying this?

Deena didn't answer, and she didn't have to, Jill's voice called from up ahead. Deena wished she were alone. She didn't know what was wrong, but she was in a mood. She looked at the hills. People spoke of skiing down a mountain, but from up here you knew it wasn't one mountain, but a chain of mountains, one attached to the next.

Getting off the lift this time, Deena was prepared. She kept her knees slightly bent, her skis in position, as instructed, and managed to get off the lift and down the mound without falling.

Wait for us, Daniel called.

She waited. There was comedy in the situation, Daniel at the hands of two southern women. He was stuck helping them. She watched them move slowly toward her; then Ann stumbled. Daniel bent to help her, and feeling his pull, Jill's feet slipped. It was better to stay away from groups. Seeing someone else fall made you stumble. She turned and started down, but her feet were too wide apart, and she struggled to bring them together. Ahead of her, in her path, a group of screaming kids were in a heap. She was going too fast to stop. She turned her head and tried to turn her body toward the right, and it helped; her skis veered right. But just when she thought she'd make it past the tangle of fallen skiers, another kid fell in front of her, her skis ran into his, and she too went down. The kid spluttered and laughed. She didn't. Avoiding Jill, Ann, and Daniel, she wound up with a pimply kid. And he was laughing too hard to make untangling herself possible. Finally she separated herself, stood, and almost fell over another kid.

Halfway down the slope, Daniel caught up with her.

This is fun, he said. Why don't you wait for us? It's more fun as a group.

Behind him, Jill and Ann were holding hands, making their way down awkwardly, but steadier. With Daniel at a distance, they didn't seem to fall as much, Deena thought. But already he was moving toward them. Wait for us, he said again. She watched for a moment, then allowed her skis and the slope to take her away.

At the bottom of the hill she stood in line for the lift, got on, and was halfway up the slope by the time Daniel, Jill, and Ann reached bottom. She would ski down, ride up again, and probably catch up with them.

Late afternoon, Daniel suggested they go down the slope together, just the two of them. Deena didn't want to; she'd had enough for the day; she was tired, her legs were sore.

Daniel insisted. One quick run before we leave. You went up how many times? One more won't hurt.

She looked at him. He was trying, but it was too late. Too late for what? Daniel would say. When it suited his purpose, he could be obtuse.

Her silence made him talkative. He chattered the whole way up.

They got off the lift together, down the mound, around the bend to face the downhill descent, and they were both still standing. They stood and looked down. Then they bent their knees and took off.

He was graceful. He turned into the bends of the slope, his long legs together, his body forward just enough. Deena started out stiffly, resentfully. But the speed and the wind thrilled her again, and she arrived at the foot of the slope exuberant and wanting to go up once more. They went up and down again. Beside her, she felt Daniel breathing in relief. For now, he was forgiven. The sun was setting and the orange gleam turned the snow a warm white. It was getting colder, and her socks were wet, but at the cabin a hot shower awaited, and also a good meal. Tonight, they'd have grilled steaks. She was hungry.

It rained in the morning, and Deena wanted to leave. There's nothing to do here in the rain, she said. We may as well get going early.

Daniel disagreed. I can think of a lot of reasons to stay. I've been looking forward to two days away from the city, I drove a long way, and

I'm enjoying this. We can do different things today and leave late, as planned. Why can't you just relax? he said.

I can relax more comfortably at home. We came here to ski and we can't do that in the rain. Besides I've had enough of skiing for now. I'm sore everywhere.

Ann stretched her legs and nodded. I can't move my legs or arms.

Then let's go, Jill said. We'll have fun driving back and maybe it won't be raining in the city.

In the car, the ongoing sound of tires on wet road, an endless ride. In the back seat, Jill and Ann were quiet. Ann yawned, Jill followed. They giggled. Daniel switched from station to station. There had to be good music somewhere. He was angry; he needed something hard. He found something, fiddled with the knob to bring it in.

Okay, he said, looking at Deena. Who's this?

She didn't turn her head. She had no idea. Who was it? The Stones? He wouldn't ask her about a Stones song. Too easy. Jefferson Airplane? She didn't care who it was. But she used to care. Their first summer together, every drive was an opportunity for a lesson on the history of rock and roll. She'd heard her first Who song in this car. The Who, Daniel said. But who are they? Deena asked. The Who, Daniel said. Who, who, who.

Well? Daniel looked at her, challenging. You ought to know this.

The Who, she said.

The Who! he said. This is nothing like them. You've heard this a thousand times. I have the album.

Good for you, she said.

No ear and no rhythm, he said, shaking his head. When she hums, she makes rock and roll sound like Jewish music, all minor chords. She inserts melody into hard rock.

Jill and Ann laughed, and Deena hated him.

"Mercedes Benz" came on and he turned up the volume. Okay, Jill. Name this tune.

Deena looked at Jill and they said it together: Janis Joplin.

That was too easy, Jill said.

I'll test you on another one, he said. But first, this pit stop. I could use a cup of coffee.

They piled out. After the bathroom, coffee, and the bathroom again, they piled back in. They were nearing the town of Nyack when Ann noticed that her purse was missing. She was frantic. All her keys, her office pass, her wallet, her paycheck, which she hadn't had a chance to deposit, they were all in her purse.

Daniel stopped in front of a reggae bar on Main Street, at a phone booth. Ann was in tears; she couldn't talk. Jill called and was informed that the purse had been discovered by the waitress, reported to the state police, and was now en-route between the rest stop and police headquarters in Stony Point.

We'll go back, Daniel said.

That's an extra hour of driving, Deena said. Ask if they'll ship the purse COD.

It's an idea, Daniel said. He turned to Jill.

But Ann didn't want to go on without her purse and Deena was overruled.

I know what, Daniel said. Why don't you stay here and wait? I can pick you up on the way back. Have a drink at the bar. The band starts up in less than an hour. Maybe someone will ask you to dance.

Deena looked at him. He was serious. He wanted her to dance with another man. If she danced with another man, he would feel better about Jill.

You're insane, Deena said.

It was just an idea, Daniel said. And not such a bad one. There are also antique shops up and down the street.

Yeah. And it's raining and they're all closed. Just shut up and drive.

He took the Thruway north and drove fast. In the back seat, Jill and Ann were silent.

They arrived home after three, after driving down the West Side Highway into Manhattan to leave Ann and Jill at their front door.

This also infuriated Deena. For her, Daniel had a policy: he didn't drive in Manhattan. But for Jill and Ann, he offered door-to-door service. It didn't seem to occur to him that it was possible to drop them off at the Fifty-ninth Street bridge, that they were perfectly capable of getting home in a taxi.

At home, Daniel turned on the stereo.

Deena had a headache. She'd had enough of his music for the day. She went upstairs and sat on her bed, grateful for her own bed. Tonight she could hate Daniel in privacy. There was something to be said for life according to the laws of menstruation. Living in close quarters with another human being you sometimes needed separation. Tonight greater distance between the two beds would be better. She pushed the beds apart. In her parents' room, each bed had stood anchored against a wall, the wide space between a Red Sea. Who went to whose bed? At thirteen Deena measured the space, four long Johnny-May-I-Cross-Your-Golden-River steps, three and a half for her mother, two probably for her father's long legs.

On the dresser beside her bed was a letter from him. She picked it up to reread it.

A seed cannot grow to perfection as long as it maintains its original form, he wrote. Growth requires decomposition.

What was that supposed to mean? His letters had grown more cryptic, and he was always quoting.

Miracle at Philadelphia was on the dresser too. She should have taken it with her upstate. With something to read, she might not have minded the rain, Daniel, or Jill, for that matter. But it was a book she had to read for work, and at the last minute she'd decided not to take along work.

She opened it, read a sentence, reread the sentence. She couldn't concentrate. She needed to do something active, not read.

Her father always wanted to know what she was reading and thinking; she would tell him. She too could fill a page with quotes. She copied out of the book an Oliver Ellsworth note on the debates in Convention: *We grow more and more skeptical as we proceed. If we do not decide soon, we shall be unable to come to any decision.* She quoted George Washington: *Democratical States must always* feel *before they can see;—it is this that makes their governments slow, but the people will be right at last.* Then Jefferson writing to Washington: *The new circumstances in which we are placed call for new words, new phrases.* She ended with comments by foreign visitors on the character of an American: *He clings to nothing. At a price, he would part with his house, his carriage, his horse, his God.*

She signed off, sealed, addressed, and stamped the letter. Her father could chew on that for a while.

She walked from room to room. It was too late to do anything use-ful. That was the problem with coming home from somewhere in the middle of the day. After sitting in one place for so many hours, you came home both tired and not tired; you weren't good for anything. You couldn't sit still and read, it was too late to get started on a pro-ject, and it was too early to go to sleep.

She went downstairs. Daniel was hopping backward on one foot, playing air guitar. She couldn't stand him this way, a teenager. He be-longed with Jill.

She walked into the dining room, then the pantry. She stopped at the doors and looked out at the patio. It was too cold and wet to sit outside. The rain was coming down again, thin and constant. Under the eaves of the house next door, pigeons sheltered, heads tucked in, tails fluttering. They wobbled, but maintained their perch.

They were always standing on an edge. They didn't require much. In the narrow space between air-conditioning units and windowsills was where they liked to mate. They cooed and moaned until chased away. But they always found another place. They adapted.

The concrete patio outside was plastered in wet leaves. In the spring she would break up the concrete and plant grass. There was enough work in this house to last the next five years, but Daniel wasn't interested. What he wanted now was to be with twenty-one-year-olds.

She went into the kitchen. On the table was Sunday's paper. She turned the pages, read headlines and ads, and in the Metropolitan section came across the Chase ad. She looked at it. In life, amidst news of political maneuverings, accidents, murders, and other dis-asters, the ad for a loan was completely beside the point. And seeing it gave her no pleasure. It raised questions: This was what she'd worked so hard for?

She dialed Karen's number.

You saw the ad, Karen said. It got really good placement. Greg says it's one of the more expensive spots to purchase. It looks good too.

Deena didn't say anything. She didn't care about placement or even design. She read the line.

What's wrong? Karen asked. Did they change the copy or something?

No, no. The ad is fine. It's me. Probably the weather.

You're home already, Karen said. How was skiing?

Karen didn't know that Jill and Ann had come. Deena had to watch what she said.

We came home early because of the rain, but Sunday was great.

Were you able to ski? Karen asked.

At first just getting off the lift was a big deal. You don't know where to put your skis. We both fell. My first time down the slope I was happy to have made it alive. The second time I started liking it. By the end of the day I was really enjoying the speed.

Sounds like you learned quickly, Karen said. How did Daniel do?

He was better than me. He knows how to use his hips.

You're both so good at things, Karen said. You're so athletic.

I don't think of myself as especially athletic, Deena said. What are you and Greg up to?

As a matter of fact, we were just going out to meet friends for coffee. Greg already has his coat on.

In the living room, Daniel was still blasting music. Deena walked in and switched off the stereo. Daniel turned around, hands halted midair, a question on his face. She had his full attention now. She spoke.

I don't want to see them anymore. I don't want to see either Jill or Ann.

Why not? Daniel asked. What did they do wrong?

Nothing, she said. It's what you're doing. If you want to have an affair with Jill, go ahead and have it. But not in my house. Not in the car either.

The car's mine, Daniel said.

Since when?

Always. It's in my name.

Fine. Give her rides in your goddamn car. But don't bring her here.

I'll call and tell her she's banish-ed.

He exaggerated the word, Shakespearean-actor-like.

Deena looked at him. He hadn't bothered denying anything. He'd taken her accusation in stride, as if every day wives told their husbands to go ahead. There was even anticipation in his face. He was enjoying the intrigue. He couldn't wait to call.

She stood in the kitchen and listened. She'd made herself useful again. She'd given him a reason to call. And how dare he call Jill in front of her, his wife? As if her knowing about it made it all right.

She walked into the living room. Daniel looked up.

Tell Jill I'd like to have dinner with her one night this week. I want to talk to her about something. It will be my treat.

Without me? Daniel asked.

Without you, Deena said. It won't kill you to be alone for a few hours.

But I thought you didn't want to see her again, Daniel said.

I changed my mind.

Daniel relayed the message, then looked up and nodded. She says it will be fun, he said. Why don't you do it on Tuesday, when I work out? I can pick you up after and give Jill a ride home.

I think we're capable of scheduling our dinner and getting there and back on our own. The end of the week is better for me.

Daniel conveyed the information, listened, and laughed.

Jill says you're right, he said. She says I deserve what I get for sticking my nose into what's not my business.

Deena went back to the kitchen. He was so sure of himself, so certain he was wanted everywhere. She knew that whatever she told Jill would be repeated word for word. And Daniel couldn't wait to hear it. The two women in his life talking about him, deciding things. He was sure it was about him they'd be talking.

They ordered a half carafe of wine, two shish kebabs, and two salads.

Daniel's name came up naturally and they laughed at the way he was always right, at his preachings about music, driving, everything.

Joni the phony, Jill quoted and giggled.

The talented ones and the hangers-on, Deena mimicked.

And *No one on the road knows how to drive,* Jill said.

You should have heard him when he was teaching me how to drive a stick, Deena said.

I can just imagine that, Jill said.

In two months, Jill had Daniel down perfectly. Laughing at him came easily to her. It had taken Deena years. She was married to him. If she laughed and ridiculed him, what did it suggest about her?

She'd taken him and the marriage too seriously; she took all of life too seriously. Listening to Jill was a relief. She was inspiring too. Knowing that Jill exercised twice a day had gotten Daniel to run daily instead of alternate days. Whether or not you considered winning the Miss America title an admirable achievement, you had to give Jill credit. She was focused and disciplined. She worked and played hard. You didn't have to choose one or the other; you could have both; you could have everything, if only you took it.

Men, Jill said and shook her head. They're impossible to live with.

What about without? Deena wanted to ask. She wondered about Jill. What was her interest in Daniel? In squabbles she took the woman's side. She sided with Ann against Mike. She supported Deena against Daniel. Looking at Jill, at her plain brown eyes, it seemed possible, maybe certain, that her intentions were entirely honest: she wanted to be a friend. And she was a good friend. It didn't matter what Daniel wanted, Deena decided. She wouldn't be a jealous wife. Jill was twenty-one; she could be a little sister. She was fun. Daniel too was enjoying himself. They could all have a good time, if only Deena would allow it. You could be happy or not in life. You had to make a conscious decision about what you wanted, and starting right now, she would enjoy herself.

But Jill was expecting something. Her eyes were wide open, her lips parted, waiting. She looked a little afraid: what would Deena say?

Deena regretted planning to say anything. If you had something worth saying, you don't plan, you just do it. Now too much was expected.

She began slowly. Sometimes you don't know what you're getting into, she said, and stopped to sip.

Jill looked at her blankly and waited.

Deena inhaled and continued. You get involved with other people and you end up in the middle of something unexpected.

Jill nodded.

Deena didn't even know this was what she was going to say. But having said it, she thought it was enough; she'd add nothing more.

Can you say more? Jill asked.

Deena shook her head. I'm not sure I know what I'm talking about.

Jill looked down, her lashes dark against her pale skin. She was pretty. And innocent. She flirted, but it was in fun. Deena felt herself wanting to lecture Jill like an older sister. Fun has its consequences. She'd learn something about starting up with married men. They weren't as safe as they seemed. Sometimes they took the flirting too seriously. Vulnerable, perhaps because neglected by their wives, they attached themselves a little too fiercely, and inadvertently you wound up in the middle of a marital crisis.

Inadvertently? Was she truly without guile? Jill would report this conversation to Daniel word for word, Deena knew, and ask for an explanation. What did it all mean?

The whole thing was crazy. She was warning Jill for a reason. She wanted help from Jill. She wanted Jill to take over for a while, to take over being saddled with Daniel.

He waited until Deena went to bed. Then he made the call.

Deena sat on the bed, listening. Even with the background noise of Johnny Carson—Daniel had raised the volume on the television— she heard his voice, but she couldn't make out the words. She got out of bed, went to stand at the top of the stairs, and hated herself for doing it. She wanted to hear what he said and he wanted to know what she said, they both needed to know what was being said, but they wouldn't say it to one another. They were married, they were man and wife, but there were things they couldn't say. The intrigue was immature, high school–like. She slid down to the bottom of the stairs, and still she couldn't make out what was being said. He'd untied the wire so the phone would extend into the dining room. She should either walk right in or not bother. What was she doing standing behind doors? She stomped loudly across the living-room floor into the dining room, flicking the television off on the way.

Daniel looked up and glared. Deena put her hand on her hip and glared back.

Just a moment, he said to Jill.

He covered the mouthpiece. Would you mind giving me some privacy? he asked.

Yes, I'd mind.

Daniel took his hand off the mouthpiece. I can't talk now. I'll see you at work tomorrow.

He hung up. Satisfied? he jeered and walked out of the room.

No, she wasn't satisfied. This was her house. He was acting as if he had a right to Jill, as if every day husbands ask their wives for privacy while they have a chat with the other woman.

She followed him into the living room. Admit it, she said. You're in love with Jill.

He looked at her. I like her a lot, he said. Is that a sin?

· · ·

At work the next day Daniel called to remind her that they had ball-room dancing that night. Deena didn't feel like dancing with him, his unfaithful arms around her. She wanted to say, Take Jill, it's what you want. But she didn't say it.

They stood facing each other, waiting for the music to start, and Daniel smiled. Deena swallowed and forced something down. This is what it's like for women who stay. They don't say anything. They absorb and swallow and soon there is nothing left to say. But they hate, how they hate. And still they stay. Somehow they stay.

The music started and they moved together. One two three, one two three. Daniel lifted his arm and stepped to the side; Deena went into the turn. Anger made her stiff, which gave her good dance posture. Daniel stepped back into place and they continued. One two three. They moved well now, and moving like this, as a team, they belonged together.

After class they stopped for dinner at the Kebab House. Deena leaned back, stretched her legs, which were tired, and sipped. Across the table Daniel was sipping from his glass. He was eying her oddly, critically, Deena thought.

You should get a short leather skirt for dancing, he finally drawled.

I thought you didn't like short skirts, she said. And leather?

He shrugged. It's just a thought. You could at least try one and see.

Deena thought she did see. Jill had a leather skirt.

The following week, when Deena arrived home from work, the house was still dark, which was strange. Daniel was usually home before her. On the machine there was a message from his mother saying she hadn't heard from them and hoped all was well.

Deena changed into her running clothes. She'd run in the morning, but if she ran again, she could sleep later the next day.

It was too dark for the track; she ran on the slate sidewalks and the hollow ringing under her feet sounded like knocking on a tomb to wake the dead, Saul asking Samuel what the next day would bring.

She passed the old white farmhouse, circled the block, ran past the old turreted Victorian, then the train tracks, and back to the street with the ancient knobby tree. She ran past their house and tried to see it with the eyes of a passerby, not an owner. An old gambrel built in the twenties. Only the front light was on; Daniel wasn't home yet. She continued running, then stopped. She knew precisely where he was. She knew where he was and with whom. She was wide awake with knowing.

This was how prophecy must feel. You know so hard it's a feeling. She could feel Daniel having drinks with Jill. She turned back and ran into the house. She was breathing too quickly and it wasn't from running. She dialed. There was no answer. But there was always someone working late in that office, Andrew or one of the other consultants. She let the phone ring and ring. She'd get an answer, she'd know she was right, she'd know definitively.

Andrew finally picked up. Daniel left, he said.

Then what are you still doing there? Deena asked.

I'm just finishing up, he said.

She could hear Andrew's hesitation.

He's on his way home then? Deena asked.

I don't know. He went out to eat with some people. He said he'd call in.

Deena hesitated. She wanted to ask whether Jill was with him, but Andrew was already uncomfortable. He knew something. Everyone at the office probably knew, which infuriated Deena. Daniel could at least be discreet. She didn't want to be known as the wife whose husband fell for the secretary. She refused to be that. She'd stop being his wife.

She hung up and spun the Rolodex, found Jill's number and dialed. No answer. If Jill was with Daniel, where was Ann?

She walked from room to room. They had this house; it was what they'd both wanted. They'd worked hard for this. They'd struggled to save, and now that things were easier Daniel wasn't coming home. She went upstairs. She came down again. She couldn't stay still. She would continue running.

She left the door unlocked and ran fast and hard, up the road, into the park. It was dark but today she needed the danger. Her heart was pounding anyway. She entered the track. She was on her third mile; she'd continue for a fourth and maybe a fifth. She could continue running forever. She wasn't feeling any pain in her legs, only something large in her chest, like homesickness, like being away at summer camp and you couldn't call your mother.

She was running in circles, matching what was going on in her head. She quickened her pace and ran without effort, on automatic. She ran round and round, a jilted woman. Jilted. A word you read but never spoke. She was living the word. Going on twenty-seven, she was learning how it felt to be jilted, and still it was an overstatement, unreal. Like falling in love or out of love. As if accidentally.

An hour later, she ran toward home, her muscles tight, her body empty. Running like that, until every bone ached, until there wasn't an ounce of strength left, was purging, like a day of fasting. You cared about nothing but the next glass of cold water. She walked the last block. Daniel was at the door looking for her. He followed her into the kitchen.

You're crazy running this late at night. Five more minutes and I would have called the police. You went to the track, didn't you? And you left the door unlocked.

She didn't answer. She drank, and it was as if she were pouring into a barrel with no throat. After her second glass, she paused. But he was finished, he'd talked himself out; now his head was in the refrigerator. If you waited long enough past questions, they didn't require answers.

She went up to shower.

Half an hour later she came down in a silk robe, the luxury of silk a statement. She'd pretend indifference. She wouldn't confront him with her knowledge. She was too tired.

From the kitchen, the smell of stewing chicken. He hadn't eaten dinner. He'd had drinks. It was no crime to have drinks after work. She stopped for drinks too. She inserted a disk into the player and pressed play.

A candle and bottle of wine were on the table. What was he trying to do, expiate his sins?

Let's eat in the dining room, she said. We'll hear the music better. I'll cook spaghetti.

The chicken will be ready in ten minutes, Daniel said.

I'll start with hot water.

Fifteen minutes later dinner was on the table, but she was more thirsty than hungry. She sipped water, then wine. She listened to the music. Exhausting herself made what came after better. To experience life you have to live hard.

How did Jill's audition go? Deena asked, turning the conversation to the very subject she'd resolved not to mention.

Daniel answered eagerly, eyes shiny. He wanted to talk about Jill. She was hoping for at least a call back, he said. She hasn't gotten it yet.

Is she upset? Deena asked.

Daniel nodded. But she shouldn't be. She's been at it for all of three months and already she's doing better than most. Her acting teacher complimented her monologue the other day. Which is all she has to do for the judges anyway.

She's young, Deena said. And every audition is practice.

Good point, Daniel said. You should tell her that. She looks up to you; what you say is important to her. I think she just has to persist. Persistence, they say, is ninety percent of success.

Deena looked at him. He believed in Jill's success. He'd never cared so much about hers. But it is always the stranger who experiences you at your best.

Daniel looked at her. What are you thinking?

I'm not, she said. I'm listening. How was work today?

Hectic, he said. But fine. We had a hardware problem that the technicians couldn't figure out. After hours and hours of fiddling with it, I came up with a software solution. We needed another bus, but the motherboard is already full. That's the difficulty with PC's. You run out of physical space. We decided finally to switch to multi-task buses; that way, whichever bus is sitting idle will be used to control the printer.

Deena, half-listening only, looked into his eyes and nodded. She'd asked the question, she ought to show interest. But once on the subject of computers, he didn't stop. He veered from one detail to the next, digressing and never coming back to the beginning. All she had to do was tune in every other minute to keep up with what he was saying, but today she didn't want to do even that.

She interrupted him midsentence. I'll call Jill if you clean up, she said, and pushed her chair away from the table.

Deal, he said, stopping as easily as he'd gotten started.

She bored him too, she knew. He called her office a soap opera. So and so and such and such, who said or did this or that, he said. I can't even keep the names straight. Todd and Ron and Sean. Aren't there people with real names in advertising?

She poured herself another glass of wine, took it into the living room, and settled on the sofa. She was in no mood to talk to Jill, but she'd agreed to call. She was always acting against herself, as if to punish herself.

Hi, Jill said simply, as if entirely innocent.

I'm lying here, drink in hand. I could use a foot massage. I took a long run.

I'm jealous, Jill said. I got home too late to run, which is really bad. I'll never get in shape this way. It defeats the whole purpose of my living here. New York City was meant to inspire me.

She didn't say why she'd missed her run, and knowing more than she was told, Deena felt again that fierce clarity, an adrenaline sharpness of danger.

How many miles? Jill asked.

Six, Deena said.

I'll have to do a double run tomorrow, Jill said. We should run together sometime. After work or on the weekend.

Or you could come out here, Deena said reluctantly. She often wished for someone to run with, but why did it have to be Jill? Jill, Jill, Jill everywhere.

Let's do both, Jill said. This Sunday here, the following one there.

That might be fun, Deena said. She paused to sip. Wine and coffee were the two worst beverages to drink after running, but they tasted great.

Daniel says you're upset about the audition, Deena said, remembering why she'd called.

Yeah, Jill said. I suck. I'm beginning to think that I'd be better off sticking to dance-aerobics for the special talent segment. Maybe that's all I'm really good at.

I don't think so, Deena said. Anyone can do aerobics. A good monologue is a much greater achievement. Even if you don't get it down perfectly, it shows greater ambition. That should count for something.

You're probably right, but I'm not feeling very talented, and this segment counts for forty percent in the preliminaries. I don't know what I'm doing wrong. Everything seemed to click. I was sure I had it. And these acting classes are so expensive.

But if you win, you won't have to worry about all that. You'll get scholarships. You'll have a choice of acting schools. Right now, you have to concentrate on winning. The judges are not expecting a Shakespearean-trained actress. By the way, which monologue are you studying?

I'm working on several different ones. My agent suggested something southern, so I'm trying a Scarlett O'Hara piece. Also a short bit from *Cat on a Hot Tin Roof.*

That's interesting, Deena said. I guess you're entering as a resident of North Carolina, not New York. I hadn't thought about it.

She pulled her toes. They needed stretching after so much cramping, first in shoes then sneakers. If legs and arms need stretching, why not toes? She rubbed the raw skin on the sole of her foot, half listening.

It's a long process, Jill was saying, and I'm what they call a late starter. I still have to enter a local county pageant. If I win they'll sponsor me for the state pageant; then the state will sponsor my entry on the national level. I have a couple of first placements in small-town pageants under my belt which helps. But I have to decide where to enter very soon, and it will determine whether or not I stay in New York.

Deena paused. If Jill moved back to North Carolina, then what? Could things go back to normal? And if she stayed?

Daniel came to the door. He stood drying his hands on a dish-towel, eager to talk, and this Deena knew she wouldn't forget. Even if Jill moved back and the whole thing blew over, some things you don't forget.

Here's Daniel, she said.

They ran together in Central Park. Jill wore pink tights with bright blue side stripes, a matching zip-up top, and a jacket that went with it, an outfit. Her hair looked the way it always looked, curled and high; it wasn't pulled back. She was disciplined that way. She worked at looking good, and the work distinguished her from others. Deena thought she would probably make it, if not as Miss America, then as something else. About herself she wasn't sure. She didn't try hard enough. She'd dressed and fingered her hair without looking in the mirror, not because she didn't care how she looked. It was some-thing else. She hadn't grown up with the knowledge that looks mat-ter. She didn't treat herself as if she deserved the best. She tended if anything toward punishment. It seemed there were women who were goddesses on pedestals, and then there were the others: she and her mother and grandmothers before her, women born to be wives and mothers. They didn't have their coffee brought to bed because they were out of bed before anyone else. They made beds, washed laundry and dishes, saw the hamper and sink fill again before they were entirely empty. The men had to eat. The children couldn't be sent to school without breakfast. It was work, and someone had to do it. These were the women who'd given birth to her, and she was destined to be one of them.

Jill was chewing gum. Hi, she said, and blew a pink bubble.

Deena laughed.

Want one? Jill asked, holding out a stick.

Deena shook her head. No, thanks.

Jill shrugged and peeled the stick, added it to the wad already in her mouth, and the scent of cinnamon filled the air between them.

Deena's mouth was suddenly stale. Why not chew gum? Why not enjoy what was offered? She'd say yes to things. Obliterate the word *no*. Jill knew the most important word in the English language. She knew the word *yes*.

I think I will have a stick after all, Deena said.

Jill smiled and held out the pack. Take two, she said, or your mouth will feel too empty.

Deena hesitated.

Don't worry. I purchased a jumbo pack last night. Ann and I figured out the other day that I average a stick a mile.

Deena laughed. At that rate, you must end up with a five- to six-stick wad. Your bubbles must be enormous.

She peeled her sticks, chewed, and spicy cinnamon filled her mouth. She hadn't chewed gum since high school and only after the school principal announced that any girl seen chewing gum would be expelled. A disgusting, immodest habit, she lectured, something you might expect from modern Jews or shiksas in the street, chewing constantly like cows chewing their cud. The principal wondered also whether it was kosher gum the girls were chewing, since she didn't know of a kosher bubble gum.

After that even girls who'd never liked gum planned clandestine gum-chewing get-togethers.

Deena and Jill entered the loop. In front of them and behind them people walked, ran, and bicycled. Deena's eyes darted. There was so much to look at. Running here was more than just running. There was people watching, touring. They passed the Metropolitan, the Guggenheim snail, then the ICP.

Is this your regular pace? Deena asked, worried that with her long legs Jill might want to take longer strides.

Jill nodded. Is it good for you? I worried you'd be faster because you're smaller.

Deena laughed and the wad of gum slid down her throat. She choked and coughed and had to stop running. Jill looked at her, concerned. She rubbed Deena's back. But the gum was already in her stomach, a rock.

I'll be all right, she said, her voice a croak.

You sure? Jill asked.

Deena nodded. It hurt, she said, but I'm fine now. We can continue.

Let's walk for a few minutes, Jill said.

Have you ever done that? Deena asked.

Jill shook her head and unwrapped another stick. In her mouth, six sticks belonged.

March

Daniel was at a conference in Nashville, and Deena was on her own. She woke to the sound of the Supremes. *Stop, in the name of*—it came through the double windows, then stretched and faded. She lay in bed hearing the words that weren't there. She could turn on the stereo and play the rest of the song if she wanted. She could play the whole album. It was a Saturday; she had no errands planned; she could do anything or nothing. There was only herself to please. But she wouldn't get up yet. She'd extend this moment, this day. She lay listening to house sounds: the groan of the water heater in the basement, the wind turning the sharp corners of the house. Then came the thud of the newspaper on the front step. A screen door yawned, open, close. Morning sounds. The morning of a day all her own. She lay spread-eagled under the covers, wanting to occupy both beds. She was warm, she was comfortable. If she didn't move, could she suspend these waking moments, make them last? But they were passing, already the first ones had passed; it didn't matter that she remained recumbent in bed. The traffic was already going from the hush of morning to the regular daytime hum, and it would continue until midnight, when the dark and the hour would once again assert a level of silence. What was the first thing she wanted to do on this gray, cold day?

At the bathroom sink, she brushed her teeth slowly, concentrating on individual teeth. Today she would do everything slowly. No one waited for her to come out. She had time enough to brush correctly and thoroughly, hard and in circles, round and round, the way you wash a plate. Teeth are no different, her dentist said. They were stones, geological, the remains of Cro-Magnon man. They had to be scraped, cleaned, drilled, and filled with what were basically primitive tools. Dentists hacking away at rock.

Daniel's mother, who at the age of twenty-three lost her molars in a fall, quickly sprouted a new pair.

Unusual in humans, the doctor said. Animals have the capability of growing more than one adult set.

Deena was certain that if she lost her teeth that would be it; no more teeth. They were weak in the first place; the surface crumbled at the slightest provocation. Already she had a mouthful of metal fillings despite a lifetime avoidance of hard pretzels, candy, and gum.

Like his mother's teeth, Daniel's were too long and crowded, one tooth bumped against the other and overlapped. The teeth of a carnivore. And she was married to this man. But it was good for the weak to acquire opposite genes. Short should marry tall, weak strong. Still, some mornings, when he was just out of the shower, his black hair wetly plastered down on his legs, he looked like a gorilla.

She put on a robe and went downstairs, her hand sweeping the smooth wood of the dark banister, her robe dusting the stairs. She wouldn't mind living here by herself, an old maid. She walked the long way, through the living room, dining room, pantry, into the kitchen. The quiet and coolness and width of the house were perfect. She wouldn't ruin it with music. She'd read the paper in this quiet, empty house. She walked back into the living room, onto the cold porch, to the front door. Already the plastic sleeve was coated with frost. She shook off the ice, took the paper into the kitchen, and did what thousands were doing at that moment. If there was sanctity in numbers, *The New York Times* would be holy, a prayer book. She read the paper every morning, absorbed its rhythms and cadences, the pyramidal structure of breaking stories: first the facts that draw, next the lesser facts, then the necessary details, followed by the less necessary, and on to the full story. Each sentence presented enough information to pull the reader to the next sentence, and also enough to make further reading unnecessary.

Deena sat with coffee and the paper, a stretch of morning with no layout for the day, no one interrupting, asking what to do. There was nothing to do. She had all the time in the world.

She cleared her throat to hear her voice. She looked at the phone, but no, she wouldn't call anyone. She would experience a day of silence. Having started as one of six children in a noisy family of eight, where everyone knew everything, and nothing was private, she'd wanted silence. In college, she liked the early morning silence of the dormitory; afternoons she went to the library. In lecture halls, waiting for class to begin, another kind of silence. You heard the creak of newspaper pages being turned, the draw of Coke sipped with a straw, a cough, but not the comfortable babble of people knowing people. Her life was growing ever more silent. Where would she end?

Alone in the house she heard the water coming to a boil, then the coffee brewing. She heard the sounds of herself, her breathing, her stomach growling. She read while she ate. After an early lunch, she went running. It was cold outside, too cold to venture into the city. Besides, she was in the city every day. Today, she'd stay home. She'd light a fire in the fireplace and eat dinner in front of the fire. But she'd have to split wood.

She brought the ax and wedge up from the basement. She'd seen Daniel do it often enough. She should know how. Where you placed the wedge made all the difference. She eyed the log, looking for center. She lifted the ax slowly, let it down, and heard the wood give. She lifted and brought the ax down again and this time the log splintered, but not cleanly. She stopped to take off her jacket. Now the halves had to be split into quarters. She placed the wedge first at one end, then the other, and it worked; she produced a cleaner cut.

She was sweating. She pulled off her sweater. It was below zero outside and she was sweating in a cotton T-shirt. She lifted the ax again and the muscles in her arm thickened. Daily wood-chopping and she'd look like Paul Bunyan. She brought the ax down on the other half log, almost hit her toe, and knew to keep her feet at a distance. If she wasn't careful she'd wind up without a toe and with the knowledge that there is a God and that he does care what you do on the seventh day. Chopping wood on the Sabbath was a sin right out of the Bible. Next would come a bolt of lightning. Or the earth would open and swallow her.

She continued more carefully. She split two more logs, quartered them, and had enough wood for the next three nights.

She carried the split wood into the house, stacked three logs to form a pyramid, pushed newspaper underneath and kindling on top, and started the fire. She continued prodding and poking until the wood caught.

Outside dusk was replacing day. A whole day had passed and she hadn't seen or spoken to anyone. She selected music for the evening, records Daniel never wanted to play. Steeleye Span. The new Vollenweider Karen had given her. In the kitchen she heated a can of pea soup and ate in front of the fire, her back against the sofa, a glass of red wine beside her. But she was wide awake, she had energy, she wanted to do something. The closets. She could use the ax to take them down. First she would reassemble the cardboard moving wardrobes from the attic and transfer all their clothes. She turned the music up and carried the glass and bottle upstairs. She was halfway up the stairs when the phone rang.

It was Daniel and he sounded subdued.

What's wrong? Deena asked.

I'm bored, he said. I worked furiously until sundown yesterday. Today I stayed in my room most of the day. Jill and Pat visited for a while. They brought beer.

Why didn't you sit in the sun. It's below zero here.

I'm not on vacation, he said. The others were working hard. I was off for religious reasons, and lying in the sun didn't seem right.

Where's everyone now? Deena asked.

They went to dinner at a lobster restaurant. I ate in my room.

You could have gone and eaten a salad. Why do you have to be such a martyr about it?

Because I told you before, a little kosher is not kosher. Besides, the hotel went to the trouble of ordering kosher meals. The least I can do is eat them. I'm meeting them at the lounge for drinks.

Good, have a drink. Lighten up.

She started with her own clothes, walking back and forth with piles of tangled hangers. Why did she have so much? More than half remained unworn. Daniel's side of the closet was rational. He had six suits for work, some better than others, and a dozen white cotton shirts. For after work, jeans, T-shirts, and sweaters. Was it possible for women to have it that easy?

At twelve-thirty the closets were finally empty and she was tired, her shoulders were sore. Demolition would begin in the morning. She went to bed.

Seven A.M. chalk dust filled the room. Deena opened the windows and continued cutting away wallboard and lathing. She could have been sitting or lying on the sofa reading. Better yet she could still be in bed. But she'd started this thing and it had to be finished.

By ten o'clock, the walls were down and only the framing remained. She stepped through, from closet to closet, and back into the room, which with its original dimensions restored looked like a room. Even on this gray day, the extra window made a difference.

She went downstairs. It was only ten o'clock, but she was hungry. She ate a sandwich, thumbed through the day's paper, and still it was only eleven. The day would last forever. When she was alone, every hour hung full. With Daniel, it took longer to get going, and longer to make decisions, and longer and longer and longer.

After lunch, she filled five garbage bags and stood eying the wood framing. If she continued working she'd have the satisfaction of having finished the job. She stood, crowbar in hand, hesitating. Contemplating the work, you see only surface. Doing it, you sink knee-deep and can't see the end. You hold your head; you regret; you continue working, and still the end isn't visible. If you're fortunate you glimpse a certain wisdom in the tyranny. You keep going, the work lasts forever, you have to resign yourself to doing this forever. Once resigned, when you have renounced deadlines and goals and it no longer matters whether you ever finish, then suddenly you do finish. You look at what you've done, and wonder why you didn't see all along that it would be good. You'd know better next time. You'd remember. You'd remember that it's faith you need.

She went down on her knees. They ached. She pushed the flat end of the crowbar under the wood, heaved, and heard the satisfying crack of its giving way. She pulled the nails. If she freed one stud the others would follow. But when she tried the next one, it stuck. She moved to another one, stepped on the crowbar for leverage, and the wood came up, but not without gouging the floor. Fixing one thing, she broke another.

She moved on to the next nail and worked more carefully. She lifted another two-by-four and discovered that the strips of flooring underneath had been pulled out for these closets. Another can of worms. They'd have to find old strips of flooring to replace the missing ones. It wouldn't be easy or cheap.

Late afternoon, the phone rang. Daniel? He hadn't called all day, and she'd considered calling him.

It was Daniel's mother.

I'm worrying about you there all alone, she said. I keep wishing you'd come for the weekend. If I'd known earlier that Daniel was going for the whole weekend, I would have insisted.

I was fine on my own. I had a relaxing day. I read and slept mostly.

Aren't you lonely? And it's too cold to go out. I've been indoors with a sweater and blanket all day.

Try splitting wood. I was sweating in short sleeves.

Splitting wood? Mrs. B. said. You're brave. And strong. Be careful, dear.

Before going to bed, Deena dialed Daniel's room, but there was no answer and she didn't leave a message. He was probably just starting to have some fun.

Monday morning, Daniel called just as she was leaving for work. His voice was strangely excited. He started to tell a story about rooms, and Deena, who was changing her shoes for the third time and looking at the clock, had a hard time following.

Pat and Jill shared? she asked. Your company can't afford separate rooms?

That was the deal, Daniel said. Jill could go along only if she shared.

Then why didn't she carry her own key? Deena asked. How did she get locked out?

I don't know, Daniel said. She just did. Anyway I was up all night. I'm tired.

But you sound better than yesterday. You're having a good time.

I am. We all drank too much and danced too late.

How are the presentations going? Deena asked.

They're fine. There were a couple of snags yesterday, but it was mostly fine. Joe's getting good feedback. I'm so tired and I'm expected downstairs in ten minutes.

Drink coffee. I have to go. I was late before you called, now I'm later.

He called again in the afternoon and again there was that sound in his voice: thrill and fear. What was he so excited about? It wasn't work. Again he talked about the rooms. Pat was angry.

But why is Pat so angry? Deena asked. What happened?

Nothing happened. Anyway I better go. I'll call you later.

She stood holding the receiver until she heard the dial tone. Something had happened. He'd called to tell her. He and Jill. That's what happened. He was telling and not telling her. How had it finally started; whose head had moved toward whose? She saw the movement, then nothing. She couldn't get them closer. She tried starting backward: the two of them on the wide hotel bed. Naked? She started at the beginning again, with drinks and dancing, Jill's arms went around Daniel's neck, Daniel's hands circled her waist. Their eyes met, Daniel looked at Jill's parted lips—

She stopped. Why did she want to know more? She shouldn't know at all. He shouldn't have said anything. Couldn't he keep any secrets? He was inept; he wanted her along every step of the way, as if to guide him and say when, and go ahead. She despised this weakness in him, the need that made him talk.

At home that evening, she went up and down the stairs, her eyes on the phone. If she didn't want to know, why was she waiting for his call? She unplugged the phone. She wouldn't care. She hadn't stopped them all along, why now? But she couldn't sit still. She couldn't eat. Upstairs she looked at the remains of the closet, what she hadn't finished. She pushed a crowbar under the stubborn stud and yanked. The wood lifted, and along with the wood came flooring. She didn't care now. She pushed the crowbar farther and farther. The wood splintered, cracked, but it came up. This was satisfying. She pulled out the next stud and the next. The sound of splintering encouraged her. She was doing something; she could work alone. She could pull anything apart, this whole house if she wanted.

At ten o'clock she stopped. She went downstairs, and poured herself a glass of wine. He was probably trying to call. Let him. Where were you? he'd demand. And why was the answering machine off? Questions. When it was she who should be asking.

She looked at the cold grate. She was in no mood for a fire. What did she want? Nothing. There wasn't a thing in this world she wanted. No, there was something. She wanted her mother and father. But she'd married Daniel.

He called at work the next day. I'm taking an earlier flight, he said. I'll take a taxi from the airport and go right to sleep. I'm so tired.

Who cares, Deena wanted to say. She didn't say it. And when she arrived home and Daniel wasn't there, she did care. Sleep, my foot, she said.

On her pillow was a gift: a miniature southern belle in a straw hat. Was he trying to tell her something? She didn't want to touch it, but she wouldn't leave it where it was. She moved it to Daniel's pillow. Then she went running.

She was running daily now, no off days. She ran with a purpose, a goal, and her body was responding. She was growing leaner and stronger. This was the cure for everything. A body stripped of extras, a body you could live in without shame made up for a lot that was missing. She was shedding slag and emerging minus the dross like a sculpture.

She ran, pushing for speed, for something extra. Without the extra, one run merged into the next, yesterday's run became today's and tomorrow's, one long run. If she didn't run an extra mile or a faster one, there was no struggle, nothing special, nothing won. She added another mile, then turned toward home.

The house was still dark. On the machine, no messages. Upstairs, two unblinking doll eyes. She turned the doll facedown, sat at the foot of the bed. She untied her sneakers, pulled off her damp socks, and rubbed her big toes, which were sore.

When she heard Daniel at the door, she hurried into the shower. She wanted and didn't want to see him. She was afraid to see him. What would he say? She remained under running water as long as she could, then she dressed slowly. He didn't come upstairs. Was he also afraid?

When she went downstairs, he was on the phone. She listened. Jill.

Can't live without her for a minute? Deena said, and walked into the kitchen.

What did you say? he said. Come back here.

Come here yourself, she said under her breath. Now she had his attention.

I should go, he said in a low voice.

She busied herself toasting bread. She'd have a tuna sandwich for dinner. He could fend for himself.

He was still talking in that voice; then he hung up. He came into the kitchen and looked over her shoulder.

I'm not hungry, he said.

He was foolish to come so close. She had a knife in her hand. She could hurt him. She turned and looked for the guilty face of an unfaithful husband. It was brown, it was the same, but different. He was someone else. He didn't belong to her.

What have I done? he asked. I just got home.

You know better than I what you've done.

I don't know what you're talking about. Did you see what I got you? he asked.

Yes, Deena said. Was it Jill's idea?

I guess you don't like it. It was my idea, actually, and she thought it was cute.

Give it to her then.

She opened the fridge. The lettuce was rotten, the cucumber soft. There was nothing to eat. She threw the lettuce and cukes out and kicked the door closed.

I guess a trip to Waldbaum's is overdue, Daniel said.

He stood hovering behind her, in the way. What did he want? Forgiveness?

Make yourself useful, Deena said. Uncork a bottle of wine.

I don't want any, he said. I've had a headache all day. I've been drinking too much.

Good. More for me.

She took her plate to the table.

I'll sit with you, he said, and pulled out the other chair.

They looked at each other. He smiled.

I noticed you kept yourself busy, he said.

She looked at him. He was trying to be friendly, but it was too late for that.

I thought you were tired. Where were you? she asked.

At the office. I wanted to check something out, a bug we were stuck on for hours.

You went to the office in jeans?

He shrugged. I spent the weekend in a suit, I needed a day off. Besides I went in late and only for a couple of hours.

He stretched his arms over his head. I am pretty tired. You should have been there. The music was good, Pat and Joe got up to dance; imagine Joe dancing. I cut in and then for the rest of the night Joe kept cutting in on me no matter who I danced with. So I asked Gary to dance. You know him, the technician who came to the club that time. He never dances, never mind dancing with a man. He didn't want to, but I talked him into it, and Joe cut in. It was hilarious.

Daniel's voice was eager, and pleasure filled his face. After years of refusing to get up for even a simple waltz, he couldn't get enough of dancing, as if it had just been invented.

In bed that night Deena lay beside him, wanting him to touch her, which surprised her. She couldn't remember feeling like this, not since the beginning, before they were married, when she'd wanted and wanted him.

She reached for his hand. No response. She tried again, and after a pause, as if he were unwilling, she felt his long brown fingers on her skin, moving knowingly. He stopped to check: was she ready? This was new, his checking. She lay still, concentrating, feeling his fingers, which were hard. He was rough, he was careless, but he knew what she liked. She breathed quickly and then it was over. He followed, a step or two behind. This too was new.

After, he moved away a little too soon, and they lay in separate beds, not talking. She went to the bathroom. When she returned, his back was turned toward her. She lay on her side, then her stomach. Still she was uncomfortable. She turned onto her side again. All these years together, desire had been low and comfort high. Now there was no comfort, only desire.

Can't you keep still? he said. I'm trying to sleep.

She went into the next room, which was empty. With the closets down, it wasn't even a dressing room. She sat on the floor and tried reading. She couldn't concentrate. Her face burned hot. For the first time since she'd known him, he hadn't been entirely willing. She felt warm, she was sweating, and it wasn't the cleansing sweat of a good run.

She would avoid wanting him. She wouldn't sleep near him. She'd make her bed here. She needed only her mattress. She'd do it now. She needed something to do. She walked into their bedroom and threw her blanket off.

What are you doing? he said. I'm trying to sleep.

I'm moving into the other room, she said.

Can't it wait till morning?

He wasn't asking why or saying don't.

She pulled and pushed the clumsy mattress, a heavy, unwilling lump, scraped her hand on the frame of the door, cursed, and he continued lying there. She heaved and shoved and finally kicked the mattress into place and then stood in a rage, not ready to surrender herself to the hateful mattress. She pulled and tucked in the sheet and blanket. She would make this her room. After seven long years, she'd once again have her own room.

The phone rang. She looked at her watch. It was after twelve. Her father? She ran downstairs and picked up on the third ring.

Daniel was halfway down the stairs.

Who was it? he asked.

A hang-up, Deena said.

He went back to bed. Five slow minutes later, the phone rang again.

I'll get it, he said, and Deena heard his voice, concerned at first, then light and teasing.

In the morning, he put on his best suit and asked which tie, this or that one.

Choose your own tie, Deena said.

I thought you liked doing it, he said.

Not anymore.

Her face was hot. This was what husbands asked their wives every morning. Throughout the world, wives dispensed tie advice to men who wore the ties swaggering before their secretaries. She was through as a tie advisor. Her previous participation disgusted her.

There was a crash and then silence. She walked to the foot of the stairs and up to the first landing. He was standing at the mirror above the bathroom sink, combing his thinning hair. He turned his head, saw her, and the comb fell into the sink. He was nervous, he was dropping things.

I knocked over the bottle of mouthwash, he explained.

At the door, he opened his briefcase and looked at the cassette in his Walkman. His hair, his body, his music—he'd become self-absorbed. He was more attractive when he cared less.

He reached into his pocket and then into his other pocket. He put his briefcase down, and searched in the inner pocket of his coat.

My keys, have you seen my keys? he asked.

Deena shrugged.

He left the briefcase near the door and ran upstairs, in a hurry now.

This was another thing wives did for their husbands. Today she wouldn't help him find his keys. She would ignore him. But already her eyes were checking the standard places. The top of the television, the mantel, beside the phone, and yes, they were near the phone, where he'd stopped first thing when he came in the night before.

He came down the stairs, irritated now.

I can't find my keys, he said. He looked at her accusingly, as if it were her fault he'd lost them.

I didn't hide them, she said. They're where you left them last night.

Daniel's eyes went to the phone, remembering now. Yes, he'd been there, he'd put them there, why didn't she say so. He took two long steps across the room, pocketed them, and said, See you later.

He called at work.

I'm planning a special dinner tonight, he said. For just the two of us.

I have to run, Deena said. And I'm tired.

Didn't you already run in the morning? But it doesn't matter. Run if you want to. I'll do the shopping and cooking. I'll set up the card table in front of the fire. How does that sound?

All right, she said. She couldn't say anything else.

Someone was telling him what to do, the right things to do, but it was too late. She knew too much. She closed the door to her office, put her face on the cool wood of her desk. She was tired. Her eyes closed. Maybe she could sleep for a few minutes. But her head hurt and her heart pounded as if she were running. She was out of breath and wide awake. She'd never sleep again. She'd die of fatigue, still sleepless.

Karen knocked at the door. Are you all right? she asked. You look tired.

Deena nodded. I didn't get much sleep last night. I think I'll leave early.

Leave now, Karen said. It's four o'clock. I'll tell Paul you weren't feeling well.

Should I? Deena said. I have this copy to write. I'll try to work for another hour.

You're sure? Karen said. Do you want some aspirin?

Good idea. I have some here, thanks. She opened her drawer, took two, and gulped down water from the perennial bottle on her desk.

That should help, she said. Thanks.

I'll leave the door three-quarters closed so you won't be disturbed, Karen said.

Deena nodded and gulped more water, hiding behind the bottle. Sympathy was dangerous. She had to hold on or she'd give herself away.

He was in the kitchen with an apron tied around his waist. Bags of groceries were on the floor, and on the table a baguette and wine.

Hungry? he asked.

She smelled cinnamon. What are you making? she asked.

Moroccan lamb stew with raisins and apricots. Served over couscous. I think it will be very good.

I'm more tired than hungry, Deena said. Maybe if I run I'll get a second wind.

Skip a day, Daniel said. Take a bath instead. Give your muscles a rest.

She wanted to skip running. Her legs were weak. Her head. It was cold out. She could crawl into bed and sleep for a month.

Upstairs she changed and splashed cold water on her face. Her nose was red, her eyes watery, and seeing herself in the mirror, they filled again. She needed the cold wind on her face. She didn't want him to see her like this.

In the living room, she cleared her throat. I'm going, she called.

She closed the door behind her and hesitated. Was he walking toward the phone right now? If she opened the door and walked in, would she find him on the phone saying that the dinner was doing the trick, she already seemed less angry?

She circled the block eight times, stretched, and was ready for a hot bath. Inside, Daniel was on the phone. Deena stood still at the door and listened.

Don't count on it, he was saying. In the history of the company, there hasn't been a Jewish VP, never mind a president.

It was his mother. He'd saved for her the details of his accomplishments, the compliments and congratulations that had come his way. Which was as it should be. Only a mother listens to the details of her son's success with pure pride.

Half an hour later, Deena took her seat at the card table he'd set up in the living room in front of the fire. Daniel served the cous-cous.

Not so much, Deena said. I'm not hungry.

He spooned the stew over the cous-cous, cinnamon and cardamom filled her nostrils, but she resisted. She was in no mood for sweet cinnamon. What she wanted was bitter herbs.

She looked into the fire and her eyes clouded. She had to stop. She looked down, fidgeted with her fork, brought food to her mouth, but she had a hard time swallowing.

Daniel was eating. No matter what happened, he was able to eat.

This is delicious, he said. This recipe will have to become our house special.

Their house. Would they continue having this house? She looked at the candles. What were they doing here, eating dinner with candles on the table like a couple?

She sipped wine. That went down. She sipped again and swallowed another spoonful of cous-cous.

Tomorrow night we have to go to Waldbaum's, he said. We're out of all basics. We haven't shopped in a month. Now that we have a pantry, we're neglecting it.

Their life together. Shopping, cooking, eating, and washing dishes. She yawned. She was too tired to respond. She was falling asleep at the table and nothing had been said; nothing important was ever said.

I'm having a hard time keeping my eyes open, she said.

Go to bed, Daniel said. I'll clean up.

Would he call to give his report now? She didn't care. She was too tired to care. She would just sleep. But upstairs, there was only the frame of her bed, a gaping hole. Her mattress was in the other room. But why should she move out of the room? It wasn't she who'd done wrong. She crawled into Daniel's bed. Tonight he could sleep on the floor.

Far away, a phone rang and was answered. Jill again? She propped herself up on her elbow and sipped water. She was dizzy. Even the one glass of wine on an empty stomach had been too much. She lay down and closed her eyes, but Daniel was at the door asking, Are you awake?

Who is it? she asked.

Your father, he said.

She sat up. Yes, I'm awake.

She held on to the banister, then the back of the sofa. Hello, she said, and wondered: was this the way to greet her father? But what were the alternatives? Should she say *Shalom aleichem* on the phone?

A giten uvend, her father said, his voice clear and strong. He was nearby, he was standing right beside her.

Where are you? she asked. You sound close.

I am in Jerusalem, he said. But I am your father. I am close to you even when I am far away. I think of you morning, noon, and night. Tell me. What news do you have?

There is no news, Deena said. Everything is always the same.

Nothing remains the same. Every minute brings change. You're unhappy, her father said. I can hear in your voice that you're not happy.

I'm just tired. I didn't sleep last night.

I received your letter. Growing more skeptical, and parting with your house and God—strange words. You are not an American, even if you are married to one. You say there is no news, but blood is thicker than water. I can feel that something is wrong. I want to see you. Mameh wants to see you. Why don't you get on the first plane and come?

They're quotes from a book I'm reading for work, Deena said.

Listen, he said. Work will be there when you return. You have all your life to work. Your mother and I won't be here forever. And today is better than tomorrow. We haven't seen you in years.

Let me talk to Mameh. Is she there?

It's too difficult for her to walk so many stairs. She tires quickly. Come and you'll see and hear her.

Deena hung up and sat staring into the blurred fire.

What do they want now? Daniel asked.

They, as if they were strangers. She looked at him. Was it for him she'd given them up?

I thought you were tired, Daniel said.

I was. Now I'm awake. They want me to visit.

Maybe you should, he said, and went back to the dishes.

She looked at his retreating back. That was a first. He wanted her to go, he was willing for her to go, which changed everything. If he were set against her going, if as usual he listed all the reasons why she couldn't go, then she would have wanted to.

At Waldbaum's the next night, Daniel walked the aisles quickly. Food shopping would not be the evening's entertainment. Whatever had happened between Jill and him, there were some positive effects.

He moved through the register quickly, and within minutes the groceries were loaded in the trunk. He turned on the engine and put the car in gear. By the time Deena realized he wasn't in reverse, it was too late. They rammed into the cement column in front of the car, bounced back, and sat shaken. The engine stalled and was silent.

They got out to view the damage. It could have been worse.

Maybe I should drive, Deena said.

I'm fine, Daniel said.

She buckled her seatbelt and eyed him, wary now. He was distracted. It wasn't safe to be a passenger with him at the wheel.

When he pulled into the driveway, the house alarm was blaring. They looked at each other. How long had it been going this time?

They left the car running, got out, and walked around the house. The front and back doors were locked; all the windows were closed. They walked into the house carefully. Deena punched in the numbers, and the screaming stopped mid-note, but their ears still rang.

It makes a lot of noise, Deena said, but no one stops to check, the police don't respond. What good is it?

I'll have it checked out, Daniel said. It probably needs adjusting.

Pulling into the garage, he misjudged, and the mirror on the passenger side snapped off.

You shouldn't be driving, Deena said.

I'm just tired today, he said.

She wondered how he was holding up at work. Another conference was coming up, this one in San Francisco. Was he just preoccupied? He hadn't mentioned Jill's name since the phone call. Was it a sign that more or less was happening between them?

·   ·   ·

Sunday morning, Daniel paced. We spend too much time inside. I'm sick of it, he said.

So go out, Deena said. I'm going running.

When she got back, he was in bed, facing the wall. She stood looking at him.

We can go to a movie, she said. It's too cold for anything else.

I'm not in the mood for a movie, he said.

Then what do you want? What would you like to do?

I don't know.

Where's Jill? Deena asked.

He turned eagerly, wanting to talk. I don't know. She won't return my calls. I don't know what I did.

Maybe she's away, visiting family or something.

He shook his head. She was down there recently. And she would have said something at the office if she was going.

He was a teenager pining and she was his soothing mother. How had she come to this?

Did you talk to Ann? Deena asked. She must know.

There's no answer, Daniel said.

But when Deena came downstairs after her shower, he was in the kitchen, putting together two heaping sandwiches.

They flew in late last night on the red-eye, slept late this morning, and then went to the gym, he explained.

He sat at the table and took a too-large bite out of his sandwich.

Deena filled a glass of water, drank, and watched him over the rim. He was restored, he was happy again, but the strain showed.

We're meeting Jill at the station in an hour, he said. We're going horseback riding.

It's ten degrees out and windy, Deena said. Are the stables even open?

Daniel nodded.

What I want right now, Deena said, is to sit in front of the fire and read.

You always wanted to do things, he said. You complained that we never went anywhere. Now we're doing them, you're wimping out. Besides Jill is already on her way. Ann also wimped out.

Horses. Their first summer together Daniel took her to Monticello Raceway. It was late June, her skin was tanned dark, and she wore white. Daniel put two dollars on a horse for her and two for himself. They both lost. He stuck with the same horse for the second round; Deena selected a different horse and won. On the third round Daniel put his money on her horse, and they both won. I think I'll keep you with me all the time, he said. As my good-luck charm.

Seven years later she was going as a chaperone, not a lucky charm. Her presence was needed to make the outing with Jill legitimate. And this time Ann wouldn't be there. She had no reason to come. It was too cold outside, it was ridiculous to go riding. Besides she'd spent the weekend with her husband, and again she'd left him. Deena wondered what that was like, what Ann was feeling.

Perched high on a horse who kept stopping to eat, Deena shivered. The wind blew and the temperature seemed to have dropped to below zero. Up ahead Daniel and Jill rode side by side. The cold didn't bother them. They were together, that was enough. They talked and talked. At home with Daniel in the same room, hours could pass in almost complete silence. They'd said everything there was to say in their first year.

Her horse stopped again; he was hungry, and she was falling farther behind. They were two unwilling creatures suffering in the cold. The horse didn't have a choice, but she did. She'd take him back where he belonged, to a warm stable with plenty of hay. She dug her heels in and tried to turn around. He didn't respond. She kicked her heels into his sides. He looked up and went on eating. Daniel and Jill disappeared around a bend. This was infuriating. Deena swung her legs out wide to get some momentum; and kicked. The horse tore away a mouthful of leaves and lifted his long neck. She kicked again. He walked. But she wanted to be galloping, not walking. She would turn around, take this horse back to the stables, and tell the management something about the way they cared for their animals.

She dug her left heel into the horse's flank and tried guiding him into the turn. He stopped walking but wouldn't turn. He'd been trained to take the path forward to the end and nothing she could do would change this pattern in his brain.

She fumed. Her fingers and toes were numb. She'd freeze sitting there waiting for the horse to finish eating.

Another rider passed her. Let the horse know what you want, he called. You have to kick hard so he feels it.

I am kicking, Deena muttered. She was tired of kicking. Her legs hurt from all the kicking. And she must be hurting the horse.

She loosened her hold on the reins and swung her heels in hard and fast, once, twice, a third time. The need for this cruelty increased her anger and made her want to do worse. She could kill this horse. She sat expecting nothing. When he suddenly started up, she grabbed the reins to hold on, and the horse slowed down. She was confusing him. She loosened her hold on the reins and the horse dropped his head and chewed. She kicked. He moved one leg forward. She pulled the rein in her right hand, and the horse turned his head to the left.

She kicked as hard as she could, and the horse started galloping and veering from the path. He went up an incline, down, and up again. She sat at uncomfortable angles, first forward then back. She gripped the saddle hard with her legs. He was going too hard and too fast for her, but she wouldn't stop him now. They'd get somewhere. He continued up and down rocks and hills, swiping limbs and brush; Deena dodged the branches overhead and brambles at her feet. The cragginess of this terrain was surprising. From the paved running paths, the park seemed flat.

They were approaching a road; she could hear the traffic, but the horse kept going, uphill, down, and suddenly came upon Union Turnpike, at a gallop. He didn't slow down. He was headed straight for the road, straight into traffic. A car would hit them, the horse's legs would buckle, he'd fall and she would fall with him. The animal was insane. She panicked, pulled hard on the reins, and the horse threw his head back and to the side, snorted, and stopped.

Two minutes later she understood what she'd done wrong. She sat on top of the huge beast, watching cars go east and west. To get across the highway, the horse had to be moving fast. The flow of traffic was constant and therefore speed was essential. You had to get across in seconds.

Daniel and Jill were way ahead, riding side by side. Were they seeing anything other than each other? It was probably better not to see. Better to allow the animals to do what they'd been trained to do.

Deena waited. What to do now? She heard voices and turned to look. There were others riding on this freezing day. She would try to get across the road with them. She sat up in the saddle and pulled on the reins. The horse raised his head. She held her breath and waited and it worked. Her horse fell in line; he was a good follower. Between two other horses, he kept moving and stayed in line. Now she didn't have to do anything. She wriggled her toes inside her boots and rubbed and bent her fingers in her gloves. She practiced sitting tall, and allowed her body to move with the movements of the animal underneath her. She could like this, riding. On a sunny day, this could feel good. She stayed with the group until they caught up with Jill and Daniel.

There you are, Daniel said.

She looked at him. His legs bowed naturally. He looked as if he'd been born on a horse. But the way she'd gotten to know him was behind the wheel of his Civic. He would pick her up, drive, then park, and they'd stay long enough to fog the windows. Our very own cocoon, he said. They banged into things: the brake, the stick, the steering wheel. One night the car started moving. Daniel looked up. Something was wrong. She straightened up, not knowing why he'd stopped, then she did know. The car was headed toward a tree. Daniel reached across her legs to pull up the brake and they laughed. Bucket seats weren't meant for this.

It was in the Civic that he finally asked. I'd get down on my knees if there were room, he said. Will you?

She laughed. This wasn't how she'd expected to be asked. This wasn't what she'd ever imagined. When things were for real this was how they came: slightly off. He'd taken her to the Red Lion earlier in the evening and she'd wondered why suddenly he'd thought to take her to a special place. They sat on overstuffed red banquette seats, sipping drinks. They finished their drinks and still he said nothing he hadn't said before. Then they were in the car again; he drove to the beach, parked, and announced that there was something important he had to say, and she wondered what now.

Later that night, alone in her room again, she decided that the car had been the perfect place; it was where they'd been together from the beginning: Daniel at the wheel, she in the passenger seat.

I'm not good at this sort of thing, he said. I love you. You know that?

She smiled, she forgave, and said yes. After that everything just happened. There's always someone waiting to make it happen. Mothers, grandmothers, sisters, and sisters-in-law—the whole female race, it seemed—were in league with caterers, florists, and photographers, the male contingent in the business. They worked together like thieves. Money passed hands. Orders were placed, invitations sent. Things got going quickly and then there was no stopping them. It would cost as much to undo. Besides, she was feeling wedding jitters, which were perfectly normal. Everyone has them.

They went to the Kebab House again. They walked through the door to their table, as if this were home and here was their table near the window, already set, waiting.

I like this place, Jill said, recognizing it.

The food is always the same but it's always fresh, Daniel said. Sort of like my mother's dinners. We always knew what we'd eat on a given night: Monday baked macaroni, Tuesday meatballs, Wednesday roast beef, Thursday spaghetti. There were no surprises.

We eat here too often, Deena said and calculated. It's my fifth time this month.

They were spending, spending, spending, and not on anything that mattered. Daniel was playing the role of generous provider. He'd paid for Jill's horse even though she'd offered to pay her own way.

He'd probably insist on paying for dinner too. Deena would gladly have saved the fifteen dollars on her horse. A tube of lipstick would have brought more pleasure. She wondered what Jill was thinking. Was it every day that men offered to buy her dinner, drinks, and more? She accepted it all very naturally, as if it were as it should be and her attempts to pay were only a courtesy.

The waitress poured water and offered menus, but they knew it; they were ready to order. Three mixed grills, three salads, and a carafe of wine. For the table Daniel ordered sides of tahini and baba ghanouj.

When the wine came, Deena leaned back and sipped.

Now I don't want to move, she said. I can sit here forever, not budging. God, I'm tired.

Jill stretched her legs and groaned. I know what you mean, she said.

By the time the food arrived, they needed another carafe of wine.

After dinner Daniel drove to the subway, dropped Jill off, and he and Deena went home in silence, which infuriated her. For Jill he made himself interesting.

It had been a long day; in the morning another week of work would begin. Deena needed sleep, but rage would keep her awake. If she ran several miles, if she was exhausted enough, she'd sleep.

Her leggings and sweatshirt were on the radiator; they were dried crisp. The inside of her sneakers, though, were still damp and her socks smelled. She put on a fresh pair.

You already ran today, Daniel said. Have you forgotten?

No, Deena said.

You're crazy. Your muscles need some rest. You'll damage something. He shook his head and turned on the seven o'clock news.

Outside she sniffed the cold and the dark. The stars were bright, overhead companions. The fresh air cleared her head. Already she felt better. She ran on the streets and sidewalks, circling the neighborhood blocks. Her legs ached, she felt muscles in unfamiliar places, and they hurt, but she liked them hurting. She smelled of horse. She would take another hot bath. If she continued running twice a day, she could call herself a runner. Whatever else she did that day wouldn't matter because all the time her muscles would be recovering, preparing for the next run. Life was all repetition. You repeated and repeated yourself. Another run, another shower, another meal. To finance this, there was work. Was that all you lived for?

In the morning she ran again. She ran to the track, on the track, and back home. It was not yet nine in the morning and already she was tired. The rest of the day went by as if without her. She showered, dressed, went to work, sat at her desk, struggled with copy, and at the end of the day, didn't know how the hours had gone by. But running again in the evening, she felt every inch of ground she covered.

Then she was too tired to eat and too tired to talk. She heard from across the table Daniel's faraway voice. She didn't hear what he said, only that he was talking about San Francisco. She was starting to think there had never been a conference in Nashville, that he and Jill had simply gone to Nashville. Too much had been said about it, too many plans had been made, it had all been too elaborate. If only he would stop telling her.

She went to bed early and woke early and found herself circling the track again. Under the rubber soles of her sneakers was the rub-berized track. Rubber to rubber. They were meant to come together. Magnets. She had to pry them apart in order to create the possibil-ity of their coming together again. She was the facilitator. She pushed for another round and another. Then she was in the subway, the office, and soon enough the subway again.

Thursday night she was too tired for ballroom dancing, too tired for anything. But she would make plans for the weekend. She would meet Karen on Sunday. They would walk down Madison Avenue. She would do what other women did. She would shop. Daniel could call Jill or not. She didn't care. She was going shopping.

Why don't you sleep over on Saturday night? Karen said.

Overnight?

It will be fun. We'll have a sleepover.

I haven't had one of those since I was twelve, Deena said.

She hesitated. She wanted to, she knew that. And why should she care about what Daniel would say? He'd gone away for a weekend, now it was her turn.

What should I bring? Deena asked.

Just yourself and a change of clothes, Karen said.

When she arrived home on Friday night, Daniel wasn't there. She ran and showered. It was after sunset and still he wasn't home. So much for integrity. She hesitated, then didn't light candles. She called Karen.

Can we do the sleepover tonight instead of tomorrow night? she asked.

Tonight is actually better, Karen said. Greg's working late today. And Madison Avenue is better on Saturdays. For one thing, more stores are open.

She heard Daniel at the door and wished she'd gotten out of the house before he'd arrived. With a note she could have avoided questions and explanations.

He took long steps into the kitchen, ran water, then silence. He was gulping. He'd had wine or beer. She stood listening. When she heard him walk toward the stairs, she pulled the drawstring of her packed bag closed. If he went into the bathroom, she'd hurry downstairs and leave.

He stood in the frame of the door.

Where you going? he asked coolly, detachedly.

She looked at him standing there with his arms folded, expecting answers, a man with rights.

I think I should be the one asking questions, she said.

Like what? he asked.

Like where were you so late on a Friday night? Where were you last week? And what happened in Nashville?

Yes, that's what she wanted to hear, she wanted to know what exactly happened in Nashville. Did they have sex? She wanted him to say it. If he confessed he couldn't pretend innocence, he couldn't stand there with his arms folded asking questions. He could stop denying and she'd stop wondering.

I believe I am the one who deserves answers, she said.

He walked out of the room and into the bathroom. She heard the water run; he was taking a shower. He wouldn't get away with that. She sat with her packed bag on the top stair. She'd wait. Tonight she'd get some answers. But he was taking his time.

When he came out with a towel around his hips, she stood in the way.

Where were you tonight and on all the other nights? And since when aren't you keeping the Sabbath?

None of your business, he said, and edged past her into the room. She followed him and stood watching.

Would you mind giving me some privacy, he said.

Answer the questions, she said.

I had a late lunch in Chinatown, Daniel said. What else do you want to know?

With whom? Deena asked.

People from work, Daniel said.

Like who? Deena asked.

None of your business, Daniel said.

Deena looked at him, a sullen teenager under questioning.

Fine. Don't ask me and I won't ask you. I'm leaving.

He stopped her at the door. Don't go, he said. My lateness doesn't make your leaving after sundown all right. I'll answer what I can. What do you want to know?

Nothing. There is nothing I don't already know. One affair is like another.

I'm not having an affair.

She stepped out.

Okay, so we kissed. That's all we did. We kissed that night in Nashville.

On his face was a smile; he was experiencing the kiss all over again.

You asked, he said.

Good-bye, Deena said. Her voice was low. They'd kissed. She'd imagined them kissing a thousand times, why did hearing about it make it worse?

She swung her bag onto her back, pulled the door shut behind her, and went down the front steps. She felt lightheaded. This was too easy, walking through the door, leaving. She walked down the driveway, turned left, and looked straight ahead, into the night, into the dark of the trees. Just now it was dangerous to see the comfortable yellow lights of other houses; she wouldn't look.

Daniel came after her. At the corner, he caught up. They walked in silence.

She shifted her bag to her other shoulder. She'd packed too much. She'd taken running shoes and running clothes, and the bag was heavy, the straps cut. If she were Jill, Daniel would be carrying it. For Jill, he opened doors, paid bills, did everything. For Deena, there was nothing. She was doomed to remain a packhorse.

If you're here make yourself useful, she said, and tried to hand him her bag.

It's your bag, he said. You're the one who wants to leave.

Then don't follow me. I'd like to walk on my own.

It's a free country, he said.

At the next corner, she waited to see which way he went and turned the other way. There was more than one way to get to the train station. She dropped behind; he went straight. As soon as he stepped off the curb, she turned left, and walked quickly. She should run; she put her bag under her arm and ran.

He caught up with her. You're nuts, he said. Give me that bag.

I don't want you with me, Deena said. You're ruining my walk.

All the more reason to stay, then, he said. His long teeth glowed.

She dropped the bag on the pavement and walked on.

He held it away from his body. He wouldn't sling it over his shoulder, and this too infuriated her. But they were almost there. She picked up speed.

At the subway, she turned to take her bag, but no, he was coming down the stairs. Her token was ready, she was at the turnstile, and finally he let her have the bag. Her hand touched his and the contact, warm skin against warm skin, stopped them. Daniel rubbed his hand, then waved. He had a strange smile on his face.

Daniel

He walked in the dark, inhaling the cold air, which hurt. It also cleared his head. He was frightened and exhilarated at once. Tonight he would live without restraint. He reached up to his head, pulled off his yarmulke, the constant cover a lid, and walked like that bareheaded under the blue-ink sky, under the stars, under the eyes of God. Already he felt better. He rubbed his uncovered scalp. With daily massaging and fresh air, his hair might grow back. He stuffed the yarmulke into his back pocket. It was made of cotton, a fine yarn, but on his head it weighed. So he lifted it, and—nothing happened. No thunder clapped, no lightning bolted, the sky didn't fall. No one cared that Daniel Binet was no longer keeping his head down and under, that he was standing straight *and tall and bare. He grew an inch, then three inches. He threw back his shoulders and walked tall for the first time since he was three and his mother pinned his first yarmulke on his head.*

First they took him to the barber. He sat in the back of the Valiant, buckled into the car seat, his mother and father in front, and they drove like that to Daddy's barber on Main Street.

If you sit straight it will look better, his mother said.

It would be like going to the doctor, who put ice-cold metal on his skin, he thought. He was only a little afraid.

But it didn't hurt. It was easy to sit straight. After, the barber lifted him up up to the sky and he flew, then landed on his feet. His father ruffled his Prince Valiant haircut and his mother bent down to kiss him. She called him her handsome prince, and he held their hands. He couldn't wave good-bye to the barber because he had his hands full; he had to lead his parents back to the car. Then he was Prince Valiant going home in the Valiant. But why did his mother talk to him in her baby voice; he wasn't a baby anymore. At home, she explained, We have the new hand-crocheted yarmulke Grammy made for you. It's lovely. Remember when she measured your head?

They used the back door even though he was a prince. Then his mother brought out the yarmulke wrapped in tissue paper: a circle of black ringed with white Hebrew letters that spelled Daniel. She let him look at it first, she named the letters, then she put it on his head with a bobby pin. He circled the room with the yarmulke on his head, first along the walls, then around the table. He sat on a chair and ate a peanut-butter-and-jelly sandwich, and all the time the yarmulke stayed on his head. Then he wanted to go out and play with Teddy, who didn't get his hair cut that day; he wasn't a prince.

Danny stood in front of his mother, and waited for her to take off the yarmulke.

Oh, she said, laughing. Oh no, you wear it all the time now.

But I want to go out, he explained.

Go ahead. It will stay on.

But it flapped when he and Teddy raced, and he fell behind—never before had Teddy been ahead, it was Danny who was fast. So he pulled the yarmulke off and, ouch, it pulled out his hair. He'd forgotten about the bobby pin; only girls wear pins in their hair; what was his mother doing to him? He pushed the yarmulke and the bobby pin into his pocket, caught up with Teddy, and ran past him, as always.

You lost your yarmulke, his mother said when she saw him. But he had not lost it; it was in his pocket. He took it out and Sugar Pops stuck to it. Teddy's mother let them have a handful, but they always took two handfuls, one for later. Mothers always said only one, but they let you have two, so that when they offered two, it meant you could have three.

It's sticky, his mother said. *I'll have to wash it. But why didn't you leave it where it was? I pinned it so it wouldn't fall off. I'll use two or three bobby pins next time. A Jewish boy never takes his yarmulke off.*

He was a Jewish boy, that's why. If he were a Jewish girl, he wouldn't have to wear it. But he didn't want to be a girl. He was a boy like Teddy, but Teddy didn't have to wear it. No one else in school had to wear it. They laughed at him, wearing it. He wanted to be like Teddy. Not Jewish. But his mother said he was and she pinned it every morning with three bobby pins and it was there to stay. She said Daddy also wears one, under his hat, and he was Daddy's big boy, and also Mommy's, and he had to wear it. So he did. He wore it to school every day. And he wore it through college, then at job interviews. Sometimes interviewers asked about it. Now, at twenty-nine, he took it off, which he should have done years ago.

He arrived home, walked to the stereo, and turned it on. Fuck the Sabbath. He turned on the television and also every light in the house.

Screw religion. It was designed to keep you down. He'd answer to no one. He'd allow no one to say he shouldn't. He'd be what he chose to be. He'd accept no burdens, not Jewishness, not marriage. They were chains; they made you a yokel. He'd been a convict with shackles on his legs and arms and brain. So many don'ts and shouldn'ts. He would say no to them all, no and not anymore and no longer.

He plugged his guitar into his amp, strummed, put it down, turned up the volume, strummed more. He'd do everything he shouldn't do on this Sabbath. He would celebrate his liberation. He was an American citizen. He would live with the liberties granted in this country. No more rules, rituals, and superstitions. That was for the Middle Ages, and this, the here and now, was the twentieth century.

He dialed Jill's number. Only when he heard her voice did he turn down the volume, using the remote controls.

What is going on? Jill asked. Are you at a party?

You might call it that, he said.

There was a pause and he could feel her worrying. She was always worrying now. We'd better cool it, she said. We have to make sure it never happens again. Distance will help, she said. And not being alone.

What did she know? It was impossible to stop what was started. It happened because they both wanted it. They couldn't change that.

Where's Deena? Jill asked. What's wrong?

Nothing's wrong. She's sleeping over at Karen's house, remember Karen and Greg? What are you doing tonight?

I just got back from the gym. I'm going into the shower. Ann is getting dinner together.

Let me have dinner with you, Daniel said. Invite me.

There was a pause. Alone? Jill asked.

Ann's there. Tell me what time?

I don't know. Just leave when you're ready. It'll take you about an hour to get here on a Friday night.

He turned everything off, set the alarm, and went out to the car. He needed movement; he was wired. He was driving on the Sabbath. His mother would be shocked. Deena too. But he was no longer little Danny. He'd held a beautiful woman in his arms, he'd kissed her, she'd kissed him, he could have done anything, she would have allowed him to do anything, but he didn't, and now he regretted it. Maybe he would have another chance. Maybe it wasn't too late. Maybe, maybe. Anyone else would have gone all the way. Without that yarmulke on his head, he too would have. It was a stamp, a yellow star, marking him a Jew. First the Jews stamped themselves, then others did it for them. Stamped, you had to be more than yourself, greater, which prevented everyday, down-and-dirty life. He'd put an end to such prevention. With the yarmulke off, he was free. It would make no great difference in this large wide world if he, Daniel Binet, had sex with a woman who wasn't his wife. The world wouldn't come to an end. And he had good reasons. Seven years was a long time and Deena wasn't the easiest person to live with. One day she liked him, the next she didn't. He never knew what he'd said or done.

He drove toward the bridge. The heavy traffic and lights on Queens Boulevard only fueled his impatience. He should have taken the Brooklyn Bridge.

He fidgeted, turned the knobs on the radio, went from rock to jazz and back to rock again. By the time he turned onto Second Avenue, he'd sobered. He was rationalizing. No argument would make what he was doing right. Still this was what he wanted and needed. He couldn't help it; he didn't have excuses, he'd be honest. He'd wanted Jill the moment he met her, and he'd wanted her because she was different. She was *young and fun and glamorous. She was both more naive and wiser than women in the city, and the combination was adorable. He loved everything about her. He wouldn't make excuses; he would just be and do and not think about what would follow. After always came, it was already coming, he'd let it take care of itself.*

He shifted the car into lower gear, precisely and smoothly, his body in tune with the wheels and the road. He was good at this. This was all there was in life: the pleasure of perfection, its beauty and the struggle to attain it. Which was why he wanted Jill. He wanted to perform as a man with a beautiful, a perfect woman. He wanted to see how Jill would feel in his arms. He would know by looking at her face and watching her mouth at the right moments how he measured up to other men. He could be a good lover. He would prove himself as a lover.

I want, I want, I want, he said aloud. The words knocked against the glass, the roof, the dashboard, then fell silent into the upholstered seats. He repeated the words and listened again. He sniffed. The car smelled like Shower to Shower. Jill? She used Johnson & Johnson baby shampoo for her hair; it was a smell he knew well. He liked her simple schoolgirl smells. Anything you could buy at a drugstore was good. Ivory, Cashmere Bouquet, Dove, simple soaps with clean scents, products tested on regular people with regular noses. He used to like Rive Gauche, the perfume Deena was using when they met. When she ran low he bought her a new bottle, but by then she wanted something different. She said she was bored with Rive Gauche and exchanged it for a bottle of Chanel, something more modern and sophisticated, she said. He never liked Chanel, and he found sophistication a turn-off. He liked natural smells, girliness. He liked Jill. I can't help it, he reasoned silently. I don't want to stop liking her. And this time he'd make love last. He was older, he'd do things differently. He didn't yet know how; he knew only that he would do anything to make it last. Maybe that's what he was on earth for: to find out if it could last. If only he could stop thinking so much. If only he could shrug out of his head and leave it on a shelf at home. He didn't want to think. He didn't want to consider the wrongs, the consequences. He would live without his stop-sign mind.

The light went to green and he drove. Now he was here he wouldn't waste time. He drove straight to the garage on Eleventh.

Walking on the street felt good. The whole world it seemed was out. It was a Friday night, the weekend was all ahead, and anticipation was in the air. He inhaled the energy. This was what he needed after a long, hard week. He needed to let loose. He needed to go out with friends. Drink, talk, laugh. This was what the Sabbath day ought to be. He was sick of the hushed silence of Friday nights and the long, immobile Saturdays. All he ever did was read and sleep. What he needed was noise, music, talk, and drink. After a night out, he could nurse his headache and think. But first the drinking and noise. You needed something to rest from.

Part Two

At Fulton Street, Deena transferred to the Lexington line via long corridors. In front, beside, and behind her people walked. She was just a part in a moving engine. She pressed forward in the crowd and inhaled the air that reeked of fuel and steam and humanity. When finally she came out at East Eighty-sixth Street, she was relieved.

She walked up Lexington Avenue, which hummed with people despite the cold and dark. At Ninety-third, Karen's block, she turned right and found herself walking downhill. It was a surprise coming upon a hill in this man-made city.

Karen's name was third in the list of names, each beside a bell, and suddenly Deena wanted her own name affixed on a door somewhere in this city. She'd never lived alone. Her name had always been attached to someone else's, family, roommates, then Daniel.

She walked up the carpeted stairs, which leaned, and liked the shabbiness of the place. Then what was she doing with a house on Myrtle?

On the counter were two glasses and a bottle of Johnny Walker.

I've never had it straight, Deena said.

Would you like some ice? Karen asked.

Deena nodded. It might make it easier.

They sat on the sofa and sipped.

Not bad, Deena said.

Karen's eyes sparkled. There's something I want to tell you, she said. I've been waiting for an opportunity.

Deena looked at her. It was good news she had to impart.

Greg and I, she said slowly and paused. Deena looked at her, her body forward, leaning into what she would say. Greg and I have decided to move in together. It will cut expenses in half. It will make it possible to save.

That's great, Deena said. Is his place large enough?

Karen shook her blonde head. No, but this is the city. No one lives in a place that's large enough. This weekend he plans to design a wardrobe for my clothes. Isn't that sweet?

He loves the idea of building something, especially if it's for you.

Karen nodded. He's going all out. He has these elaborate ideas for saving space. He's very creative.

Deena nodded. Marriage was in the end just settling. Having given up her romantic notion of being swept off her feet by a creative director who worked at the latest hot shop, Karen was ready to accept Greg. Which was fine. He worshiped her. And she seemed happy enough; she was ready to join forces with him; they would save together. Deena didn't question or argue against this joining. She merely nodded and congratulated.

So tell me what's going on with you and Daniel, Karen said. I know something's wrong because you called me on a Friday night and you traveled on the Sabbath.

Deena looked at her. There wasn't much to say. A kiss. Daniel kissed Jill. She didn't know more. Did it last a minute or five minutes? Were they sitting or standing?

She sipped and swallowed.

I don't know what's going on, Deena said. She shook her head. No. That wasn't true. She knew what was going on, but she didn't know how to say it. It wasn't what Daniel was doing that was the matter. It was what she was feeling. She hadn't planned to care. She shouldn't hurt.

We're having some problems, Deena said.

I thought you might be, Karen said. Is Jill involved?

Deena didn't answer. She was ashamed of the ordinary details. The secretary, the office.

It's strange, Karen said. I always thought you and Daniel had a model marriage. I tried to visualize myself in such a marriage—you know, to make it happen.

Deena nodded.

Karen shook her head. I can't say I didn't notice signs, like when he visited you at the office. I was surprised because he'd always seemed so strictly religious.

It's more than Jill, Deena said. It's me. I don't know what I want.

Karen nodded. Give yourself time. Don't let anyone rush you. Which reminds me, she said and looked at her watch. We should go out before it gets too late. I thought we might want to rent a movie. And I should buy some things for tomorrow morning.

At the video rental, they agreed on something quickly. They'd both missed the new version of *Cousin, Cousine*. Karen suggested popcorn and Coke for dinner and Deena looked at her. Popcorn for dinner?

At the corner store they purchased milk, Coke, tissues, and microwave popcorn.

Walking up the stairs again, Deena said, I think I should get myself an apartment for a short time. If you hear of anything.

You can stay with me, Karen said.

It might be for a week or two. I don't want to impose on you, Deena said.

I spend so many nights at Greg's, Karen said, you'd have the place mostly to yourself. I was planning to place an ad. Until I find someone, you're welcome to it.

I'll feel better if you allow me to pay something, Deena said.

We can figure all that out later. I'll have to come up here for clothes.

Was it possible it could be so easy? She could just move out, get away for a while. She wouldn't make any long-term decisions. She would move with just an overnight bag. She'd plan a week at a time. The rest of life could wait.

If she'd brought more, she could have avoided going back. It would be hard to leave again, but she had to return. Tonight she would sleep here, tomorrow night at the house, and Sunday night here again. Her life was changing. Ordinary, everyday life was over.

.   .   .

She slept unexpectedly well. And as soon as her eyes were open in the morning, she was hugely awake and alive. She lay on her back and watched the sun come up full and round above the buildings across the street, then up higher in the sky. She was happy; it was good to be here. She had a morning of being here.

Karen's eyes were closed, and without opening them she reached behind her for her sunglasses and put them on. Good morning, she said. Did you sleep well?

Mmmm, Deena said. It's lovely here in the morning.

Sometimes it's too bright, Karen said, and picked up her remote control. Do you watch *Pee Wee?*

No, but I guess I will today, Deena said.

Everything in the apartment was white. The television was a fourteen-inch white Sony. The telephone-answering machine, also white, was the new Sony model, with a large round light like a full moon.

Karen cackled over Pee Wee's antics. This was the way to start your day.

They were ready to go, they were at the door, when Karen pulled an ashtray from a shelf and lit an old roach tucked into a ladies' cigarette holder. She inhaled twice and offered it to Deena, who declined.

Deena was surprised. She hadn't thought of Karen as a pot smoker. And before 5 P.M. it seemed dangerous or decadent, she wasn't sure which. Was it as bad as drinking before noon? She didn't know much about marijuana, but she wondered why Karen needed it. Was she bored or was this something she did regularly on Saturdays?

On Madison Avenue, Deena felt underdressed. Women here looked like they were going places. She was wearing baggy jeans. In the windows, sale signs beckoned.

It's a good time to buy, Karen said.

Deena tried on a soft black sweater that ended in a flare like a short dress.

You ought to buy some things, Karen said. It will make you feel better. It's what every woman would do. Charge her husband's credit cards to the max.

Deena hesitated. With house expenses and all the recent sprees, spending was already at the max. Besides, if she spent, it would be she who'd end up paying, not Daniel. Still, she'd wanted to buy; she'd planned on buying. She looked in the mirror. The sweater didn't qualify as a good piece. Already it showed signs of pilling. It wasn't even one hundred percent wool. In her closet at home there were already too many such purchases. Impulse buys. She had enough junk to last a lifetime. She'd wait. She'd buy something that would make a real difference.

They continued walking. At a drugstore they each bought a booklet of powdered paper, made in China.

Are you hungry? Karen asked.

Starving, Deena said. If she ate now, she'd have to wait a couple of hours before running. She wasn't sure if and when she would run. She didn't know how this day would end.

They ordered burgers and beer. Karen ate quickly and more than usual. The pot had given her an appetite. After eating, she took the booklet from her skinny purse, tore out a page, and rubbed it on her nose.

Good idea, Deena said.

On the back cover, under a paragraph of Chinese characters, was a paragraph titled *Mode of Use*. Deena read aloud. *Rubbing lightly face and neck with a sheet torn from the booklet will remove grease and oil from the skin, leaving a thin film of perfumed powder which whitens the skin and enhances the natural beauty of complexion.*

They laughed. Deena rubbed a powdered paper over her nose and chin, and they looked at each other pale-faced. This was fun. She couldn't remember having so much fun.

On their way home, they passed the store again and Deena debated. She hadn't purchased anything else. Should she just get the sweater? Did she need it? Did she deserve it? She suffered too much over every purchase. Yes, no, maybe. It gave her a headache. But if you don't spend money, shopping is a bore. You need the added edge; your money has to be on the line. But first she had to get rid of things. To start from scratch, you have to get down to scratch.

Daniel woke with a headache. Where was Deena?

He closed his eyes. He needed water. He looked at the alarm clock. It was past noon and he was late for something. The car. It was still in the city. They would charge him for an extra day. Everyone wanted his money. Let them. What he wanted to do was cry.

Downstairs he looked up Karen's number and dialed. The machine answered. They were out. They were all against him; they'd banded up against him as if only he were at fault, as if Jill hadn't flirted, as if Deena hadn't encouraged him. They were blaming only him. But hadn't Jill's head moved a little toward his?

His stomach rumbled; he was hungry. He hadn't eaten anything substantial since lunch yesterday. You may not like this, Jill said when she opened the door. We ordered a platter of cut-up vegetables for dinner, and Ann is in the kitchen making a yogurt dip. We're both auditioning on Monday so this weekend has to be all exercise, diet, and plenty of sleep, which means no late nights. We're not going out.

He stayed an hour crunching on carrot sticks and sipping sparkling water. Jill was beginning to sound like Deena. He could take only so much. He took a cab downtown to the club on MacDougal, ordered a scotch, and checked out the women. Tonight the good-looking ones weren't there. They were all home drinking mineral water. He ordered another scotch, finished it too quickly, and decided to walk. He walked east, stopped for another drink. Then he was stopping at every bar. The garage was on Fifty-sixth; he kept walking and stopping for another drink, and finally he was too drunk to drive. He took a taxi home and discovered too late that he was five dollars short. He apologized, he tried to get the man's address, but the driver wouldn't give it to him. He didn't believe the money would arrive in the mail. He cursed and pulled away, tires screeching.

On Karen's machine, there were two messages from Daniel: in the first he said he was taking the train into the city and would call again when he arrived. The second announced that he'd arrived and would try again in an hour or two.

Karen came in with two glasses of water.

I think I'll head back now, Deena said. If Daniel calls, tell him I went home.

You're welcome to wait for his call, Karen said.

Thank you, but I should go. I'll call you later tonight.

I'll be at Greg's. Call me there.

Deena stuffed her clothes into her bag. She didn't want to go. It would be so much easier simply to stay. If only the move were already in the past, a solid fact, unchangeable no matter who said what, or what was promised.

At the door they leaned into each other, touched lightly, and parted. If only it could be this easy to part from Daniel. It was strange. On the occasion of her separation from Daniel, Karen and Greg were coming together, as if people had to take turns being married, as if in this world quotas of single people and couples had to be maintained.

At home, she emptied the leather suitcase and looked into her cardboard wardrobe. There was nothing there she truly wanted, nothing she especially liked. She looked in the mirror. How could anyone have so much, and none of it worthwhile?

She looked at the pile of clothes she'd worn all week. If she washed and packed everything in this pile, she'd have the clothes she really wore, none of which was hanging in the closet.

She packed her black jeans, two shirts, and several T-shirts. She packed a jacket to wear to meetings. She folded her long raincoat. Into a duffel bag, she would throw her running clothes, sneakers, and shoes. She eyed her line-up of shoes and decided on only the brown lace-ups, which she wore every day. She added a black sweater, and she snapped the one working clasp on the suitcase shut.

There was still the whole evening to get through. She went running. It was growing dark but it didn't matter. She knew every inch of the way. She knew where there were puddles when it rained and where the lip of a pipe protruded enough to catch the toe of her shoe and send her sprawling. She knew precisely where under the concrete tunnel the echo of her thudding sneakers would begin and where it would end. She came out of the tunnel with the sound of the wind in her ears, into the half-light again, then into open park. A month ago she'd calculated the number of days before she would reach her thousandth mile on this track. In five months she'd run over five hundred miles. Running twice a day, she would have been at a thousand sooner. Now she wouldn't get to a thousand, at least not here.

He hadn't eaten all day and there was nothing quick in the house. He stood in front of the open refrigerator. It was empty, not even a yogurt to tide him over. She didn't do a thing. She didn't shop, cook, or clean. All she did was run. Every time he turned around she was out running.

He looked at the clock. It was hard to believe it was only Saturday night. So much had happened since Friday.

It was after seven. Only the Korean market would be open. Carrot sticks for dinner last night, and more of the same tonight. Rabbit food. That was all he was offered in life, nibbles.

He put on his jacket and went out. He looked toward the park, but there was no sign of her. She was verging on insanity, running twice a day.

He walked the aisles of the Korean market. Heads of romaine, oak leaf, Boston. Bunches of rosemary, parsley, cilantro. He bought lettuce, a tomato, and two cukes. He needed more than that. He passed the pizza place on the corner and stopped. A couple of slices would hit the spot. With pizza, salad would be welcome.

The place looked like a bar, red brick and neon. He looked up and down the street. No one would see him enter. He reached up to take off

his yarmulke; it wasn't there. If he stopped wearing it altogether, he
wouldn't think twice about going anywhere, doing anything.

Inside the smell of pepperoni. His stomach turned. But he didn't
have to eat here.

He ordered three slices to go.

Toppings? the man asked.

Daniel hesitated.

The pie was fresh out of the oven. He could eat the three slices him-
self and Deena would want at least one.

Make that five slices, Daniel said. Two garlic, two olive, and one
plain.

The box was warm in his hands. He opened one side, picked off some
cheese, and chewed. Mmmm. He was hungry and it was good. Kosher
or not, pizza was pizza.

Deena was in the shower when Daniel arrived. When she came
downstairs, pizza and salad were on the table. She was hungry.

He opened a bottle of wine. Despite all, there was this: eating and
drinking together.

This is good pizza, she said.

What's with the suitcase upstairs? he asked.

I'm moving, Deena said.

Where? he asked.

To Karen's place. For a week or so.

He nodded. Maybe that's best. We probably both need some time.

.   .   .

Greg picked up when she called to confirm the move.

I heard, he said. I'm sorry. Is there anything I can do to help?

He spoke too tragically, as if someone had died. In the meantime she and Daniel had eaten dinner together. He'd even agreed that she move out.

Karen says to tell you that we can pick you up at your house in the afternoon, if it will help, Greg said.

Deena hesitated. She didn't want to seem helpless. Daniel will drop me off, she said.

You're sure? Greg asked. Call tomorrow if you change your mind. Here's Karen.

How are you feeling? Karen asked dramatically.

Deena frowned. She wanted privacy; she wanted the whole thing done quietly, without drama and talk.

Daniel called about an hour or so after you left, Karen said. He was asking all these questions. He wanted to know what you'd said, and claimed it wasn't all true. I told him you'd said very little, that I had nothing to do with it, and that he should talk to you. Has he called?

He's here now, Deena said. We had dinner together. We've agreed to try this separation for a week or two. He will be out of town anyway. This way I won't be alone at the house. It's working out pretty well.

She was making things up as she went, giving the whole thing a veneer of normalcy, like Daniel's mother, who in the middle of a bitter argument with her daughter would pick up the ringing phone and answer with perfect propriety, listen and respond, and after a calm good-bye, turn to resume the spat.

Is tomorrow morning still good for you? Deena asked.

Of course. Greg was saying this is sort of a godsend because it forces us to move faster. But the circumstances are unfortunate. He was really angry at Daniel. You should have heard the names he called him.

Deena protested. It's not exactly what you think—

Karen interrupted. I know. I told him that. Listen, about the apartment. I'll try to pack as much as possible and give you enough room in the closet.

I'm not bringing much, Deena said. I have one suitcase and a duffel bag for running clothes. Even if you leave everything there, I'll have plenty of room.

She couldn't sleep. She turned left, right, onto her stomach, and back onto her back. She sat up and let her head fall to her knees. She was tired, she had a headache, but she couldn't sleep. She walked to the bathroom, swallowed aspirin, lay down again, but from the next room she could hear Daniel snoring. She'd never fall asleep with him snoring. She closed her eyes, and counted off every passing minute. When you're awake, the hours of the night double and triple and you remember all the sleepless nights of your life.

She tried reading and couldn't. She went downstairs and turned on the television. The blue light and the voices hurt her eyes and her head. She turned it off. She dropped her head onto the arm of the sofa and closed her eyes. She was exhausted. The base of her neck hurt. She felt stiff. She was falling asleep, she was almost asleep, almost there, then she sat up. The wide moon was at the bare windows. She walked onto the porch and opened the front door. It was cold. She put on a sweater and stood in the frame of the door, then stepped out.

Moonlight illuminated the newspaper smudges and grease stains on the door. Why hadn't she painted this door first thing? She'd taken possession of the house through this door, in the morning she'd leave by way of it, and still it was dirty. She'd paint it right now. She'd paint by moonlight. On the porch were cans and brushes. She had a choice of linen white and pink. She'd use pink.

She opened the can, stirred the paint, dipped the paintbrush, hesitated. Where to begin? Anywhere. Somewhere. One must begin.

She started at the bottom, in horizontal strokes, right to left and then back. She stepped away to look. In moonlight it was a blue pink. She continued painting, stepped back again. The door looked bottom heavy, pink below and white on top; a woman with wide hips. The paintbrush was heavy. She dropped her arm. She was exhausted but she had to finish; she would leave this door without hips.

When she stepped back again to look, the moon was setting, and the light waned like a warning: going, going, gone.

She hurried, dipping frequently and painting in quick strokes. In the dark, the door seemed shrouded, not the bright pink she'd started with. She had one panel left, the last panel. She stopped. Above the doors of her parents' home, a large square was always left unpainted, so that coming and going you stepped under the shadow, as befits a people in exile, her father said. With the temple destroyed, pure, full joy couldn't and shouldn't be.

She'd leave the panel unpainted, a reminder of what was.

She was tired. Her lids were heavy. She would finally sleep, but first the paintbrush needed washing. She couldn't sleep yet. She'd wash the paintbrush and seal the can. She was sleepwalking now. She had to walk through the door carefully, without touching the wet paint. If she didn't clean the brush, Daniel would have something to say about the significance of tools. White trash don't take care of their tools. His voice, the voice that knew the value of things, that worked for the dollar, that paid taxes, that knew and understood, oh, everything. He was good, he was perfect, he was right. He was barbaric in his rightness.

She walked across the yard, into the side yard, wrapped newspaper around the wet brush, and dropped it into the neighbor's garbage can. No more paintbrush. No carelessly-left-to-dry-out paintbrush.

Inside she stepped on the paint can and heard the satisfying slide of the lid. Closed. She'd done something right. Then to the sofa. She leaned back, pulled the folded blanket up to her nose, and slept.

The newspaper landing on the front step woke her. Where was she? What was she doing on the sofa? There was something she had to do today. The paper was at the door. The door. It was still wet. She sat up. Day had finally come; she could finally move out. She was strangely excited about the whole thing. For two weeks she'd live by herself in New York City. It would be an adventure. Then she'd come back to the house. She wasn't giving up the house, only leaving it for a short while.

She drank coffee, thumbed through the paper, showered, and still Daniel was in bed.

She walked into their bedroom.

I know you're awake, she said. It's after ten. I want to leave here in half an hour.

What does it have to do with me? he asked.

If you don't want to drive, then I will.

No, you won't, he said. It's my car.

I happen to have a set of keys, remember?

Okay, okay. I'll get up, he said. It's Sunday. Can't a person get some sleep around here?

He took his time. He looked at different parts of the paper. He hadn't even showered.

If you're not ready by eleven, she announced, I'm leaving without you.

At eleven, she decided to call a car service. She didn't need his favors. She didn't need his car.

I said I'll take you, he roared. What's your hurry? Can't you go running or something?

Karen's white Toyota was parked in front of her building and Greg was loading things into the trunk.

There's no parking, Daniel said. And I'm not paying for a garage.

Greg came to say hello. I waited ten minutes to get this spot, he said.

I'll unload, Deena said and got out. She tapped on the hatch, but Daniel didn't respond. She walked around to the driver's side, and opened the door to reach in.

It's open now, he said, and moved to pull the lever.

Greg took the suitcase, Deena lifted the duffel, and slammed the hatch door closed.

Greg hesitated. Is Daniel coming up?

I guess not, Deena said.

Tell you what. I'll lock the car and come up with you. Karen's up there, packing.

She followed Greg up the stairs, worrying about the weight of the suitcase on his shoulder. She should have packed in something lighter.

Karen met them halfway. Is there more? she asked and took the duffel from Deena.

Greg led the way into the apartment and carefully set the suitcase down. Is this a family heirloom or something? he asked.

It is beautiful, Karen said. She turned toward Deena. How are you? Where's Daniel? Did he drive?

Deena nodded, feeling Greg's eyes on her face. Last night he was fine with the idea of this move. This morning he's in a mood. I don't know why.

Greg shook his head. He wouldn't even open the hatchback. He just sat there.

He's angry, Deena said.

Greg walked to the window. He's gone, he announced.

But why should he be angry? Karen said. You're the one who has a right to be.

Deena shook her head. They didn't understand. She didn't either, but she knew that Daniel wasn't entirely in the wrong.

Part Three

Her first day at work as a single woman, Deena arrived forty minutes late.

Everything took longer than expected. In the shower, she spent ten minutes reviving two plastic Florida flamingos, which were pink and limp, in need of air. Then, drying herself with Karen's oversized towel, she knocked several pieces in a collection of windup toys off a shelf.

She went to work thinking about the significance of toys. Clinging to bathroom walls were rubber gorillas, lizards, and orangutans. On adult beds and dressers, stuffed bears and dolls. Even at work people had toys. The walls of her office were bare; her desk was all utility. Was that what was missing from her life?

But when she arrived at her office, she liked the bare walls. Today the sameness steadied her. Enough in her life had changed. She inserted a sheet of clean paper into her Panasonic and typed. It was good to have this specific thing to do, this copy to write, and she worked until she was stuck. Then she went to get her first cup of coffee.

Delaying things—the coffee, the roll she'd bought on her way to work—made them better. This could be her credo for living: delay as a tactic.

She passed the kitchen, walked to the end of the hall, and turned back. Offices should have long hallways for pacing. If you could walk without encountering anyone, you could think your way past the next sentence.

Karen was in the kitchen getting her coffee.

Good morning, she said, her eyes wide and calm. I worried when I didn't see you at your desk. Were you able to sleep?

Straight through, Deena said. I didn't set the alarm, thinking I wouldn't need it, and I overslept.

It's the Dux. Ever since I bought it, I've been sleeping well. You don't expect a mattress to make such a difference, but this one does.

Deena listened to the drawn-out words, slow and unthreatening. Some days Karen's attention to dailyness irritated; today she liked it. Today nothing was more important than having slept well.

There's something peaceful about your place, Deena said. The whiteness maybe. The music.

Karen nodded. I'm playing a new Windham Hill tape. You want to bring your coffee into my office?

Only for a minute, Deena said, knowing she shouldn't. I want to finish some copy before lunch.

In Karen's office the music was already playing, and Deena sat listening. It was true, the music, the white surfaces, they soothed.

I forgot to tell you, Karen said. You're welcome to anything in the closet. Borrow what you need. I know you didn't bring much.

I live in your apartment. I listen to your music. If I wear your clothes, I'll simply become you. Good thing you're blonde and I'm dark.

Karen laughed. Don't worry. You'll remain who you are.

It was drizzling after work, but it was the first time she could walk all the way home. She purchased a three-dollar umbrella on the street.

Walking, she stopped at windows to look, but didn't enter. She paused in front of North Beach Leather and debated. A leather skirt? But she was enjoying the walk; it was good just to walk and see and nothing more. Another day she might do more. After packing and unpacking twice in six months, after leaving behind most of what she owned, buying anything else seemed regressive.

At Ninety-third, she went up the slanting stairs, and yes, this was the door, these were the keys, they fit, how strange that she had keys to this place. Inside, she closed the door and stood leaning against it. Was this where she'd slept so well? It seemed unlikely now.

She opened her duffel bag and took out running clothes. It would be a wet run, and her feet were tired—she'd walked forty blocks—but she hadn't run yesterday either.

She ran toward Fifth Avenue, then south. She wasn't sure where the entrance to the park was. At Ninetieth, she found an opening, entered, and settled into an easy pace. Her first time here alone she wouldn't push herself. She corrected herself. She wasn't truly alone. In front and behind her people ran, rode, and walked. She was in a crowd and the companionship was pleasantly anonymous. Her shoes and socks were wet, and water dripped down her forehead, into her eyes. Still, coming around full circle, she wasn't yet ready to stop. She ran a last lap around the reservoir.

On her way home, she stopped at Gristede's for a steak. It would be easy enough to broil a steak and microwave a potato, dinner for one. She bought milk and cereal and coffee for mornings. She bought Comet and Windex. She stopped at the liquor store for a bottle of red wine, and finally arrived at Karen's carrying two full bags. She'd spent thirty dollars for only one person.

In the bathroom, she threw the blow-up flamingos into the sink, scrubbed the tub with Comet, rinsed and filled it. The hot water soothed her sore legs. She floated with her eyes closed and heard the phone ring as if from a distance. Was it this apartment or next door? She listened. A male voice—one of Karen's friends? She continued floating and the water lapped at her lips, then her nostrils. This would be her second night in this apartment alone, but in the city you were never truly alone. Even behind this dark door in this brown building she wasn't alone; above and below and across the hall were others. She was one of a million in the aggregate of city residents, alone and not alone.

She wrapped herself in a large towel. She had a good night ahead. She'd turn on the oven, prepare the steak for broiling, chop onion, wash the potato. But first she'd pour herself a glass of wine. She'd sip while cooking. She was talking to herself in her head, noting every moment, commenting on everything she did, step one, two, three. If she continued living alone, this could become a habit.

She sipped wine, chopped onion, remembered the phone call,

and went to press play on the white answering machine. Daniel's voice was loud.

I want you to move back, he said. I don't know why you're being so dramatic. Nothing happened. I didn't have an affair. Call me and we'll talk. I can come pick you up.

Talk? She was just beginning to enjoy not talking. And she wasn't a yo-yo he could yank back and forth, as if the move had been up to him. She'd moved out, now she'd stay out for as long as she wanted. Why was he so eager to drive into the city to pick her up?

She picked up the phone and put it down. She'd cook and eat as planned. Telling him could wait. She chopped half the onion and then decided to chop the rest. She put the onions on top of the steak and put the steak under the fire. Broiling was a single person's cooking style.

She was just cutting into the meat when the phone rang. She chewed and swallowed and waited for the machine to pick up. Daniel's voice again, saying he was leaving the house, that he'd be there in half an hour. She put the plate on the floor and picked up. What do you mean be here? she said. You weren't invited. I'm not coming back tonight. What do you think this is, a game?

I knew you were there, Daniel said. Where else would you be?

Out, Deena said. I might be out running, or having drinks with someone, or seeing a movie. Ever heard of that?

What are you doing for dinner? he asked, his voice suddenly thick. Had he been crying?

She paused, and looked at her steak. The juice was turning white.

Let me take you to dinner, he said. Even if you don't want to come back with me. I can pick you up in half an hour. There won't be much traffic this late.

My dinner is in front of me. I just broiled a steak.

Dessert then, he said.

No, Deena said. I'm staying in. I didn't move here in order to go out with you. Besides I have to be at work early tomorrow and it's after nine already.

Why is everyone so mean to me? What did I do? I'm trying to be nice. You moved out. I should be angry.

What are you talking about? I moved out for a good reason.

In that case, he said, his voice clearer now, angry. In that case, why don't you cut up my bank card and Visa and mail me the pieces. Open your own checking account. And send me a check for half this month's mortgage and half the credit-card bills. Why should I pay for everything?

Why? she said. I'll tell you why. Because most of the spending was for your sake. It was you who wanted to go dancing, skiing, horseback riding, everything all at once, and it was you who insisted on paying for Jill and Ann. Did you ask them for payments?

What about your costs? Daniel said. You could at least pay your own way, Miss Independent. I can't carry the mortgage plus other expenses on my own.

Divide the bills in four and I'll pay one quarter. I'll pay my way. I always have.

She hung up and paced. In the end, what you talk about is money. She would go to the bank first thing in the morning and open her own account. Her next paycheck would be entirely hers. She should have done it years ago. She had her own AmEx. She'd apply for a Visa. She'd live on only her own earnings. She could afford this apartment, and it was comfortable enough for one person. In Jerusalem, she'd grown up, along with five siblings, in just two rooms and a kitchen. It was amazing how little one really needed. She could live in one room. She'd moved in with only a suitcase and a duffel, and it was enough. At the house, half the rooms remained unlived-in, most of her clothes were unworn; it tired her to think about them, but she was always acquiring more. She'd change that. She'd learn to live with less.

The thickened fat on the steak disgusted her. She took the plate into the kitchen, wrapped it in foil, and put it into the refrigerator, which was filthy. It was a surprise to find Karen's kitchen and bathroom so dirty. Her office was so neat.

Deena leaned back on the sofa and tried following the music. She couldn't. Her head was spinning. She stood. She needed food to absorb the alcohol she'd been drinking. She turned on the light in the kitchen and roaches scurried. She switched the light off. She could see enough without it. She took the steak from the fridge and put it in the microwave. This time she'd eat in bed. The newspaper and several magazines were already there. Near her pillow were the remote control and some of her books. When the bed was all yours, you brought everything into it.

She heard a voice speaking Yiddish, which was strange. She'd stopped dreaming in Yiddish years ago. When she spoke it, her voice went several octaves higher and emerged squeaky from somewhere high in her head. Then why was she suddenly dreaming in it?

She fell asleep again and this time she was a child, and the voice of her mother spoke, saying, Go to bed already, tomorrow's another day.

· · ·

When she emerged from the elevator after work, Daniel stood there, in his hand a tall red rose.

She hated red roses. You'd think he'd know, she thought, but she hadn't known until now.

Let me take you somewhere, he said. To a quiet place.

What for? Deena said.

To talk. On the phone you hang up on me.

I don't want to go anywhere. I want to walk home and run.

Then I'll walk with you, he said.

She felt ridiculous with the rose in her hand. Here, she said, giving it back. I don't want it.

But I bought it for you, he said. It's the longest stem they had, the most expensive one. I didn't buy it on the street.

The mention of money reminded her of the roses he hadn't bought. And now it was too late; she didn't want anything from him now. She wished he wouldn't try so hard. He was suddenly too anxious to please.

Slow down, he said. We'll enjoy this walk more if you slow down.

But she couldn't slow down. She was too agitated.

Why do you have to be so hard about everything? Daniel said. Forget your run for one night. Let me take you to dinner.

Stop trying. I don't want to forget my run, and it's too early for dinner.

Then a drink.

She fumed. One way or another she always paid for things. He bought a rose, and therefore she had to sit across a table looking at him. Not to do it was mean. But flowers wouldn't change her mind. She'd moved because they needed the separation, he'd said so himself. But if he kept calling and visiting, it was no separation.

Where's Jill? she asked. What's going on with her?

I wouldn't know, Daniel said, his voice shaky. She's not talking to me. No one wants to talk to me.

That's why you're here, Deena said.

He stopped walking. What do you mean, that's why? Daniel said. Can we just sit somewhere for half an hour? I'm asking for a half hour of your time.

She led the way into a coffee shop. Daniel resisted. This place is greasy and too bright, he said.

Greasy? She looked at the counter. She often stopped here for coffee. She liked this place. She liked the counter and the hard orange of the stools. Coffee shops were all the same, bright lights and straightforward service. Daniel wanted dimmers and shadows, but for the conversation she wanted to have, fluorescents were perfect. In love, you saw through rose tints. Breaking up, you were clear-eyed, sharp.

Two coffees arrived, along with the bill.

I resent your choosing this place, Daniel said.

She shrugged. You don't have to eat here. You wanted to talk.

You're not giving us a chance, he said.

A chance for what? Deena asked.

You could have stopped me, you know. You could have put an end to the whole thing in the beginning. But you didn't. You made friends with her.

What did you want me to do, scratch her eyes out? Besides, you were having fun. I thought she was good for you. I still think so.

·   ·   ·

In the morning she sat up, a five-year-old worrying about the bed-clothes and mattress. But only her face and pillow were damp. She touched her face. There'd been sounds—hers? When you slept alone, there was no one to tell you.

It had been a good day at work, no disturbances. Jill and Daniel were probably talking again. The copy for the Volvo ad was approved without changes. With no other assignment on her desk, Deena felt an unusual ease.

Outside, the days were growing longer, spring was coming, it was finally April. At Sixty-sixth Street, in front of North Beach Leather, she hesitated, then entered.

She took into the dressing room a size four and a six, tried the six first, and liked it. It was large enough to rest on her hips. But when she came out of the dressing room, the saleswoman shook her head.

That's not how it's meant to fit, she said. Try the four.

In the dressing room, Deena zipped up the four, buttoned the waistband, and quickly sucked her stomach in.

Much better, the woman said.

It feels snug, Deena said. I feel fat in it.

Leather stretches as you wear it. At the end of the night, the four will still look good.

Deena looked at herself in the three-way mirror. If she lost a couple of pounds, the skirt would feel better. If she gained a few, the zipper wouldn't close.

Wear it around the house for a while, the woman advised. You'll get used to the feel of leather and it'll stretch.

But she'd purchased enough pairs of leather shoes thinking they'd stretch.

This is much softer than shoe leather, the woman explained.

For the next twenty blocks, she carried the North Beach Leather bag and wondered when she'd wear the skirt. She wasn't dancing anymore; she wasn't living that lifestyle.

At home, she put on her running clothes but she didn't want to run. The walk uptown tired her. But she'd bought a size-four skirt. She had to run.

An hour and a half later, after running and showering, she sat, stood, and walked in the leather skirt. It was scratchy.

She ate dinner, read, and finally, tired of so much constriction, undressed for bed. In bed, she became aware of a burn on her lower back. She looked in the mirror. Below her waist was a red scratch. The tyranny of tags. She cursed the skirt, Daniel, then Jill.

Thursday passed quietly, no calls. Deena worked, ran, ate; the mechanics of living. With or without Daniel, her days went by in much the same way. Two weeks ago life without him was unthinkable, today living with him was difficult to imagine. They'd lived together seven years, they'd even come to look alike. Some days looking into Daniel's face, seeing her own face reflected in his brown eyes, she'd note that the outer corners of their eyes took the same downward slant. You become what you look upon, like Jacob's spotted sheep. A theory of evolution. If she continued to live alone, whom would she come to reflect? She'd be careful this time. But already she was living in Karen's apartment, wearing Karen's clothes. She hadn't chosen.

The apartment had been available and she'd taken it. It had been mostly circumstance, no choices. Life happened; it was arbitrary. You merely responded to what was there.

Friday night there was a message on the machine from Daniel. I called here, he said, because I wasn't getting through at work. Listen to this. Joe is offering me a bonus, a weekend in Florida, on the company bill. He says I look like I could use it. I'm sure you could too. I reserved two seats for a late flight tonight. I have to confirm, so call me as soon as you get in.

She could think of nothing she wanted to do less. She went running even though she'd planned to take the night off.

When she returned, there were two more messages from Daniel; the first was angry. I'm leaving on the ten-o'clock flight, he said. The least you could do is call to say yes or no, you bitch.

During the second message, he apologized and sobbed.

She picked up the phone to dial, hesitated, put it down. He was crying a lot. He needed taking care of. Joe was right. Daniel needed time to collect himself, he needed help, and it didn't look as if he would get it from either of the women in his life.

Karen called to ask if she wanted to join Greg and her for brunch.

Deena didn't. She was uncomfortable around couples. And their pity made her feel like a victim.

I want to stay in bed half the day, rest and read, she explained. It's my first full day here. I also need a good, long run.

She went out to buy the paper, came back, and read it.

She went out to buy lunch, came back, and ate it.

She went running, came back, and showered.

Everything she did went too quickly. She started a thing, finished it, and still there were hours to fill. She could have run the loop twice. There was nothing and no one to hurry for, she was doing nothing else, but she'd gotten bored. The track was new, there was plenty to look at, still it seemed to her that all she ever did was run. There had to be more to life. She was living in New York City.

She read and outside it grew dark. She turned on the lamps and continued reading. She cooked dinner, ate, and read more. She undressed for bed. Tomorrow she would do more. She'd go places, do things.

She listened to music and fell asleep thinking about tomorrow. Then the phone rang. It was after twelve; it could only be Daniel. He needed her. The phone rang again and this time she picked up.

Fly down here, he said, his voice a drunken imperative. There's an early-morning flight. You'll be here before noon.

You're drunk, Deena said.

So what? he said. Alcohol might do you good too. You coming?

I didn't move out so that I could take vacations with you.

Bitch, Daniel said.

You're very persuasive, Deena said. I don't know why women don't fall over themselves for you.

They do. You should see me in action. I'm good. At the bar, these two women—

Is that what you called to tell me?

I called to invite you here, Daniel said.

The answer is no.

Why not? What did I do? I want to know. I held back. Don't I get any credit for that?

There was an interruption, she heard a female voice, then Daniel's response. Hang on for a minute, he said. She hung up quietly.

The phone rang two minutes later and Deena disconnected it. I am a bitch, she thought.

In the morning she opened the windows wide, stuck her head out, and breathed deeply the moist, rippling air. The humidity felt good on her winter-dry skin. In the park, the ground would be soft and everywhere people would be swarming, prisoners of winter released for the day. She wanted to join them, but not on foot and not running. She'd ride. She hadn't ridden since fall.

Karen's bicycle was a heavy old clunker. It bumped and bounced down the stairs. Carrying it back up the stairs would be harder, but right now the sun was out and she was going down.

In her backpack, she had a sketch pad and the Colette book she'd found on Karen's shelf, *Retreat from Love*. Was that what she was doing? She'd read and find out. Living alone, she had time for everything. She had too much time.

The tires were low and she had to walk down Lexington to the bicycle shop for air. Then she pedaled to the park and entered. The bicycle wasn't built for speed, which was fine. She didn't want to race past trees, pedestrians, the world. What she wanted today was a slow ride that allowed for seeing. She would see how other people lived. She sat on a bench and watched a man and woman walk briskly, arms swinging with the rhythm of their stride. European, she thought. At six years old she had decided that she would never swing her arms so hard and grotesquely, like grown-ups. Children, she noted, didn't move their arms at all. They simply walked. She would always walk like that, arms straight and still. Even when she was a mother. But today she admired the couple's swinging arms, the vigor in the swing. These people were alive, they walked with purpose, they had somewhere to go.

They passed out of sight, and then, for a while, Deena focused on younger couples out for the day, walking slowly, stopping, leaning. She lost patience watching their languor. She'd languished similarly long enough. Now she wanted to stride with some knowledge of where she was going.

But she had nowhere to go. And no one to go with. Unless she was riding or running, doing something active, she found herself uncomfortable alone in public places. As if everyone knew why she was alone. It was silly; she should get used to being alone, but she couldn't bring herself to take a table for one at a restaurant or café.

She rode home slowly. She was tired. She would take a nap. Then maybe the Calder show at the Cooper-Hewitt. She turned the corner, coasted halfway down the hill, and saw Daniel leaning against her door. She braked hard, thought to turn back, but it was too late; he'd seen her. Her heart thumped. What was she afraid of?

I've been waiting here for over an hour, he said.

Deena shrugged. I didn't know you were coming, she said. What happened to Florida?

Riding is a good idea, he said. I wish I'd thought to bring my bicycle. I could have brought your Fuji too. We could ride together in the park.

But she didn't want her Fuji. Or maybe she did want it. She didn't know. The ride would have been more fun with company. But then why were they separated? Why was she living here?

What happened to Florida? she asked again.

I was lonely.

What about all those women in the bar? she asked, then shook her head. Don't tell me. I don't want to know. I want to go upstairs and take a shower.

Let me come up and wait for you, Daniel said. I'll take you to lunch.

No.

We lived together seven years, he said. What are you afraid of?

I'm not afraid, Deena said, but she was. If he came upstairs, if he moved toward her, would she be able to stop him? Besides, the purpose of this apartment was to not be with him.

I thought you'd want to see my tan and hear about the seafood I ate. I tasted shrimp for the first time and it was delicious.

She looked at him. When they first met he was darker than this. It was June, school was over, and she wanted to put her hand on his browned skin. Clinging to it was a thin Indian cotton shirt and she wanted to be that shirt. Then, mornings, she lay in the sun trying to match his brown skin. Evenings, he picked her up in his Civic and they rode with the windows down, the wind cooling her sunstruck skin.

But on a New York City sidewalk, at the end of a long winter, pale skin was appropriate, beautiful even. His tan was offensive. He looked sleazy, she thought, a swinger. Without the yarmulke on his head, with the bald spot exposed, he was without dignity. He picked up women at bars, ate shrimp. Religion had given him character. Without it, he was a weak, undistinguished man. And all along her father had said this. There's no depth there, he warned, no deep attachments. Merely a follower of rules.

Deena looked at Daniel with distaste and he looked back unhappily. Underneath the veneer of excitement about his tan, the shrimp, and women, was a weak, confused man. He needed her.

Wait for me in a coffee shop, she said, yielding.

I can't wait any longer, he said. I need some movement. I'll take a walk or go somewhere. In an hour, if I'm still in the area, I'll call you.

She nodded. She understood. He would call Jill. If she was home and willing to join him, Deena wouldn't hear from him. Now he was impatient to go, she could safely put the key in the lock and walk up the stairs alone. She steered her bicycle up the step.

You need help with that? he asked and lifted the rear wheel. And he held the door as she passed through. All because she'd said no. That's what it took to get a man to hold doors for you. She turned to see if he wanted to come up, but no, he stepped back and lifted his hand to wave.

An hour later he still hadn't called and she went to the Cooper-Hewitt.

Calder's wire sculptures reminded her of her mother's one-minute drawings. She'd ask for a duck and in a minute she had a duck made of one continuous line. Or a flower. A tree. Deena walked home planning to make a duck out of a wire hanger.

There were no messages on the machine. She poured some of Karen's scotch, wet her lips. Burning butterscotch. She could get used to drinking this. She sipped again, and listened to the first notes of Vollenweider's *Winter Solstice*. She had the whole evening ahead. She'd eaten a late lunch; she wasn't hungry. What could she do?

Daniel said he was lonely. She was too, which was unexpected. When she was living with Daniel, time alone had always been welcome.

She poured more scotch, sipped, and closed her eyes. This was the way to listen to music: eyes closed.

When she stood again, she had to hold on to the back of the sofa. She was thirsty, she needed water, but the tap water ran brown and she'd forgotten to buy a jug.

In the refrigerator, there were several cans of V8. The vitamins would be good for her. She'd have to remember to replace it. That and the scotch. She pulled off the foil seal and gulped down the juice, which tasted of metal, like all canned food. She ate the remaining half of the Reuben sandwich she'd had for lunch, and bent and flattened a hanger. But the wire didn't easily release old bends or accept new ones. She would have to work with a lower gauge and a pair of pliers.

She was feeling queasy, was it the scotch? She undressed for bed and let her body sink into the mattress, the floor, and below, into the apartment beneath. She couldn't move, her arms and legs hurt; they were stiff. She lay unmoving, eyes closed. She swallowed. She'd sleep it off. What else could she do? She wouldn't drink again. That's what people said about drinking alone. You didn't stop. You went too far too fast. But she wasn't like that. She knew how to stop. It wouldn't happen again. She wished the queasiness would pass.

An hour later, she awoke in a sweat. Her legs and arms were far away; where were they and how could they hurt so hard from such a great distance? What was wrong with her? She had cramps. Her stomach felt swollen. She couldn't stay on her back. She turned over, but it didn't help. She crawled onto the cold, hard floor. That was better. She pressed her face into the floor. Her shoulders, elbows, wrists, even her fingers hurt. Hips, knees, ankles, she felt only the bone, there was no flesh. She was poisoned, her body was done, she couldn't move. This is what happens to a woman who lives alone: she dies and no one knows for days, maybe weeks, until a bad smell is reported. But she wasn't dead yet. She lifted her head and crawled. In the bathroom, she tried standing and couldn't. Her stomach heaved. She retched. The V8. And the scotch. She wouldn't drink again. She couldn't move. She leaned against the sink, washed her face, and brushed her teeth. She sat on the edge of the tub and waited. Better to stay here and wait. She stuck her finger down her throat. That was better. She brushed her teeth again, went back to bed, and slept for a minute.

The alarm clock rang. Her head weighed fifty pounds. She pressed the snooze button and closed her eyes. It rang again and the sound hurt. She turned it off and slept. But something was still ringing. What was it? She had to answer. Hello? she wanted to say, but it was hard to say it. She tried again, hello, and woke to the sound of her voice. She sat up and her hands went to her head, which needed holding up. Karen's voice was on the machine. It wasn't a dream.

It's eleven o'clock, Karen said, and I'm calling to see if you're there, if you're all right. Deena hurried to the phone, picked up.

I was asleep, she said. I'm not feeling well. I was sick during the night. My stomach is upset.

Do you want me to come over? Karen asked, her voice warming, concerned. I'll bring wonton soup.

Deena looked at the half-empty bottle of scotch on the floor.

No, she said. Not right away. I just need sleep now. I'll call you when I'm up again.

All right, Karen said. I'll tell Helen. Take care of yourself. Get some rest.

She swallowed aspirin and went back to bed. Why did her arms and legs still ache? And her stomach? She slept, woke, slept, and woke again. Where was she? The room was white, a hospital. Even with her eyes closed, she saw white walls coming closer. She was in a hospital bed, she couldn't get out of bed, there was only this bed and the walls were coming closer. She had nowhere to go. She lay still and felt the walls lean toward her. She closed her eyes again and this time roaches were all around; at her sides, circling the crown of her head, along the length of her legs and feet. If she moved, they'd crawl under her. If she turned right or left, she'd squash them and they'd crunch. She didn't move.

She thought she heard the phone again and opened her eyes, startled. But it was quiet. She looked to the right, then left. She lifted the covers. No roaches. She touched the sheets, smooth cotton. She closed her eyes, then cracked one to see the time. One o'clock. She should get up, call Karen. She had to go out to buy a small bottle of scotch, just enough to refill Karen's bottle.

What happened? Karen asked. What did you eat?

I had a V8, Deena said and laughed.

Not those cans in the fridge? Karen said. They're ancient. I've had them since my first year at SVA. The assignment was to redesign the can. I should have thrown them out a long time ago. They're at least five years old.

Deena walked to the fridge. The expiration date was May 1980.

At work there was news: Paul Herz had been given notice.

I didn't want to tell you yesterday, Karen said. You were sick.

Is he in today? Deena asked.

Karen shook her head. He came in late yesterday, made calls, did some packing.

Who announced it? Deena asked.

Ron, Karen said. He went from office to office. He said we're a strong group and that we'll continue to grow. He was positive about the future. Technically he's now the head of the department.

Deena worried. The timing of yesterday's absence wasn't good. Seen as dispensable, as a remainder of the old rule, she'd get shafted too. She couldn't afford to lose her job now. She was on her own. She had rent to pay; she had to live. Already she'd spent too much despite intentions to strip down to essentials. Every day there'd been something. The leather skirt, a basic black sweater, running tights, a towel, a special toothbrush. She had to keep working.

After lunch, Ron came into her office and closed the door. Deena looked up, afraid. Was this it? He sat.

You've heard? he asked.

Deena nodded.

I know you were close to him, he hired you. I'm sorry.

He looked at her. I understand you're having some personal difficulties, he said slowly. If there is something I can do to help, let me know.

She nodded and mouthed thanks.

He wasn't done; he had more to say. But I should warn you. It's been noticed that you've been late a lot, and yesterday you weren't here.

I was sick, something I ate, didn't Karen tell you?

He shook his head.

I moved recently. My life has been complicated.

He nodded. Sometimes it's better to take a week off, do what needs to be done, and return in better shape. We have a new business pitch coming up and I'll need some teams working weekends. Not this weekend, probably the following one. Are you up for it?

Definitely, Deena said. It will be good to be busy on the weekend.

Good, he said and stood. Hang in there.

She stayed till eight that night, kept her door wide open and her radio on. It wasn't that she had so much work to do, but it would help to be seen at her desk. Tomorrow morning she'd make sure to be in before nine. Even if she spent the first two hours reading the paper or a book, it would look good if she was at her desk before the others. Ron came in at eight every morning.

She didn't drink all week. She read, went to bed early, and woke up at seven. She was healthy; she was fine. She was sleeping again, and work was once again boring. She resented all the hours at her desk doing nothing. She had no new assignments. She read the paper cover to cover every morning. She read three books.

People are working on their portfolios, Karen whispered. I saw Kathleen sneak out with hers. She was wearing a suit.

I'd better take a look at mine, Deena said. If there are layoffs, I'll be the first to go.

Behind the door of every art director's and copywriter's office was a black portfolio containing his best work. From every assignment that landed on your desk you asked one thing: that it produce a piece good enough for the portfolio. Deena closed her door and lifted the case onto her desk; she knew without looking what was in it and that none of it was good enough. The mock campaigns that had landed her this job were better than the work she'd produced in three years here. Nothing stood out. Not one headline announced a major talent.

. . .

Sunday night the phone rang and it was Daniel.

Move back, he said. I demand that you move back tomorrow.

I'm not taking orders, Deena said.

I'm warning you, he said.

About what?

He didn't answer.

What happened to needing time?

I did. I needed to think things over. Now I want you to move back.

Just like that? First you needed time, now you don't. Well, I'm not moving back at the snap of your fingers.

Never? Daniel asked.

She didn't know. She wasn't certain. She liked the idea of being single, but she was also lonely. She wanted company, but not necessarily his. In truth, she didn't miss him. She did miss the house. Karen's brown, dark kitchen hurt.

You know, she said slowly, I could have forgiven you the whole affair, but not the way you treated me.

She stopped. She could say this better when she was angry. She had to harden herself against him. She had to remember his voice saying, Do you mind and None of your business. She had to remember his trips to Manhattan for Jill, his generosity, the doors he held open. And how uncaring he'd been when he turned to her.

So you're not coming back? he asked again.

What happened with Jill? Deena asked.

I don't know. She's not talking to me. She says we need distance.

His voice trembled and Deena bit her lip. She didn't want him to cry.

That's why you're calling me, she said.

So what? Daniel said. Is that so terrible?

In the morning she showered, dressed, and walked to the subway. This was becoming routine; in just a few weeks you could get used to anything. Life was all habit.

On the street, she walked with a bounce. People smiled and she smiled back. The sun was out and everyone was happy.

On the platform, it was unusually quiet, with only the sound of a saxophone. People stood listening quietly. There was no rush to the middle or end of the platform, so that getting off the train you'd be at the exit nearest your destination. It was by this precise knowledge of which car to be in that you knew a daily rider from a visitor. Today they were all visitors.

At work, there were five messages. Daniel, Daniel's mother, her father calling from Jerusalem, Daniel again, and Jill.

Her father called here? What time was it there? And what was wrong? He'd gotten the number from Daniel. Why not Karen's number? What was Daniel up to?

She dialed his number first.

That got your attention, he said.

What are you talking about?

Your father called last night and I told him where you were and why. I was angry. You keep hanging up on me. I didn't know what else to do.

What did you tell him? That you're having an affair?

Stop saying I had an affair. It's not true. Maybe you want me to have one. Some people are saying that you were just waiting for an opportunity to leave me. That you always wanted to leave me.

Some people? Deena said. Like who? Your mother?

You could have stopped me, Daniel said. If you minded, why didn't you have a good fight over me instead of that dinner when you said nothing that made any sense?

Maybe I don't think you're worth a fight.

Why not? Daniel said.

Deena didn't answer. She didn't know why not. Because she didn't love him? Because it was true that she'd wanted to leave him and the opportunity presented itself?

You know, Daniel said, you're not a very nice person. You're not forgiving.

And who said that? Your sister?

Yes, as a matter of fact. It was Celia. She says you're very proud. You should have consulted her sooner.

I told your father I was no longer responsible for you. That you're on your own in the city.

Responsible? Since when were you responsible for me?

You know what I mean. Anyway I knew when I was telling him that it was a bad idea, he was never on my side, but I wanted to get you into trouble. I wanted you to have to answer to someone.

Well, you got what you wanted. Now you can call your mother and ask her not to call me.

I did, Daniel said. She says you need to discuss things with some-one, that they are your family. She says I deserve a second chance.

Tell her I have my own mother and father. Besides, she's your mother; she should talk to you.

She does. Believe me. She gives advice as if she has experience in such situations. When I pointed out to her that she's not exactly an expert, she had a story to tell about old Dad. Want to hear it?

I'm at work. And I still have to call my father. Good-bye.

Ten minutes later she was on long distance to Jerusalem.

You're not losing any great goods, her father said. Merely a boy from the nations of the land, nothing special, no genius. You can do better even now. Get yourself a divorce and come home.

Someone knocked at the door.

I must go. I'm at work.

Work, money, America. What do you need it for? Give it up and come home.

It was Karen. What's happening? she asked, handing Deena two more message slips. Helen says you're getting a zillion calls.

Daniel told everyone. His family and mine. I just talked to my father, who is delighted. He never approved of Daniel. His mother wants to talk about second chances.

Does she know about Jill? Karen said.

I don't know what Daniel told her. He didn't tell my father the truth.

Listen, Karen said. They all have their own agendas. You need to think about what you want, what's best for you.

What was best for her. Did anyone know for sure what was best?

I know that I'd better get some work done, Deena said.

Karen nodded. That will help.

Helen came to the door. It's Daniel's mother again. She begs you to please, please take her call.

Deena sighed.

Good luck, Karen said.

When Deena picked up, both Daniel's parents were on the line. This was a family emergency and they acted together. But it was Mrs. B. who did the talking.

Daddy and I feel that you are as close to us as one of our children. We wish you'd felt comfortable calling us in the very beginning. We will do anything for you. We'll help you in any way we can.

I don't think there's anything you can do, Deena said. Right now, I'm not in any mood to give Daniel second chances. Telling my father wasn't brilliant. As you can imagine, he recommends a quick divorce.

You're right, that wasn't smart, Mrs. B. agreed. Your father was against him from the beginning. Daniel says he put the idea of divorce in your head before the two of you were married. That's very irresponsible. The power of suggestion is a dangerous tactic to employ. Every marriage has its difficulties that require working through. Your father is a grown man; he ought to know better.

Mr. B. spoke. You experienced opposition when you married Daniel. You ought to consider whether you don't owe it to yourself to honor that struggle with another effort. Right now you're angry and hurt, that's understandable. Daniel is confused; he doesn't know what he's doing. You both need some time. In the meantime Mom and I hope you'll feel comfortable calling us.

The two of you were always such good friends, Mrs. B. says. When you're in pain, it's easy to forget the good things. And I want you to know we love both of you equally.

Deena shook her head. They didn't deserve this; they'd worked hard to do what they could for their children. And there was only one thing she could do for them: remain married to Daniel. That's what they wanted, therefore that's what they advised. But it was her own father's advice that remained in her head. Divorce. She hadn't dared to say the word aloud until now, but her father had said it, thereby making it possible.

When she finally hung up, she put her head on the desk. What had begun in privacy was now completely public. First people at work found out. That had been hard enough. Now it was a family matter.

And there were other complications: she wanted Daniel to keep the house. It was possible, she thought, that after a year or two of living separately, they'd want to remarry and she'd move back to the house. Considering divorce, she was already contemplating remarriage. Odd thinking, she knew. Still, she didn't want to sell the house to a stranger. If Daniel purchased her share, the possibility of her living in it someday remained. Maybe Sergei could work something out. He'd performed for her at the closing. He'd pushed the seller into a corner and saved them another four thousand dollars.

Not a lot, he said looking into her eyes. But enough for a great leather sofa. Or maybe velvet is more your style.

Sergei. A Romanian with a touch of gypsy, Jew, and everything else. He'd grown up in Hungary, France, and Italy, had a knowledge of borders, and knew how to cross them. He was a lawyer you wanted on your side.

She put her hand on the phone to call him and hesitated. Why was she calling him? What did she want? After the closing, he shook her hand and said not to hesitate to call, and in his eyes and in the hands that held hers she thought there was more than an offer of lawyer's services. That's what she was calling for.

She dialed and, yes, he was in, the secretary said. Then he was on the phone saying, I thought I'd never hear from you again.

Deena took a deep breath. She didn't know how to say it, where to begin. She should have planned before calling.

It can't be that bad, he said.

Daniel and I are separating, she said.

I'm not surprised, he said gently. The two of you are night and day. What do you want to do?

I know I want Daniel to keep the house. About other things I don't yet know. It's all so recent I haven't had a chance to think.

I don't usually do divorces, Sergei said, but I will for you, if it's what you want. Do you want to have dinner with me tomorrow night? I'll try to advise you. There are things you can do now that will be to your advantage later. Where shall I pick you up?

She gave him her office address, then worried. What if Daniel showed up?

As if he could feel her transgressing, Daniel called. Let me take you to dinner tomorrow night, he said. Think of it as a date.

I'm already going out to dinner tomorrow night, Deena said.

Anyone I know?

A client, though it's none of your business, Deena said.

A man? Daniel asked.

I'm not answering any more questions, she said.

Walking up Madison, she saw herself reflected in a window and stopped. Her hair. It had no style. What had been a close crop no longer was. It had grown in crazily. She rang the bell at the first salon she came upon, and walked up a flight of stairs.

She didn't have an appointment and she didn't know a name. She asked the receptionist to recommend someone. Who cuts your hair? Deena asked.

Burton. He might take you between two appointments.

The receptionist looked at her. Your hair, she said and stopped, not wanting to insult.

Deena laughed. I know. And I only just noticed.

Fifteen minutes later she sat in a chair, wearing a black kimono and sipping cappuccino. This haircut would cost, she didn't know how much, there was no price list anywhere, but the cappuccino was a sure sign. She responded to Burton's capable hands on her head. She didn't want to care how much it would cost.

Do you have something specific in mind? Burton asked. A style?

She hadn't thought about it, not until he'd asked, but now she knew.

I want long hair again, she said. In the meantime, whatever will look good.

He made suggestions and Deena nodded. Anything would be an improvement. An assistant led the way to the sink and Deena leaned back, let go of her neck and head, and concentrated only on the luxury of having her hair washed.

So did you just break up with some guy? Burton asked.

Deena looked up, startled. Is it that obvious?

He put his hand on her shoulder and smiled into the mirror. Don't worry. It's just that women tend to go for a drastic change when they're breaking up with someone. They either cut their hair real short, or they let it grow. Sometimes they just change the color.

Deena laughed. I cut my hair short two years ago, before I knew there'd be any change. Suddenly I'm sick of short hair.

Then you've met someone, he said.

At work she was suddenly popular.

She had lunch with James and Al, two other copywriters. They took sandwiches to the East River and asked one another what came after advertising. That was the thing about advertising. It was temporary. There had to be something better after.

James wanted to write screenplays. It was what he did after work. Al was thinking about sitcom comedy.

I'm sick of desks, Deena said. I want to do something physical. Maybe I'll take up ballet.

James laughed. You won't do that.

Watch and see, Deena said.

In the afternoon Gary Ross, the AE on Volvo, stopped in to say the client liked her copy. He was surprised it was a woman, Gary said. He suggested my inviting you out to lunch, but I think you'll have a better time if you go out with someone of your own choosing. Just send me the bill.

That's thoughtful of you, Deena said. Thank you. Maybe I'll take James and Al tomorrow.

He stood leaning against the wall. So what is it you really want to do? he asked. You're too smart to stay here.

Deena looked at him. The last time I heard that was in a prelude to getting sacked. I read too much of what came across my desk, my boss said. And it was just a temporary secretarial job.

Gary Ross laughed. You were too smart and he felt threatened. Plus he probably had a few secrets.

After work, when Deena walked out of the building, Sergei was already at the curb, leaning against his black Mercedes. He came toward her like a gangster, his long black leather coat fanning wide behind him, and kissed her on the lips. She hoped no one at the office was seeing this.

He took her arm and led the way around to the passenger side, keeping her on the inside, away from traffic, then opened the door and held it.

A man who opened doors. Wasn't this what she wanted?

He pulled up in front of an Italian restaurant on Second Avenue.

Will this suit you? he asked. This early it should be quiet. We can talk undisturbed.

Without looking at the menu, he spoke in Italian to the waitress, who disappeared and quickly returned with a bottle of white wine, a basket of steaming bread, and in a glass dish peppered olive oil for dipping. He knew this place; he'd been here before.

He poured the wine, lifted his glass, and looked at Deena with a question. To what?

Deena looked down and shrugged. He was making her uncomfortable with his long, deep looks. He was behaving too romantically. Was he just trying to make her feel better?

To beauty, he said. Dark-haired beauty.

She looked into his dark blue eyes. The pupils were black. To beauty? He was a married man. He had a daughter. Did it matter?

Sip your wine, he said, and tell me what happened.

Deena sipped and waited. She sipped again. I don't know where to begin, she said.

I know one thing. It wasn't you who had the affair.

Deena shook her head. How do you know?

He laughed. A thousand ways. The way you dressed today, for example. You're wearing a jacket, as if this is all business. When you called me, you wanted more, then you ran scared. Are you afraid of me?

Deena nodded and looked into the large white plate in front of her. She fiddled with her knife.

But why?

The antipasti arrived and Sergei paused to fill first her plate, then his. He ate.

Mmm, he said.

Only after he finished what was on his plate did he pick up the conversation. Tell me why you are afraid of me, he said.

I think I'm more embarrassed than afraid. I called you right after some difficult conversations. I was overwrought. I didn't know what to do. Maybe it was a mistake to call you.

Sergei wiped his lips with his napkin. Well, he said, his voice suddenly more businesslike. Since then, you've had some time to think. What is it you want now?

Deena cringed. His crisp, all-business manner was worse. She preferred his flirtatious, love-making approach. She needed him to be good to her. That's why she'd called.

I take back what I said. I am afraid and confused. I don't know what I want. You seem so experienced, that's what makes me afraid of you, I think.

Sergei laughed. If your husband had been more experienced, if he were a better man, you wouldn't be here talking about divorce. It's not because of the affair that you want to leave him. That's beside the point. You're hurt because he mistreated you. As long as I am good to my wife, as long as I continue to take good care of her and of Isabella, she is satisfied. She doesn't care to know more. She shouldn't know.

Does your wife also have affairs? Deena asked.

Maybe, he said. I don't ask her. It isn't important.

He stretched his legs and sipped wine. You and I, he said, the two of us, should go to the Bahamas for a weekend. I know you will look good in a bikini. You have all the right curves. Tonight we can go dancing.

Deena looked at herself.

Not in those clothes, he said.

The food arrived, and they ate, but with his eyes on her, she swallowed very little. If she continued eating like this, drinking more than eating, she'd feel better in the leather skirt.

You still haven't told me anything, he said.

There isn't much to tell. And you seem to know without my telling.

But I don't know how you feel, what you want. I don't know the important things.

Deena looked at him. You're right. What I minded most was how good he was to the other woman.

Sergei nodded. That's the worst mistake a man could make. He's getting what he wants and at home he is a bastard. That's bad character.

The waitress came to take the plates.

You don't eat very much, he said. Will you have a cappuccino? Or espresso?

Espresso, Deena said, and Sergei looked up at the waitress and mouthed, *Due.*

After dinner he drove uptown, turned onto Ninety-third, and pulled into a spot right in front of her building. He was someone for whom spaces opened. And he was accustomed to things going his way. He backed in efficiently, turned off the engine, and then they were out of the car, and in front of her door. He took the key from her hand, opened and held the door for her, then followed her up the steps. What was she doing, bringing a man she didn't know very well up to Karen's apartment? She hadn't allowed Daniel in, why Sergei?

Inside, without waiting for her to show him, he walked the length of the place, from the door to the windows, and from the windows to the kitchen and bathroom. Now he knew where she lived. Deena stood watching.

I am subletting this from a friend who moved in with her fiancé. He nodded, stepped behind her, and helped take off her jacket. Then he stood back to look, and she felt looked at.

That's much better, he said. I was right. You will look good on the beach. Do you have a bikini? You'll need only the bottom half.

She shook her head. I didn't pack much, only necessities.

Without the jacket what you're wearing is quite fine, he said. A skirt would be better. Do you have one?

She nodded.

Show me, he said.

She opened the closet, stepped in, and located the leather skirt. The sales tag was still attached because she'd been debating whether to keep the skirt. She managed to tear it off before stepping out. She didn't want him to know it was new.

Perfect, he said, feeling the leather with his fingers. Let's see you in it, he said.

Did he want her to undress and dress in front of him? She delayed, looking for a pair of stockings. Did Karen leave any?

Come here, he said, his eyes on her face.

She came and he took her hand and brought her closer.

This, he said, his fingers on the clasp of her belt, is what you're afraid of.

He worked quickly and then stepped back.

Sit, he said, and she sat.

Open your legs, he said, and she looked at him and opened her legs.

Now, tell me what you want.

She shook her head.

Say it, he said.

He looked at her, nodded, and waited. He wanted her to say it; he'd get her to say it. You want? he prodded.

You, she mouthed, looking into his blue eyes.

He took her hand and led her to the bed.

When Sergei left, she pressed play on the machine, which had been blinking all night, demanding to know how, after moving out because Daniel was having an affair, she could explain what she was doing with Sergei.

It was Daniel. You're never home, he complained. What's going on?

She didn't call back, but what if coming home one night with Sergei she found Daniel waiting? He had a way of showing up when you least wanted him.

At her desk the next day, Deena spent the morning on the telephone comparing futon prices. Karen wasn't sleeping well on Greg's spring mattress; her back and neck were stiff. If Deena purchased a Dux, she could have it delivered directly to Greg's place and they could avoid the trouble of moving the old Dux downtown.

My Dux is practically new, Karen said. I bought it less than a year ago, and it hasn't gotten much use.

Deena nodded. She didn't care about that, but she didn't want a Dux mattress. If finally she purchased a bed, she wanted something better than foam. At lunch she took a train downtown and tested futons. She sat and lay on four-, six-, and eight-inch-thick futons. She tried all-cotton, alternating layers of foam and cotton, and a combination of wool, foam, and cotton, which was more comfortable than any bed she'd ever slept on.

She decided on queen size. She'd gone from twin to full (Karen's) to queen in one month. After twenty-seven years of single beds, she'd have room enough for anyone. Her nights would never be the same. She wasn't the same. These days she was having a hard time knowing herself.

Karen was insulted. The Dux had made all the difference for her, and it cost less than a futon. And what's wrong with full size? Queen means you'll have to buy all new sheets, she added. Isn't money an issue?

She shook her head disapprovingly. Deena's behavior had changed. She came late to work, went for long lunches with the boys, and now this bed. It could have been simple. For $99 she could have had a Dux and saved both of them the effort of switching mattresses. It was inconsiderate of her. Singlehood wasn't doing much for her character.

On her way home from work, Deena stopped at Conran's and charged a set of all-white, all-cotton sheets. Another $69 expense. She worried. Karen's antagonism was dangerous. The futon would be delivered tomorrow morning, Deena would be late to work, and Karen wouldn't cover for her.

The machine was blinking again.

Daniel's voice was loud. I thought you should know, he said. I'm filing for divorce. I have to. You were out all last night and the night before. I don't know what to think. The local rabbi advises a quick divorce to minimize the sin. Now I know why you hang up on me, why you won't move back.

A divorce. As easy as that. She wouldn't have to ask for it. She wouldn't have to wait. All she'd had to do was sleep with another man. The rabbi advised and Daniel agreed. He was a victim, a man sinned against by his wife, which couldn't be allowed. Daniel wouldn't be the husband of a wife who slept with other men.

There was also a message from a Rabbi Hirsch in Brooklyn, who was calling at her father's request. He left a number and asked that she call when she arrived home, even if it was very late. Call anytime during the night, he said.

Deena played the message again and wrote down the number. What could she say to this rabbi? That she was having an affair with her lawyer? Besides, what her father wanted was a divorce and it looked as if she wouldn't even have to ask. She could tell the rabbi that and he would relay the information to her father, who'd be delighted.

A woman answered. The wife? Then Rabbi Hirsch was on the phone, introducing himself and speaking calmly.

Encouraging divorce is not a stance I usually take, he said, but I agreed to help your father, who is a dear friend and fine scholar.

Deena explained that it looked as if the proceedings had already started and that it would probably go quickly.

That's very good news, Rabbi Hirsch said. I'll pass that on to your father. Is there anything else I can do for you? If you need someone to talk to, please call. Perhaps you will be more comfortable talking to my wife. It will give me great satisfaction to help in some way.

.   .   .

The futon arrived at nine-thirty as promised, and Deena was at her desk at ten.

What's going on? Susan came in and asked.

Helen followed. Yes, what's going on? You have three messages. Daniel's mother, his brother, and one from a man with an accent. He flirted with me on the phone.

Deena smiled.

Who is he? Susan asked.

Karen came in. Who's who? she asked. Did the futon arrive?

Deena nodded.

Hold the details on the futon, Susan said. Tell us about this guy. She took the pink slip from Helen. Sergei. Sounds real Jewish.

Deena laughed. He is, as a matter of fact. He's the lawyer who handled the closing on the house.

Oh yeah, Susan said. The lawyer. If you saw yourself in the mirror you'd know not to lie. Now the new bed makes sense.

Karen eyed them. I hope you're not bringing this guy up to the apartment, she said. I hope you're not doing anything dangerous.

He's a lawyer, Deena said.

Sounds like more than a lawyer, Susan said.

Ron stuck his head into her office. Ten, fifteen minutes late is understandable, he said. Half an hour is not.

Give her a break, Susan said. She met someone and she had a bed delivered this morning. That goes together well somehow.

Anyone I know? Ron said. Maybe we should warn him.

I have to run down to the bullpen, Karen said and left. Deena wondered about her. She no longer wore her short skirts and heels. Today she was wearing baggy khaki pants and black flats.

The phone rang. Will you all please leave, Deena said, her hand on the receiver.

I'll bet he's a hunk, Susan said.

Women, Ron said and left. Susan and Helen rolled their eyes and waved.

It was Ben, Daniel's brother.

Daniel is incoherent, Ben said, so I thought I'd talk to you. What's going on? He's filing for a divorce. I thought you guys were going to try and work things out.

He paused.

This is none of my business, he said, but Daniel says you're sleeping around. I'm not asking whether or not you are, but if you're doing it just to get him back, it seems to me you're hurting yourself. I think my brother needs help. I suggested a shrink, but you know Dumbo, he wouldn't hear of it. It might be what you two need, a marriage counselor. The least you could do is talk this thing over, give it another chance. I'll do anything to help.

Thanks, Deena said, but no thanks. The more I see him in action, the less I like him. I don't want to be married to the guy. Let him file for a divorce.

Sergei stayed over Friday night. In the morning the buzzer woke them.

Karen, Deena remembered. Karen and Greg were here to pick up the Dux, on which Deena and Sergei were sleeping. They'd gotten back too late to make the switch, and the new futon was lying on its side, still wrapped in plastic.

What time is it? Sergei said. It's too early for anyone to ring on a Saturday.

They're here for the bed, Deena said. I forgot about it. She pulled on a robe, Karen's. Sergei walked into the bathroom. Before she could finish stripping the sheets, Karen was at the door, inserting her key in the lock. Despite the rent she was getting, this was still her apartment.

Deena unlatched the chain, and there they were, fully dressed and carrying black garbage bags.

You didn't answer the buzzer. I thought you weren't here, Karen said, looking past Deena into the apartment.

If only Sergei knew not to emerge from the bathroom. But his suit, shirt, tie, and shoes would give her away.

Did we wake you? Greg asked. We called before we left, but the machine answered. Karen said you probably weren't here.

I turn off the ringer at night, Deena said. I didn't hear it.

It's after ten, Karen said, looking at her watch, and Deena felt like a slug. She was sleeping away her life. She was on the road to ruin, going down fast.

The bathroom door opened and Sergei came out holding Karen's strawberry-pink towel around his waist.

On Karen's face was pure disgust and Deena wished she were anywhere but right there. She should never have brought Sergei into Karen's white apartment. But he was there, a naked man with sleep still in his face. He couldn't be ignored.

Deena introduced him and watched the men shake hands, Greg dressed and bustling, Sergei wrapped in pink, chest and legs exposed. He looked ridiculous.

Karen, who was standing in front of her closet, didn't put out her hand or acknowledge the introduction. She put her head into the closet.

Deena went to finish stripping the bed. I'll take these sheets to the laundry and bring them to work when they're ready, she said.

Actually, Karen said, I'll take them as they are. My towels and robe too.

Let me wash them for you first, Deena said.

Karen shook her head. We have the car here now.

Deena nodded. If you like I'll pay for the wash.

Sergei didn't speak. He didn't hurry either. He gathered up his clothes, took them into the bathroom, and they heard the water in the shower. Karen's face showed disbelief. He was showering in her tub, using her towel. This was worse than finding Daniel on the doorstep. And she could have avoided it; this was her punishment for not purchasing a Dux. But why was Karen so angry? The apartment had been a favor, but it wasn't free. After rent there was even $150 profit in it for her. Deena thought it had something to do with the baggy pants and sweaters Karen had begun wearing. Where were all her short skirts and tiny tops? The emerald ring was on her finger, her fingernails were perfectly done, but still she looked frumpy.

She'd been working late on freelance projects, Deena knew, trying to stash away money for a house. Were they still planning a wedding on a cruise liner to Bermuda, with Greg in a pale linen suit and Karen in a long forties dress and hat?

Have you scheduled the Bermuda trip? Deena asked, attempting to ease the tension.

Greg responded. Now that we've told our parents, things have become complicated. My mom wants us to stop in Florida for a reception so she can introduce Karen to all her yente friends. Then Karen's family wants to do something in California. It's turning into more than a romantic cruise for two. We should have eloped.

You still can, Deena offered and laughed. Elopement via cruise liner.

Greg, Karen said, will you help me with this?

Sergei came out, dressed and ready for the day. In front of Greg and Karen, he cupped Deena's face in his hands and touched her lips with his lips. I'll call you when I can, he said and, with his long coat thrown over his shoulder, walked out.

He seems nice, Greg said and smiled.

Karen frowned. Start loading the car, she said.

Deena looked at her watch; it was almost eleven. Sergei was gone. Karen and Greg were leaving. She had no plans, and the day stretched long and empty.

Monday Deena got to work at eight. She'd start the week off right. She'd get her life in order.

Ron came in. He was always early.

I'm glad you're here, he said. I want to talk to you before the others arrive. Listen, this is difficult. I like you. You're smart. You're talented. But I'm going to let you go. I'm holding off filing the paperwork because I want to give you as much time as you need. I'll give you a month if you need it, which means the paperwork won't be filed for another two weeks. I didn't want this to come as a surprise. I want you to have time to do what you need to do. Use this office as you need it. Finish up the projects you're on. You won't be assigned anything else.

He stopped talking, breathed deep. He'd said everything he had to say. Now he waited. Would she say anything?

She sat stunned. She'd been warned, she'd tried, but it had been too late; the decision to let her go was made when Paul was let go. He'd hired her, she was a remainder of the old management, she had to go. She understood this now. She understood that her absences and lateness had served to relieve consciences, but they had also nailed the lid. It didn't matter that for three years she'd worked steadily. What mattered was the last month.

Is there anything I can do to make you change your mind? she asked.

He shook his head. I believe this will be for the best. You don't truly belong here; you don't like the work. Think of this as a challenge, urging you on to something you like better. And if I can do anything to help, let me know. He stood tall and pulled his pants up by the buckle of his belt. A man adjusting his pants. As if he'd had them down, and now he was back to business.

For the best. That's what people said when they gave you bad news, like it was you they were thinking about. Right now what she needed was a steady income to make living alone possible. What would she do without a salary?

He pulled the door closed behind him, and Deena sat looking at the white door, at her tan coat hanging on the white door. Next, Karen would come in and tell her to move out. But she'd paid this month's rent; the check had already been cashed. The apartment was hers for the rest of the month, after which she'd find another place, to which only she had the key. She turned the newspaper on its back. This morning she'd start with the classifieds. She suddenly needed both a job and an apartment. And she needed friends. Right now the whole world was against her. Thinking this, she realized she sounded like Daniel.

There were rentals on the East and West sides of Manhattan, also downtown, Chelsea, the Village. She didn't know where to begin looking. She couldn't concentrate. The words blurred. She turned past the classifieds to the main section and paused before a Tower Air ad offering a $249 flight to Lod Airport with a brief stop in Paris. For $500 she could get away for ten days. She did have family, and they wanted, they begged her to come. She had a place to go. She sat looking at the 800 number. There was nothing and no one to stop her. No job, no husband, and Sergei hadn't called.

Minutes later she was taking out her American Express and doing what her father wanted her to do: she booked the first available flight to Jerusalem. She'd get away fast. After seven years of absence, she'd arrive without a husband, and every family acquaintance would know of a handsome, rich, and altogether wonderful widower whose four, six, or eight children are no problem at all, the grandparents have been taking care of them, soon enough the older ones will be married and out of the house, and the younger ones will be good help with, God willing, her own newborns.

Would she stay here behind a closed door all week? It would be better if she could get on the plane tonight and avoid this office. If she could get a flight tonight, she'd have just enough time to pack. She'd avoid planning and shopping, questions and doubts. If only she could put on her coat and leave without cleaning her desk. But no seat was available, and ahead was a whole week. Evenings she'd pack, unpack, and pack again. She'd change her mind about going and change it back again.

There was one thing she should do before leaving: get her portfolio into circulation. She was in no mood to interview, she didn't care if she never wrote another ad, but she had to earn a living. Two portfolios would cover more ground than one. She would have to spend money laminating another set of mediocre ads. She had to call headhunters. She looked at the phone, picked it up. She needed to tell someone: Daniel. She dialed the first two numbers, hesitated, and hung up. Why was she calling him?

She lifted her black portfolio onto her desk, quickly selected the best of the worst, put them into a large yellow envelope with card-board backing, and called Mr. Laminate, who picked up and delivered. She'd do things as quickly and painlessly as possible. She took the addressed and sealed envelope out to the front desk and returned to her office feeling better.

It was a start. She'd managed something. Next she'd call a head-hunter. It was only three and a half years since she'd walked the streets with her black box. It was too soon to have to do it again, and this time there was a difference. She was no longer the promising young beginner on the scene. She'd had a chance to prove herself. This time she'd be a hack pounding the pavements along with other mediocre hacks. At fifty she'd be Paul Herz. If she could find herself having done so little in three and a half years, why not twenty or thirty years later?

Paul had taken all his books on the Constitution home to Connecticut. Deena hoped he'd set himself up at a desk and continued reading. Maybe it didn't matter that his idea of a rewrite was ill conceived. In the meantime he'd developed an interest in the subject and he was learning. She hoped he wasn't too unhappy. She should have taken him out to lunch on his last day; she should have stopped into his office more often. But like everyone else in the business, she'd stayed away. As if bad luck rubbed off. She was an ingrate. This man had given her a first chance, he'd hired her, and he'd stayed late one night to help with her first assignment. They had long conversations then. They talked about the writers they both liked, and what was true writing. He complained about his son, who'd dropped out of college. His daughter also didn't finish, and he wondered why it was that both his children were so unthrilled by education.

How did your parents get it right? he wanted to know. How did they manage to raise three sons and each one a scholar? Even you, however much you try to deny it, tend toward that tradition.

She left work at noon, ran, and what a relief it was to be running. Whatever happened, there was still this. She could run. No one could take this from her. She ran the full loop, circled the reservoir twice, stopped to stretch, and walked home.

At six, she ran again. It was crazy but she didn't know what else to do. Besides, this was the way she was used to ending her day, and this was the time of day there were runners on the track worth watching.

He brought pink tulips. It was spring and Sergei brought pink tulips. Deena ran water into Karen's glass vase, set it down on the floor beside her new futon, and stepped back.

It looks like a magazine photo, Sergei said.

They kissed and kissed again. She was kissing more in two weeks than she'd kissed in years. With Sergei, she'd turned into a kisser.

She told him about her trip, but not the job. Unemployed, she was all risk.

Ten days is a long time, he said. I'll miss you.

Deena looked at him, pleased that for once she would be leaving. She wanted him to feel what she felt when he left. She missed him more than she should. When he came, he was with her for a few hours, then he was out of her life for several days. And she didn't know when he'd be back. He came when he came.

Two hours later they went out for an early dinner.

After dinner, Sergei walked with her up the stairs to her door and said good-bye. Deena stood at the window, watched him leave, and continued standing there, looking at the black street. She turned back to the room, but there was nothing she wanted to do just then. It was only nine o'clock and here was the sofa, there the bed, the chair at the desk, but she didn't want to sit or lie down. She walked the room. He was going east, he was turning onto the bridge, then the Long Island Expressway. He was going home to his wife and child. Tonight he'd be a father and husband. Would he eat a second dinner with them? After dinner they'd watch the news together and when it was time, take their daughter up to bed? Did he read to her? No, his wife would do that. His Parisian wife. Was she dark-haired, like Sergei, or blonde? A photograph of his daughter would reveal something about his wife.

She had six days and nights to get through. Then the flight and ten days in Jerusalem, where there wouldn't be the possibility of seeing him; there'd be no expectation. Also she would never be alone, she wouldn't have much time to think about him. Which would be easier. It was only loneliness, she sometimes thought, that made her miss him so much.

Nights now she heard the sounds of the old city and felt warm cobblestones under her bare dusty feet. Without boarding the plane and flying across the Atlantic, she was there. When she closed her eyes she found herself walking up the long flight of stone stairs to her parents' apartment. She climbed and climbed—there had always been too many stairs—and woke up before she reached the landing and front door.

She had to get to the door and through it. She closed her eyes again and walked through the door to the first room, which was cool and dark and large. She touched the dark oilcloth on the table in the center of the room, and her fingers followed the sweep left by a wet sponge. Her mother's wiping-up. A bowl of salted herrings was on the table as always. It was past noon, the meal had been eaten, and everyone was asleep in the next room. She could hear their breathing. She walked around the table and toward the door, and awoke still walking.

Her portfolio went to DDB Needham, a shop once known for its creativity, now it was known for size.

The large shops are where the high salaries are, the headhunter said. At your level, you should be worrying about getting your salary up. But I wouldn't send you to just anyone. The creative director at DDB is looking to hire a hot crop of young writers and art directors. He thinks there's room for a creative pocket within this larger, corporate shop. If you have an art director you like to work with, tell her to send her portfolio to me and I'll send you out as a team.

She couldn't ask Karen. And there was no one else she wanted to work with.

Wednesday night she climbed stone stairs again, reached the third landing, and walked past neighbors' doors. There were more than she remembered, and they were all closed. The chairs beside the doors were empty. Why was no one sitting outside? Where was her mother?

. . .

Ron suggested that Deena write and send an office memo announcing her ten-day trip to Jerusalem.

You won't come back, he said. Once there, you'll wonder why
you're living here.

Susan, Helen, James, and others agreed. If you could live in
Jerusalem, why would you stay here?

Deena shook her head. What did they know? What did they know
about the life of a woman in Hasidic Jerusalem?

If you decide to stay, Susan said, call us. You can reverse the
charges. The company will pay.

Ron rolled his eyes.

We can pack your stuff for you and ship it, if necessary, Karen
offered.

Why were they all so quick to give her up? Why were they so
eager?

She needed the long black skirt she'd left at the house. Black stockings. Another pair of shoes.

Sergei offered to meet her there early afternoon on Friday; he advised taking as much as possible. Afterward they'd go out to dinner,
and then, who knows, he said, as if the possibilities were endless.

Before leaving she dialed the house to make certain Daniel wasn't
there. A surer way might be to call at his office, but she didn't want
to do that.

On the downtown 4, she met Paul Herz, as if thinking about him she'd conjured him up before her. He looked tired and old. He was working as a headhunter, he said, and gave her a business card.

When you're ready to move on, Paul said, send me your portfolio.

Deena pocketed the card, glad to have his address. She would send him a note to say what she hadn't said all these months. She'd tell him about her trip to Jerusalem. Maybe she would leave her second portfolio with him.

Keep in touch, Paul said.

I'll do that, Deena promised. She wanted to say more, but Paul was in a hurry to get away. He seemed embarrassed.

At Fulton she transferred to the J, which emerged from the underground tunnel, crossed the Williamsburg Bridge, and rode east on elevated tracks. She missed this ride through the streets she'd known: Keap, Hooper, and Rodney. Then Hewes, Havemeyer, Rutledge. She'd moved for college, then her family went back to Jerusalem, but purchasing a house, she'd returned to the old J and M line.

After Williamsburg, the tracks turned a sharp left onto Metropolitan, and the buildings went from brick and brownstone to wood and shingle, from connected to stand-alone houses, small to larger lots. And it was like coming home after a long trip. Things were both familiar and not. Sergei's black Mercedes on the corner was not. When he saw her, he got out and came toward her.

Deena looked at the house anxiously. She didn't want a confrontation.

He put his arm around her. Come on, he said. Do you have a list of what you want to take?

Deena shook her head. I won't need a list. I'm taking only what's mine.

It's all yours, Sergei said. Since you cannot take furniture today, you ought to take stereo equipment, silver, whatever. I keep telling you: In the final settlement the one in possession of the object has the advantage. It's easier to keep what you already have.

Taking the stereo equipment will infuriate him, Deena said. That's one thing I won't touch.

You should. Didn't you purchase it together? Think of what you'll need in your new life and take it.

Deena looked at him and shook her head. He didn't understand. She didn't want to pull apart the house; she wouldn't strip Daniel of his things. She didn't want to end her marriage that way. She wanted it to end, and no more.

Sergei looked at her, his blue eyes hard, mercenary. I'm your lawyer, he said, and I have to advise you. If you don't take what you can, you'll regret it later. I've seen it happen too many times.

I don't have anywhere to put these things, Deena said. And I'll be moving again soon. Besides, there will be other opportunities. Right now I just want what I need for the trip. And maybe some of my books.

Then let's get it over with quickly, he said. Do you have the keys?

Deena felt in her bag for the keys. She had them; they were on her key chain along with her office and car keys. House, car, job. She'd lost all three, though for a while she still had the keys. Soon enough she'd be asked to relinquish them, which she wasn't doing willingly. Give up all that nonsense and come home, her father wrote. But she no longer had to choose. She had nothing to give up. She'd been chewed up and spit out.

She didn't care about the car. She'd hardly ever driven the Civic anyway. She'd stopped driving regularly when she gave up her old lemon, the Le Car. But she missed it. She missed riding with the windows down and the volume on the radio up, cruising up and down blocks, going nowhere, just going. She never knew how the drive would end. Once Kenny the mechanic pushed her home. Another time he towed her. There was always something wrong and it was always costly. The gas tank cracked one day. The radiator another. On cold mornings, the battery was dead. She'd gotten stuck on every highway at least once.

Getting stuck, her father said, is also an adventure. Think of it that way and you won't get so aggravated. You'll be a few hours late and the world won't end. There is a reason for everything that happens in this world. He retold the old story of his father, who, detained by authorities because he was a Jew, missed the morning train to Lugoj and escaped a fatal derailing. That, her father said, should convince anyone that there is a divine plan.

And was standing here in front of the house with Sergei also preordained? Was her phone call to his office and everything that followed meant to be and therefore forgivable? Where does free will come in?

Well, Sergei said, looking at her. Are we going to do this?

Deena nodded and walked up to the front door, which was not pink. It had a fresh coat of high-gloss white. She couldn't say she blamed Daniel, but what was the hurry? The house would belong entirely to him soon enough. She knew suddenly that he would also repaint the pink room. He'd erase every sign of her. He'd choose his colors from the colonial-paints brochure. The woodwork would be brick brown, the walls a creamy beige. He would make this house his.

She stopped at the door and inhaled. Her ribs hurt. She was forgetting to breathe.

Relax, Sergei said and put his large hand on the base of her neck. She dropped her shoulders. It was good to have him here.

She turned the key in the lock and hurried to deactivate the alarm, but the red light remained on. She tried again: 3-5-9-7, her dorm-room phone number, on which she and Daniel had spent hours talking. It was the pin number for his bank card too. The alarm blared and it was loud. Sergei hovered over her.

He changed the code, Deena said.

She stood thinking, index finger poised: 6-9-6-9. The alarm stopped. Then for seconds the silence was as unbearable as the noise had been.

She turned her head. She'd known, somehow she'd known.

Sergei looked at her, questioning.

He went from my number to Jill's.

Sunday night she ran in the streets of Jerusalem, on cobblestones and dirt paths.

What are you running from and where to? the voice of her mother asked. You're going in circles. You want to do some running around, I'll give you things to do. There is laundry to hang, trays to take to the ovens. But first put on a pair of shoes.

Deena opened her eyes and saw that it was true: she was barefoot. Her sneakers were where she'd left them the night before. She was exhausted, every muscle ached, she was running too much, she was bordering on insanity; still she would run again this morning, which would be all right since for the next ten days she wouldn't. Her sneakers were staying here. She had to stop the craziness somehow.

She ran the loop twice, extending this final run, then stretched in the sun, and how good it was to be in the sun. She didn't move, and for long minutes nothing mattered. She remained in the sun. If only it would stand still and she could keep this day, this moment.

Daniel called. I've been informed you're leaving town, he said.

Who's doing the informing? Deena asked.

I called at work. You weren't there, so I asked for Karen.

It's a shame, Deena said. A few more hours and you would have missed me.

Don't you care at all about me? he asked. I was in North Carolina this past weekend. I went to visit Jill and met her family.

Jill moved home?

You sound surprised, Daniel said. I wasn't. Ann went back to Mike, and Jill didn't want to remain here alone. Besides, she switched agents, gave up on the Miss America idea, and is concentrating on film. She's planning to move to California. Anyway, I met her whole family. They live in a trailer park. I felt like I was in some down-and-out movie or something.

That's interesting, Deena said. Jill gets credit for trying to make something more of herself.

True, Daniel said. So you're finally really going?

Yes, I'm really going, Deena said.

Well, say hello to the old man for me. And you can give me a call when you get back.

·   ·   ·

Sergei showed up at the airport, carried her bag, and led the way to the VIP lounge. He ordered two glasses of wine, tipped his glass toward hers, and they drank.

The first time you walked into my office with that undeserving husband of yours, you had on a short skirt without stockings, and I wanted nothing so much as to feel the skin on your legs. I wanted to get you on a plane with me to Bermuda. Will you allow me to do that?

Which one? The skin or Bermuda? Deena asked and laughed. She was beginning to understand his way, his flirtatious compliments. They were light, they were quick, they could apply to anyone. Still, they made her feel good. He knew what to say when.

Both, Sergei said. But I'll wait until you get back.

She got a window seat as requested, and hoped the two seats beside her would remain unoccupied. But the plane was filling. A woman with a child in her arms walked by and Deena let go of her held breath. Then a Hasidic man came down the aisle and took a seat three rows back. Just when it seemed she'd have all three seats to herself, a clean-scrubbed man stopped, looked at the stub in his hand, and smiled apologetically. He was good-looking; he'd be all right, especially if he sat near the aisle and the space between them remained open. A Frenchman, she decided, looking at his gold cufflinks and watch. Less flashy than Sergei, but clearly European.

He turned the pages of his newspaper and Deena noted his too-small hands. She looked at his shoes, also too small. He was tall enough, five-ten probably, but he had the hands and feet of a smaller person. He felt her eyes on him and looked up.

Are you visiting Paris on business or pleasure? he asked.

Neither, she answered. I'm taking a connecting flight to Israel. I'm visiting family.

Israel, he said, interested.

Have you been there? Deena asked.

He shook his head. No, but I may go there sometime soon. He paused as if to let the information sink in. My business is in wine and there has been talk of the Carmel grape, which is grown there. It's not very good, at least not yet, but the climate seems right. Someday they may produce a good crop. Do you drink wine?

Deena nodded. Too much, she said.

He held up a finger. One doesn't drink too much, he said, just too fast. Do you like red or white?

Mostly red.

He nodded. In that case I have something for you.

He took out his wallet and found what he was looking for.

Was he giving her his business card? She put her hand out reluctantly, but he didn't hand it to her, not yet. She read his name, which didn't seem French. Peter Thrippen. Dutch maybe. He turned to the back of the card, leaned toward her to show her, and she inhaled his aftershave, which wasn't unpleasant.

This chart will tell you which was the best year for a particular grape. If you like a Rhône, for example, you look here and it shows you that 1978 was an exceptional year for this grape. Now you know that it is worth paying more for a Rhône bottled in '78, but not for a bottle from '75, which was a very bad year. See, it rated only a four.

That's very handy, Deena said, relieved that it was more than a business card.

Yes, he said, and put the card in her hand.

Thank you. She turned to the front of the card and asked, You are Peter Thrippen?

He nodded.

Are you Parisian? she asked.

Not originally. I am from Luxembourg, but I live and work in Paris now. What about you? Where are you from?

She stuck to the easy facts: born in Jerusalem, moved to Brooklyn when she was twelve, but her family returned to Jerusalem. If she were telling the whole truth, she would turn around and point to the Hasid several rows behind them. But that would raise more questions. The plane had not yet taken off. Would they do small talk for the next seven hours?

She turned a page of the magazine in her lap and Peter Thrippen quickly returned to his newspaper. He could take a hint. Deena hoped she hadn't offended him.

After a twenty-minute wait on the runway, the engines finally roared; they were preparing for takeoff. The Hasid was probably praying. With him on board they'd have a safe trip. They were going faster now, the engines were working harder, they were climbing, and she felt herself thinking light, thinking that every passenger on the plane was doing what he could to help get off the ground, and that maybe this really was how planes made it up into the sky, by the power of collective will.

An hour later dinner was served, and Deena noted that Peter Thrippen wasn't above drinking the screw-capped bottle of wine offered on board, despite the fine wines he'd known.

What do you think? he asked.

Not terrible, she said.

He nodded. It's from California. For an inexpensive wine, it's good.

After dinner, the movie *Airplane,* which she'd seen before. Only Tower would show this movie on board. She declined the headphones. Julie Hagerty's fragile helplessness was difficult enough to watch the first time. She read.

The plane quieted down; people watched or slept. Deena got up to stretch her legs and use the bathroom. She checked on the Hasid; did he have everything he needed?

To get back to her seat, she had to wake Peter Thrippen. It was like sleeping on the inside; during the night you had to climb over the other person. She hesitated. How should she wake him? Peter Thrippen stood to let her in; he hadn't been sleeping.

He offered her a blanket from the overhead compartment, which she accepted. She lifted the armrest on her right, pulled her knees up, and hoped she could remain in this position awhile. She would try not to fidget. She closed her eyes and didn't think she'd been sleeping, but a movement nearby woke her. Peter Thrippen was reaching overhead for a pillow. He brought down two and, seeing her eyes open, bent toward her, pillow in hand. She lifted her head and he tucked it in for her, then he tucked the ends of her blanket tight around her shoulders and looked into her eyes. Would he kiss her? He was a stranger; she didn't know him. All he'd done was give her a blanket and pillow. And a business card.

He smiled and moved away, and Deena closed her eyes. What was the matter with her? First Sergei, now Peter Thrippen. After years of fidelity, she was a faucet opened. She was prepared to kiss anyone who was good to her. Sitting near a stranger for a few hours, eating, drinking, reading, then falling asleep side by side, you developed a level of comfort. This wasn't so different from marriage. You live with a person, near a person, he becomes part of your life. Any change in the pattern, a separation for even a short time, quickly turns you into strangers again. Days after her separation from Daniel she couldn't imagine ever living with him again. A few evenings with

Sergei and he became more important than Daniel. Intimacy seemed merely a result of proximity. If she and Peter continued to live like this several days in a row, if in sleep her hand wrapped itself around him, and on waking it was he who saw sleep still in her face, they'd come to feel married.

After the movie, people stirred. Peter Thrippen stood to stretch his legs and Deena took the opportunity to get up too. She stood in line to brush her teeth and wash her face, as if eight hours had passed and now it was morning. When she returned to her seat, Peter Thrippen made room for her and they continued standing. They'd have to sit again soon enough. Deena looked at her watch. They'd been in the air for five hours, but it seemed like days. Everyone on board was restless, the seats were empty, the aisles full. Then carts with peanuts and drinks were rolled out, and passengers, suddenly docile, returned to their seats. Minutes later, they were all munching peanuts, snacking en masse, a picnic in the clouds. Deena smoothed the emptied foil and looked at the ingredients. There was no sign to indicate that the peanuts were kosher. The Hasid wouldn't eat them, he wouldn't be subdued with food. Eating kosher had political advantages: you escaped certain controls, which is what for centuries kings, pharaohs, princelings, despots of every variety, knew and feared.

After cleanup, duty-free goods were brought around. Deena looked at her watch. Only an hour had passed since the last time she looked. Peter Thrippen opened his *New York Times* again. The Hasid walked past them to the front of the plane, then back. Stretching his legs probably. Were they the only two people on this flight going on to Jerusalem? It wouldn't be easy to sit again. There would be an hour between the two flights; she'd make sure to stand and walk that whole hour. She'd have to say good-bye to Peter Thrippen. Already she missed him. And she missed the beginning of this flight, when it had seemed endless, when life on earth was on hold, and nothing mattered. She was no longer in America; she'd relinquished her foothold there. But she wasn't in Jerusalem either. She was afloat in the middle of nowhere, in limbo, where Dante places Abraham, Isaac, and Jacob. It would be good to stay awhile, neither here nor there, not east or west. Up here her choices were clearer, an either/or: Peter Thrippen or the black hatter several rows behind.

When she closed her eyes, she sank into the cold Atlantic. On a ship, miles away, were Daniel, Karen, Susan, Paul, Ron, and yes, Sergei and Peter. Everyone. They waved good-bye and the engines revved, the horn blew, *au revoir, auf Wiedersehen*. Why were they leaving her?

Wait, she shouted. Wait for me. But they'd turned away, they were going back to New York. She tried again, she used all her breath and her arms. She waved so hard her sockets hurt. Someone turned and waved and she waved back; they shouted good-bye and good-bye again, taking turns the way departing ships do, tooting back and forth, once, then again, tooting mournfully, and moving farther off all the time. When the shout of good-bye came again, from a great distance this time, she responded with a tired toot, a ship answering. She was hoarse; she had no voice left. She had to save her strength and learn to live in the water. She would become a fish. She swayed in the wake of the ship, then the gallon waves, asking, Now what?

The voice of the stewardess answered: Coffee or tea?

Coffee, Peter Thrippen said.

Deena sat up, put her tray down, and received a cup of black coffee. Breakfast followed. Was anyone hungry? It seemed as if they were being fed every hour.

Is it morning? Deena asked.

In Paris it is, Peter Thrippen said. We'll be landing in an hour. Were you able to sleep?

Deena nodded. And dream, she said.

That's good, Peter Thrippen said. You'll feel better all day.

Deena looked at her watch. It was 2 A.M. Eastern Standard Time; she'd slept only an hour or two, but she felt fine. Maybe an hour or two a night is all that's necessary; the rest is indulgence. She lifted the shade on her window and saw only clouds. Soon she'd see land, then more sky and clouds. Hours of flying, eating, sleeping, and more flying. She looked at Peter Thrippen. Who would take his seat?

If you should find yourself in Paris, he said, you could ring me. My telephone is on the card. I could show you around a little.

I would like that, Deena said. I should have planned better. I could have stopped in Paris for a few days.

Perhaps you still can. If you want, I will ask for you when we land. Probably there is another flight to Jerusalem at the end of the week. You could request a seventy-two-hour visa from customs. You will have to say it's an emergency, that you are ill.

Deena nodded. She didn't have to decide; the airline's schedule would determine whether or not she could stop in Paris.

When the plane landed, she walked the long corridors at Peter Thrippen's side. He passed through customs quickly and went to the information desk.

She was given a three-day visa; she could stay or go; she could do anything. There was no one to say yes or no; in Jerusalem they didn't know she was on her way, she was expected nowhere, she was free.

What about Peter Thrippen? Would he expect something in return? He'd offered a ride into the city. Did he know of a hotel she could check into without a reservation? Up ahead of her was the black back of the Hasid, walking firmly, assuredly. He knew where he was going; he had no questions and doubts. In his hand he carried the requisite velvet bag, which held his prayer book, a book of Psalms, and the smaller cloth bag in which his tefillin were zipped up. If she followed him down long corridors, to the gate, and continued following him, she'd end up where she'd started, where she was born. Lost, you retraced your steps and returned to the beginning. She would continue walking behind him, keeping his back in front of her, seeing nothing and no one else. She quickened her pace to keep up with the black back. There was an hour to takeoff, what was the hurry? He turned a sharp left and went through a door.

The men's room. That's what.

She stopped and there was Peter Thrippen coming toward her with a smile. He had good news. She walked toward him. She was either following or walking toward a man, it seemed to depend merely on who was there.

There is a flight to Jerusalem every afternoon except on the Jewish Sabbath, but probably you knew that, he said. Deena nodded.

You must ask at the reservations desk whether your ticket will allow these changes. I don't know about the charge, Peter Thrippen said. In the meantime I will go to pick up my car from the garage.

Deena nodded again and went up to the desk. There were people ahead of her, also Americans with questions.

She was suddenly afraid.

We're getting older, her father liked to say. We will not always be here to visit.

She hadn't heard her mother's voice in months.

She doesn't want to talk to you through wires, her father said. She wants to see you sitting at her table again. She wants to talk for uncounted hours, not timed minutes. It's been seven years.

Three months before the wedding, Deena visited for ten days and returned to find Daniel waiting at the airport, saying he'd missed her. He kissed her and she felt that it was right, this new life of hers here, so far from family.

Seven years later she was visiting again, and again without Daniel. But she was dallying. Her life had been one long dally. Seven years of Daniel. Several weeks with Sergei. Hours with Peter. What would come next: minutes with another stranger? There wasn't just one man for her. There were a multitude of men, each different, each with something new to teach her. Relations for the short term, meant not to last.

For every soul that's born, another one is provided, her father said. Eve was made for Adam; Adam for Eve. There is someone in this world meant for you. But finding him is not an easy task. You must pray.

The Hasid emerged from the men's room, turned left, and walked toward their gate. What was she doing standing here in line? She too had a plane to catch. She picked up her bag and ran to catch up with the moving black back.

Daniel

She didn't call.

Two weeks passed and still no word. He called her office and spoke to Karen, who said they were beginning to wonder too.

Apparently, Karen said, Deena was let go before she left. Ron announced it a week ago.

That explains why she went so suddenly, Daniel said.

Two more weeks passed and she still wasn't back. Karen called to ask whether he'd be willing to store Deena's things at the house. The company will pay for delivery, she said, but we need an address to send them to.

What things? Daniel asked.

At the office there were her typewriter and books. At the apartment, the old suitcase full of clothes and her running shoes, which was a surprise. Why wouldn't she have taken them? Karen asked.

This was his cue to say what he'd heard, but he had nothing to add. Deena hadn't called him.

The new futon, Karen said, can remain at my apartment. My current tenant is using it.

Deena purchased a futon? Another thing about her he didn't know.

It's a long story, Karen said.

Daniel thought he heard something in her voice. Something had happened between them.

She had more to tell. About two weeks ago Ron got a postcard saying that she was staying longer than she'd intended. He hasn't heard from her since. But there were calls from a headhunter; Deena had left her portfolio, so she was planning to come back. Also, Karen said, Helen says to tell you that your lawyer has been calling.

Sergei Traub, Daniel said. I wonder what he wants. I'll give him a call.

How are you holding up? Karen asked.

I'm quite fine, Daniel said. I'm seeing someone, her name is Sabrina and we get along, but already she's questioning the seriousness of my intentions. Are you and Greg married yet?

Karen laughed. Not yet, she said. That hurricane that tore through the Caribbean hit Bermuda too. We heard that the place was in bad shape so we postponed the whole thing for fall. There's no hurry really. Summer is beautiful here, and we're taking that share in East Hampton again; we just want to relax.

Daniel laughed. Ten years from now, you'll still be planning to get married.

That's what people are saying, Karen said. *But if we are, it will mean we still want to do it, which is good, isn't it?*

I guess, Daniel said absently. That's how women were, he thought. Once they had you, they weren't so hot and bothered. Only a year ago Karen was turning thirty-five and frantically pursuing marriage. Now she had the engagement ring, it seemed the wedding could wait. Maybe that's all they need. Solid proof that they've snared a man.

But Deena had never wanted the ring. It was his mother who'd insisted on his buying one. He was so young then, they both were; that had been half the problem. What would happen to her now? The Jewish divorce papers had been sent to her parents' address in Jerusalem. She was essentially single again. Would she marry a Hasid this time? It was what her father wanted, and that man was persistent; he could wear anyone down. But it was hard to imagine Deena as a Hasidic wife, or that she would have left him for a Hasid. It would be like having your wife leave you for another woman. You couldn't think of the other person as a rival.

There was something strange about the whole thing, about her going back and staying. Was she being held against her will? If only she would write or call. He would help her if she needed it. He wanted to help her.

Part Four

The bowl of sunflower seeds was making the rounds again. It had been refilled three times, and still everyone sat cracking *papites,* not because they were hungry, but because it was a way to extend the meal. In front of each person was a pile of expertly cracked shells. Even the children were good at it.

Deena's pile was small and sloppy. She'd lost the skill to extract the seed cleanly without chewing. Her mother poked her in the side and demonstrated. Deena nodded. She knew to keep the seed between her front teeth, she knew to apply only so much pressure, but somehow she wound up biting down too hard, then sucking on the salted shell to extract the broken halves.

Give her a week, and she'll be as good as us, her sister said.

Her father cracked a handful of shells and passed the whole seeds to her. You don't eat enough, he said. A woman needs some fat.

You'd think there is a shortage of food in America, her mother said.

In America, Deena said, I look like I could lose ten pounds. I exercise every day and still I'm not thin enough.

With the black kohl around your eyes, her mother said, you look like a hunger victim. You ought to know better. You don't need *cosmetica* here. It doesn't impress anyone.

All she needs is a good night's rest, her father said.

What do you do for exercise? her older sister asked.

I run, Deena said, and nodded confirmation. They stared at her.

In the streets? her mother asked. People don't look at you?

I run in the park. Hundreds of people run there. It's perfectly normal.

How far? her brother asked.

Five, sometimes six miles.

How many kilometers is that?

Deena shrugged. Her father calculated. That's a long way, he said. It must take more than an hour. But you were a weak child, you need fresh air. It's certainly better than inhaling the corrupt atmosphere of a gymnasium.

Gymnasium. He said the word the old European way, making it seem more foreign and desirable than any college gym or exercise club she'd experienced.

Historically, he continued, one could say that the gymnasium represented the largest threat to the Jewish faith. Jews are descended from Jacob, a man who dwelled in tents not fields. The state of Israel, founded as it was by people seeking to turn themselves into a nation that works and defends the land, stresses physical conditioning. Which means that the very lifestyle of the kibbutz is a threat to the character of the Jew. Kook and his men tried to take our children and convert them into young, healthy Edomites, hairy, red-faced Esaus.

Deena looked at her father, the fact of the physical man whom she hadn't seen in seven years. He looked older and more fragile than she remembered; his beard had gone white.

Her mother too looked frail. Her sisters, only in their twenties and early thirties, looked as if they were in their forties. In their child-bearing years, their breasts were heavy with milk, bellies newly de-flated or just expanding. They laughed at themselves, at how fat they had become, but what can we do, we are only human and this is what happens when you bring life into the world. What else is there? What does one work for? For the pleasure of sitting at the table with your family and cracking *papites* late into the night. They weren't slaves to tomorrow, they were free. Tomorrow would come soon enough. In the morning, the roosters in the courtyard would wake them, and they would be tired, but they would get up, send the children off to school, prepare the midday meal. The day would pass, the sun would set, and there would be another night in which to sleep.

Her brothers looked like their father, beards grown in and point-ing, eyelids fat with too much studying and too little sleep.

She was tired too. She looked at the beds pushed against the walls in the room. She could fall right asleep. Even with all the laugh-ter and talk she could sleep. But there was no private place, no sep-arate room. She couldn't take off her clothes and climb under the covers. She would have to wait until the table was cleared and folded, and the room prepared for the night. With only two rooms and a kitchen, every space was multiple purpose. For the next ten days, she wouldn't be alone for a minute.

They asked about the house and she passed around the pictures she'd brought.

She carries pictures of her house the way a mother carries pictures of her children, an aunt said, laughing.

Be happy she isn't showing pictures of her dog or cat, her mother said.

A typical American house, her sisters agreed. Small and specialized rooms. A special entrance room, then a room to sit in, no tables, no beds, just a salon filled with large white couches and chairs. They call it a living room, as if what's done in the other rooms isn't living. There's a dining room for the evening meal. For breakfast there's another room. The kitchen is usually small. On the second floor, there are more rooms. A room to sleep in and a room for dressing, even their clothes have special rooms. There is a baby room for the only child, and a guest room. In the basement is the laundry room and also sometimes a den for anything and everything, as if the anything and everything hasn't yet been provided for.

They laughed. There aren't enough hours in the day for a person to live in most of these rooms.

Her father spoke. Much about life and family can be learned from a house, he said. First, a good, firm foundation is required. You don't begin to build without a reliable foundation. The rest of the structure can be only as good as what's beneath it. One thing depends on the other. If the foundation crumbles, the structure will fall; if the structure falls, the roof caves in. One cannot survive without the other. Human beings are also like this; we are a dependent people, we need one another. A man needs a wife, a woman requires a husband; children, like scaffolding, must have solid footings. Young parents depend on the grandparents, and so on. The Torah sets the great example. Before first man, God created the world. Before woman,

man. When man and woman build a home, they are attempting their own small, imperfect version of creation. But humans make errors, they commit sins. After the pain, one repents and tries again. . . .

His voice went on and Deena smiled. It was for this that she'd come. And it was also this that made it possible for her to reenter her own life.

Her mother shrugged and smiled back. Her brothers and sisters nodded. Yes, there he goes again. But if he stopped talking, they'd have to worry. If in his letters he no longer lectured and quoted, Deena would know something was wrong.

When she was eleven, her legs suddenly grew and they hurt. Of all pains, her father said, these are the best kind to have.

There were others that also brought rewards. Bringing forth life, her sisters suffered too. Before he could become a great and blessed nation, Abraham had to leave his land, the country of his birth, and his father's house. Go forth for yourself, by yourself, into yourself, God said, addressing all men.

She'd gone forth, and she was coming to know herself, and she would continue this knowing.

And on her return trip, perhaps she would stop in Paris.

The author of the critically acclaimed international bestseller *The Romance Reader*, **Pearl Abraham** grew up speaking Yiddish in a Hasidic home. She teaches writing at New York University, and lives in New York City.